The Girl Left Behind

Walter Eugene Lane

The Girl Left Behind
by
Walter Eugene Lane

All rights reserved. Copyright © 2016 Walter Eugene Lane

No Portion of this book may be reproduced or transmitted in any form or by any means, electronic or mechanical, including, but not limited to, audio recordings, facsimiles, photocopying, or information storage and retrieval systems without explicit written permission from the author.

This book is a work of fiction. Names, characters, businesses, organizations, places, events, and incidents are the product of the author's imagination or are used fictitiously. Any resemblance to actual persons, living or dead, of locales is entirely coincidental.
V.6e
www.walterlane.com
ISBN: 1535057548
ISBN-13: 978-1535057547

DEDICATION

Unto all who love His appearing.

Chapter One

Golden sunlight fell upon the neatly trimmed lawns and modest, well-kept homes of the neighborhood. The gentle beams came down like peaceful rivers of light pouring from a benevolent heaven glinting off the windows of the ranch houses, A-frames and split-levels lining the tranquil streets of this homey, sleepy community. The light reflecting off the glass made them look like twinkling eyes in the face of each abode. This was one of those planned communities so popular decades back; to Susanna, it seemed a bit retro. It was the kind of planned neighborhood with large, curving brick walls on each side of the road leading in and branded with a stylish sign with raised letters. The sign on the right curved wall here read: *Welcome to Cloverdale*. As Susanna Kelly drove past it, the sunlight warmed her bare arms.

 The scene through her dad's car windshield was like a diorama of suburbia with green grass surrounding houses of colorful vinyl siding with touches of brick showing here and there. The curved brick walls receding in the rearview mirror were like a fading memory.

 She glanced at the yard on the right as a man laboriously pushed a lawnmower, his back bent with the effort. In the yard to the left, a kid played fetch with a bouncing dog, the Doberman chasing the round plastic disk with unbridled enthusiasm. This was an ordinary morning; yet wonderful in its own way. It made for a nice drive to work. It was a pity, she thought, it was to be one of her last.

The warm air through the car windows was scented with honeysuckle and pine from the trees and bushes growing throughout the community. Nice walking weather, she thought, promising herself a nice jaunt later, her sneaks resting comfortably on the backseat ready to go. The sidewalk traffic—a few ladies taking their sweet time going nowhere and a few men walking dogs—was sparse, most people no doubt at work, or on their way, by now. A distant echo of laughter came from ahead, children playing somewhere; it was a fitting musical score for the quaint tableau surrounding her. She thought that if it wasn't for the marring visage of the occasional potbelly here and cigarette-befouled mouth there, this could have made for a very pretty picture. The thought made her smile.

Now that the hard part of the drive, getting through Research Triangle traffic, was over, she savored the pleasant trip through Cloverdale and took her time getting to Albert's place. When she entered college, she struggled with the decision of living on campus or just continuing to live at home. Her mom was all for her staying, making arguments, one or two very good, to support her position. She pointed out that staying at home would reduce her living expenses—having a dorm room, paying for meals—and give her a quiet place to study without the distractions of a lot of noisy dorm mates. She loved her mother dearly, but at eighteen Susanna was at an age she wanted a change and looked forward to spending time with other smart, young people. She explained to her mom that living on campus would make getting to classes so much less of a hassle. And the thought of driving to campus every morning, fighting the horrors of Triangle traffic, did not appeal to her. She moved onto campus at the beginning of her first semester just over three years ago. Even though by taking this job with Albert she ended up, all this time later, wrestling traffic a few days a week. Still, the twenty-one-year-old did not regret her decision. She'd loved the past few years on campus.

Again, she inhaled deeply the aroma of honeysuckle. It reminded her of when she was a kid and the honeysuckle bushes that grew at the very back of her parent's yard on the neighbor's property. The bushes and small trees growing there and to each side of the yard had enclosed her backyard like a hidden fairyland—a fantasy attractive to an imaginative little girl who by twelve had already started writing her own stories in a notebook. But it was all gone now; all of it cut down years ago to make way for a large storage building and a vegetable garden. Her mom still lived in the house but the fairyland was gone.

Approaching the middle of Curtis Road, she passed that house with the really nice car, an expensive German luxury model parked in the drive. It was the house where, she believed, some preacher lived. To her, the car just seemed out of place with the house and the neighborhood in general.

At the middle of Curtis Road—an avenue that has been around many years before the housing development came along—she again looked over the wonderful, two-story house constructed of cream-colored stone blocks. Each day when she drove by on her way to Albert's house, she slowed down and admired its elegance and stately grandeur. It belonged to the Curtis family whom this road, according to Miss Jensen, was named after. A century before, the Curtis family had been the road's only residents and this house stood in solitude before *progress* came along and gave it so many neighboring homes—welcomed or not. As she understood, the Curtis family had owned all the land around here decades back but it had been sold off over the years for some reason. Well, money was the reason, but did they need it or just want more of what they already had plenty of?

The lawn was three times the size of any other around. The immaculate deep green grass covered a large quadrangle enclosed on the back and both sides by stately lined stands of lush trees, popular and oak—no cheap pines here. It was all the product of planned landscaping; that was obvious. She could see from the road how the trees shaded the entire backyard with a welcoming, cozy shadowiness. This was the prettiest property in the whole neighborhood (maybe the whole town); far more upscale than any other property in the community. She wondered if she would ever have a chance to look inside.

She often wondered what kind of house she'd have someday. She often thought about the future and what it held for her, what kind of job she'd get or if she'd get married soon. She was single right now and that was okay. For now, her attention was focused on school and she didn't need the distraction of a heavy relationship. But maybe someday before too long she'd meet the right guy.

Right now the only future she could actually visualize was graduating. A couple of years is not all that long. Then it would be time to start job hunting. Exactly what kind of job she would pursue she didn't yet know. She hoped there would be offers, but she knew the kind of job she wanted, something in publishing, would probably not be found around here. Another mystery of the future:

where would she end up? The future stood afar off beckoning, making big promises—promises she hoped it would keep.

Further down, she saw Miss Jensen working in front of her house. She was on her knees digging with a hand trowel in the flowerbed beneath the bay window left of the door. Miss Jensen knew her mom a little. Years ago, they had worked together for a couple of years in an insurance office, the one that had been managed by Albert in fact. Susanna honked a greeting and pulled over.

"Good morning, Miss Jensen!" She spoke loudly to be heard through the passenger side window.

Smiling, Miss Jensen looked up and waved. The plump red-haired lady of fifty-five seemed comfortable in her blue jeans and short-sleeve checkered shirt. The work attire suited her.

"What you up to?"

Miss Jensen raised her arms and stretched. "Trying to get these ol' weeds out." She pointed down to the flowerbed. "Rough work for an old girl!" She laughed.

Susanna smiled. "It looks beautiful. I just love Black-Eyed-Susans. Maybe it's the name. So close to mine."

Miss Jensen grinned.

"By the way, my mom says hello."

"Well, you tell her hello back."

Susanna waved goodbye and pulled away. The two-door compact she piloted over the suburban streets rolled along smoothly. When her father had it he kept it well maintained and she tried to do the same. The new tires added just last week gripped the road firmly and turned quietly on the blacktop. Her dad would be pleased with how well she was taking care of the vehicle. She still missed him and thought of him often when she drove it.

Passing the brick ranch house two doors down from Miss Jensen's, the home occupied by a family named Bergner, so Miss Jensen had told her, she noticed a Hosey Cow standing in the yard, its tail pouring water back and forth over the lawn. With all its square angles, it looked like a lawn implement designed by Picasso.

Albert Carson's house was not far now. The book she had helped him with was finally done and only needed the usual final proofing any book requires before publication. That meant these drives to his house would be over by the end of the week and she would be looking for another part-time job. She hoped she could find one quickly.

She reached for the radio and repeatedly punched the scan button trying to find a weather report. The street to Albert's house was coming up and she let go of the button and took hold of the wheel with both hands. She made the sharp right turn and the houses and lawns of Curtis Road became a momentary blur replaced by the sights and sounds of Cucumber Street, its sights and sounds much the same as the other.

These new street names! She shook her head. *Housing developers must've really had a sense of humor back in the day. Or they just ran out of ideas.*

The radio scan stopped on a Johnny Cash song. His deep voice sang a lyric, *It's going by the book*. The rock arrangement of the tune was so different from other songs she'd heard by him. Five or six kids were playing tag in the yard of a split-level just to her right. They stopped and glanced in her direction. She waved and continued on towards Albert's place just on the left a few doors down. She pulled across the street and parked in front of his two-story colonial as she'd done three mornings a week for the past six months. Albert's red SUV sat in its usual spot just in front of her.

His book had been a big project. Bible prophecy was a complex subject and Albert had a vast amount of material for her to correlate, all of it lying around in disorderly notes and general chaos, and put into book form. He was a fine scholar and, she thought, a true expert in eschatology, but he was definitely not a writer. For several weeks, he had tried on his own to put some chapters together, coming up with nothing but confusing and over-technical pages. At last, he decided he needed help in putting his exhaustive material into a form accessible to the public and, indeed, in the actual writing of the book. Susanna was glad he answered her ad in the university's student newspaper offering editorial services. She thought it was funny how so many good scholars were such bad writers.

She truly wanted to help him achieve his vision. Not that she believed a word of the subject matter. To her, the whole end time thing was like science fiction without the science. She was strongly entrenched in her agnosticism; so much that it was almost a faith—a faith of faithlessness. All she was sure about was that she wasn't sure about anything. But she'd been glad and grateful to get the work and put her studies of English and literature into purposeful work. Editorial and writing jobs were not plentiful in a mid-sized town like this or even around the university. And for a college student trying to make a few extra dollars, this wasn't a bad gig. It sure beat washing dishes in the school's food hall.

Her phone rang. She dug it out of her shoulder bag lying on the passenger seat and glanced at the screen. It was her mother.

She quickly put the phone to her ear. "Hi, mom!"

Eloise, her mother, a plump woman of fifty-three, had worked until she took early retirement three years ago.

She quit in order to stay home with her husband who had suffered a light stroke and needed extra attention. Eloise Kelly had taken good care of him. Susanna recalled the many times she'd seen her helping her dad through his daily activities. She was glad she too was able to help out now and then. It was sad when he passed away last year.

"Hello, Susanna," her mother replied. "I wanted to let you know that your Aunt Fran is in town for a few days and will be staying at the house. I want you to come to dinner this Sunday. She's dying to see you."

It was from her mom she had mostly developed her agnosticism. Her dad rarely spoke of religion one way or the other but neither spoke outrightly against it. However, neither of them saw the point of it.

"Sure," Susanna said. She looked forward to having dinner with her aunt, but she wasn't interested in another religious discussion if that was on the menu. It was the kind of discussion that often came up when her Aunt Fran was around. "Usual time?"

"Yes, dear."

For half a minute, they chatted about nothing in particular and hung up. Instead of her bag, she put the phone in her shirt pocket wanting to keep it near.

Before getting out of the car, she adjusted the rearview mirror and looked herself over. Her full brown hair, short and straight, reflected a healthy sheen. It was cut perfectly in a Dutch Boy hairstyle and crowned her head like a well-fitted diadem. She stroked the bangs covering her forehead with her little finger and watched them bounce back to exactly where they had been. Her warm brown eyes set slightly apart were clear and pretty. All makeup was in order, not that she used or needed much; her naturally fair complexion provided all the coloration she needed and her clear, smooth skin was flawless. *Like butter*, her mom often observed.

Out of the car, she made sure her white blouse was tucked neatly into her blue jeans. Before walking up the brick steps to Albert's door, she looked over the quiet neighborhood showcasing nice homes, neat lawns and clean sidewalks. To her, it seemed like they were presented with an almost sentient pride. Again she thought about that walk. The temperature so mild, the honeysuckle so inviting, she decided the morning was far too nice to spend all of it indoors. She knew she still had a little while before absolutely having to go in. *He's probably working on a video anyway,* she reasoned. She opened the back door of the car and sat down and changed out of her flats into her sneakers.

As she walked along, passing the homes of the neighbors, her footsteps made a soft padding against the concrete of the sidewalk. Like before on her frequent walks around here, she noticed the way this street seemed to flow along, the unmarked black asphalt, curving round in a wide, gentle sweep banking slightly at the center. It cut through the neighborhood like a black river running through it. She imagined herself tossing in a coin for good luck and it disappearing into inky blackness. She smiled.

Three doors down from Albert's, she approached Mrs. MacNaverder's house and stopped for a moment to admire the huge bed of yellow tulips that had come in so nicely, the lawn under the large window glimmering with gold. Just then Mrs. Mac, as everyone called her, came out the door.

"Morning, Susanna!" her voice rang. The slender, pixyish gray-haired woman stepped over to the newspaper lying on her neatly manicured lawn.

"Hi, Mrs. Mac," Susanna returned. "The tulips are beautiful!"

"Yes, I'm really pleased with how they've blossomed." She reached down and picked up the paper. "How's Albert's book coming along?" She tucked the paper under one arm.

"We're pretty much finished. Doing some proofreading now."

Mrs. Mac nodded as if she knew what proofreading was. "Does this mean you won't be around much longer?"

Susanna shrugged. "'Fraid so. Too bad." Losing a job sometimes meant losing friends too. It was one of the odd quirks of life.

"Well, we'll sure miss not seeing you around." She brushed away a fly from her face.

Susanna's smile fell away. "Yeah, me too."

Mrs. Mac's face lit up. "Hey! I'm having a cookout this Saturday around two. Come if you can."

"Yes, I'd loved to. Could I bring something?"

"Oh no. We'll have plenty of everything. Some nice homemade ice cream too!"

Just then they heard a dog barking from inside the house.

Susanna smiled. "Sounds like Buddy wants his mommy."

"Oh, that dog!" Mrs. Mac huffed. "Let me get in there before he has a conniption." She waved. "You take care, now. See you Saturday." She went back into the house.

Across the street, Mr. Davies stood watering his lawn, the nozzle of the hosepipe gushing water profusely in a wide arc. A few drops made their way across the narrow street and rained down on her.

He pointed the hose at the ground. "Oh, Susanna, I'm so sorry!" He twisted the valve and stopped the water flow. "Are you okay?"

She laughed. "No problem, Mr. Davies!" She wiped the moisture from her brow. "Lawn's looking good!"

"I'm really sorry about that."

She smiled. "No problem."

He truned and resumed watering.

She'd been coming around here for so long that many of Albert's neighbors, not just these people, knew her by name. She was going to miss seeing them. She turned and continued on her way.

After Mr. Davies' house the neighborhood street hit a sharp decline and Susanna slowed down a bit. She walked in a leisurely fashion and thought about the many times she had walked her dog around her own neighborhood. She wished Bosco, her standard poodle, were here now; she missed him on days like these.

Two doors down from Mr. Davies lived the Madisons, a young couple in this older community. They had moved in about two years ago as Susanna recalled Dora Madison saying. Robert Madison, Dora's husband, had transferred down from New Jersey to work at one of the big companies in Research Triangle Park.

Susanna crossed the street and approached the walkway to their door and stopped in front of the house. She hoped Dora might catch sight of her and come out and speak. She liked talking to the people in the neighborhood, but most of them were much older than she. It was nice talking to someone not that much older; someone she could relate to better. She looked over the brick ranch house; its new blue metal roof looked like a clean, freshly laid tablecloth. There was not a sound coming from inside. She knocked softly on the door in case Dora was sleeping late, perhaps not feeling well.

***

Her husband off to work—finally—Dora was able to get started on her morning chores. She quickly pushed the vacuum cleaner across the bedroom carpet as if she was training for some kind of vacuum cleaner race. But that was not the reason for her haste. She wanted to get the noisy vacuuming over so the house could return to quiet, albeit a deceptive quiet. If that Milliner woman came to the door again, she wanted her to think no one was home.

The breakfast dishes waited in the sink and she was impatient to get to them; the fastidiousness instilled by her mother nagged at her. Her husband endured her near-obsessive meticulousness with good grace and usually with a smile. After all, this was Dora, his very own brunette beauty that he pursued for a year and kept at until, finally, she agreed to marry him.

She moved quickly and finished the bedrooms and hastily dragged the vacuum into the living room and began there. She glanced over her shoulder and looked out the front bay window. No one was coming. So far, so good.

In less than three minutes, she was done and pushed the vacuum cleaner back into its spot in the hall closet. As she closed the door, for a moment, she felt like she was hiding R2D2 from the Imperial Guards. Maybe the Star Wars marathon last night with Robert, all three original films, was a bit too much. She dove into cleaning the kitchen floor moving over the tiles with an elegance worthy of at least a silver medal if this had been an Olympic event. The smell of stew beef cooking on the stove filled the room. Stew beef was one of the Southern things she'd picked up on since moving down here. That and southern style cornbread—no blessed sugar added to ruin it—were two of the surprises she found to her liking since living in the south. The killer humidity in the summer, however, was not so great.

She heard a gentle rapping at the front door. It made her think of Poe's *The Raven*. Not answering immediately, for fear it just might be Mrs Milliner, she stood very still and almost held her breath. Lately, Cheryl Milliner had made a habit of dropping by. Odd, since Dora barely knew her and in no way considered her a friend. Her objection to Cheryl Milliner was that she was so objectionable.

Cheryl Milliner was the type who loved to express a detailed opinion on everything. That included how Dora should do her housework. After her young life with her mom, she didn't need any more housekeeping advice. She now considered herself an authority on the subject.

Also, Mrs. Milliner talked a lot about religion. Dora was not a religious type but she had no objection to others embracing it. She did, however, have a problem with people trying to shove it down her throat, especially from someone whose own sincerity was by no means certain.

The last time she had been around, she said, "You know about the Rapture, don'cha?" She spoke so emphatically the curly, blond wig on her head moved slightly out of place. "It's happening soon and holy people like me will be going to heaven. Now, people like you will be left down here to face what's coming."

Dora had just stood looking at her, biting her tongue. The Milliner woman seemed to use religion, not as an expression of faith, but more like a weapon to attack others. But she couldn't bring herself to outright tell her to get out and stay away. She was too kindhearted for that and felt a little sorry for the older lady. She thought it must take a lot of loneliness to drive someone to this kind of bitterness.

She carefully moved into the bedroom and looked out the window. She was delighted to see Susanna standing outside.

After a moment, Susanna turned away and started back toward the sidewalk.

"Yo, Susanna!" She looked again at the house. Dora was peering out of an open window. She held the curtain back with an arm. "Hold on a minute!"

"Okay!" Susanna replied and stepped back onto the walkway.

Dora came out of the door, smiling. The pretty, short-haired brunette, her dark, gleaming curls combed back from her smooth face, walked up to her. She was robed in a red terry cloth bathrobe but wore blue canvas sneakers instead of slippers on her small feet. Susanna wondered if she had just started getting dressed for the morning just as she came by. She knew some people who put on their shoes first when getting dressed; her cousin Linda did that.

"I'm glad I saw you. I was keeping low in case of Mrs. Milliner."

"Oh, has she been around again?"

Dora shook her head. "Not for a couple of days now. Maybe she got tired of me and moved onto a fresh kill."

Susanna laughed.

Dora's eyes brightened. "Oh, Did Mrs. Mac tell you about the cookout Saturday at her place?"

"Yes. I'm going. Looking forward to it." Just then it struck her that this upcoming cookout was almost like a going away party for her. The thought made her a little sad. The thought that this was her last week working here was bittersweet.

Dora smiled. "Good, I'm so glad I'll have someone to talk to who's under sixty."

Susanna grinned. "So how's Robert?

"Oh, same as usual; more trouble than he's worth!"

They chuckled but Susanna knew Dora's husband meant the world to her—well, most of the time at least.

Barking came from inside the house. Not the yapping of a toy something or other, but the resonant bark of a big dog—a *real* dog as Susanna's father would have said.

"How's Horatio today?" She folded her arms and balanced her weight a little on one foot. Bad posture, her mom would have said, but more comfortable just the same.

"Big and ugly as ever. Why I married a man with such an ugly dog, I'll never know."

Susanna smiled broadly. She always enjoyed Dora's sense of humor. At college, she had gotten to know many of the students from up north. Yankees as her grandmother used to call the transplants. Carpetbaggers, her grandfather had called them.

Dora placed a hand on Susanna's arm. "I gotta go. Got something on the stove." She backed up a step. "I'll see you on Saturday." She turned and went back inside.

Susanna turned and continued her walk. She moved at a steady pace, not wanting to keep Albert waiting too long, waving to people standing outside their homes now and then. She crossed Coffee Lane and continued toward the intersection ahead. Back when she first saw the sign she had wondered, *Coffee Lane? Wonder if it leads to Non-Dairy Creamer Street?* At the end of the street, it intersected with Collins Road, a street that sounded refreshingly like a real street. Here, she turned around and headed back.

As she approached her car, she noticed in the yard across the street that the Davidson place had become a galactic battleground. A group of kids, they all looked under ten, boys and girls, were engaged in fierce swordplay using plastic lightsabers. A little girl in a white Princess Leia costume, no doubt gotten from the same toy store as the plastic lightsabers, kept shouting, "Galaxy far, far away!"

Susanna opened the back door of the car ready to put the black flats on again, the shoes that took her two minutes this morning to decide upon from the many boxes crowding her dorm room. A former boyfriend had once asked her why she had so many shoes. She just looked at him as though he were speaking Klingon. *I don't know why guys don't get this!* Looking at her feet, she decided the sneaks were just too comfortable to remove; and besides, Albert didn't care what she wore. She got her shoulder bag from the passenger seat and closed the door.

After walking up the brick walkway to Albert's door, yellow buttercups in bloom on each side of the steps, she stood there knowing she would not be doing this much longer. She felt that bittersweet pang again. All good things...

With the sound of galactic chaos at her back, she lingered a moment in front of the outer storm door of the elegant red, six-paneled door, its cut-glass fan lights gleaming. She thought about the first time she had approached here, how excited she was to be putting her studies to useful, practical purposes. Now, the regret that it was coming to an end was so strong, it seemed like an actual tactile sensation. She really liked Albert and was going to miss him. She opened the outer storm door and took hold of the brass door-knock. She gave it a little rap to let Albert know she was coming in.

Chapter Two

Albert Carson came out of the bedroom and headed for the stairs. The blue pullover shirt and tan slacks he wore were typical of the way he dressed, often the kind of clothes he wore on casual Fridays at the office when he was still working. His black walking shoes padded softly on the carpet as he carefully took each step. At the bottom of the stairs, he looked down at the framed picture on top of the small table there. He stared at the photo of Liz and himself, stared at it longingly, a faint smile on his face. He set it back down and headed for his study.

He sat down, and with some trepidation, faced the computer. Even though he'd made a couple of these recordings already, as he sat in front of the camera mounted on top of the monitor, he still felt a little uneasy. He did every time he made one of these. To him, the experience was just *foreign*—like entering a room full of people you don't know, or worse, going to a *party* full of people you don't know. That was a mistake he promised himself he'd never make again. Like most people in the neighborhood, he'd had a computer for a long time; he used one at work as well. But that was for simple data entry. Other than that, he was not all that tech savvy, not like the young people these days; not like Susanna. It was she that showed him how to make these recordings or, rather, videos as she said they were properly called.

He stared at his paunch belly reflected in the glass of the turned-off monitor, not a flat-screen but an old CRT type. He had watched a video on the Internet that suggested turning the monitor off when recording a video so the light from it wouldn't reflect off his eyeglasses, or illuminate the face unduly. But the text he would be reading was on the computer and he really wasn't worried about the other concerns.

"Medium of our age," he mumbled as he turned it on.

He wanted to get his viewpoints on prophecy out there and he hoped this was a good way to do it. He already had a simple website set up with articles on the subject of the end time, a subject he felt he knew quite well. Having studied very prayerfully and intensely for decades, he had gathered together his thoughts into notes hoping to share his insights in a book. Susanna had already explained that there were tons of prophecy videos on the Internet and his would be just another drop in the bucket lucky to get a handful of views. But he knew for sure no one would see them if he didn't post them. *Post a video*; another term he learned from Susanna. At least he could warn *somebody* of the Great Tribulation coming upon the world. He looked at the Bible on his desk. *If people only knew how close it is, and how bad it's gonna be.* Then he thought, *People so often say the world is going to Hell. Little do they realize that Hell is coming to the world.*

He knew results from his efforts on the book would not be immediate if there were any at all. There was still some time before the book actually got into print or published as an ebook available through the Internet, a suggestion by young Susanna. He had no delusions about book sales either, and he knew he'd have to self-publish. That was okay. He wasn't writing for money. Besides, he didn't need it. He'd done well in his business career, regional manager for an insurance company, and he had retired comfortably by the age of fifty-nine.

He did this book out of love of God's word. In fact, he was going to talk about that this morning in a recording, rather, video. He was going to explain why the God of love was going to pour such wrath on his creation: the planet and its population. This seemed to be a sticking point to a lot of people. He hoped the video would provide at least some explanation. However, he wasn't so naive as to expect that anyone would actually believe it, but it gave him satisfaction to know he'd at least made it available.

But first, he had *this* video to do. With the mouse pointer, he clicked the start button on the video software and let it run a few seconds for pre-roll, the way Susanna had shown him. She would help him with any editing the video needed before he posted it to the web. He opened the document containing the notes he wanted to share.

"In this video, I want to talk about the Rapture and the opening of the sixth seal." He glanced down at the notes on the screen. "At an unspecified time before the sixth seal is opened, the Rapture will occur." He leaned forward a bit. "Let's keep in mind that the seals, trumpets, and vials are symbolic images the book uses to help us reference the events in Revelation. There will be no literal opening of seals but I use that terminology as reference points as the book of Revelation does." He sat back again. "Before the time of the sixth seal, in a moment, the dead in Christ will rise and with them, the living saints will meet Christ in the air to be taken to Heaven by Him."

As he clicked to the next page, his body slightly shifted. "When the Rapture occurs, the timeline of the Tribulation begins. The days specified in Revelation and Daniel can then be counted, and the countdown to the return of Christ can begin. The key to understanding the Book of Revelation is to understand the chronology of the Tribulation events. This is why it is so important to correctly establish the start point of the earthly judgments. These judgments in Revelation are presented in chronological order. They are neatly grouped together in three listings. First are the seven seals, the first five being pre-trib as is the Rapture. Then come the seven trumpets, and later the seven vials or bowls as they are called in the New International Version.

In this chronology, we are not told outright just where the Rapture fits. Indeed, the Rapture is not even mentioned in the book of Revelation." He pointed to the camera. "Remember that Jesus said in Matthew twenty-five verse thirteen, 'Watch therefore, for ye know neither the day nor the hour wherein the Son of Man cometh.' This is still true today. Those engaging in date setting are in error, but we are given some indications as to where to place it in the Revelation chronology. We know it happens before the Tribulation begins, but a more exact point of view is that the Rapture is itself the starting point of the seven-year Tribulation. When the Rapture takes place the Tribulation begins. The book of Revelation is in chronological order; this point is fundamental to understanding the book of Revelation and the timeline of the Tribulation events."

Albert looked thoughtfully into the camera. "But just what is the event represented by the sixth seal? It is my firm belief it is a major asteroid strike." He nodded. "When this happens the world will know the great day of God's wrath has come and many will seek shelter in underground bunkers and caves in accordance with Revelation six verses fifteen, sixteen and seventeen. And it's also prophesied in Isaiah two and nineteen, 'And they shall go into the holes of the rocks, and into the caves of the earth, for fear of the LORD, and for the glory of his majesty, when he ariseth to shake terribly the earth.'"

Again, he glanced at his notes. "When the asteroid strikes, immense earthquakes will rock the globe and possibly trigger volcanic eruptions around the Pacific Rim, the Ring of Fire as it's called, fulfilling the prophecy of the first trumpet. Due to the asteroid strike, every island and mountain will be moved—shaken. The meteor impact will create a mushroom cloud—the heavens departing as a scroll. The impact will launch dust into the atmosphere and ejecta into space. The dust will darken the sky and blot out the sunlight; the moon shall appear as being blood red. The ejecta, rocks, and debris that will be thrown out by the blast will be pulled back down by gravity and ignite in the atmosphere, creating a fiery meteor storm—the stars falling from heaven. To ancient people, all the objects in the sky, except the sun and the moon, were stars; that's why John called this falling debris stars. This creates a global emergency, perhaps giving the Beast the opportunity to seize control over the world—the start of the one world order, or if you prefer, the New World Order."

He waited a moment and looked thoughtfully into the camera. After he closed his notes, he clicked off the recording software and sat back. Taking a deep breath, he got up and headed for the kitchen.

Through the window over the sink, he admired the beautiful glow of the sun against the lawns and houses on the street behind him. His lawn, neatly trimmed, just mowed yesterday, looked like a golf course green. *Be a great day to get in a few rounds,* he thought. A scripture came to mind: *This is the day that the Lord hath made; we will rejoice and be glad in it.*

"Amen to that!" he softly whispered.

Quickly, he prepared a simple breakfast and finished it in no time. Comfortably, he sat at the kitchen table with a cup of coffee, the egg sandwich settling down nicely. Albert recalled the great breakfasts his wife used to make every morning before he left for work in the Triangle. He missed the meals but the morning commutes to the Triangle he in no way missed. Driving Interstate 40 to Research Triangle Park, to him, always felt like some kind of vehicular Russian roulette. He took another sip of coffee, percolated in his old style stove top percolator. It was laced with artificial sweetener from a small pink pack. He smacked his lips in satisfaction. Finished, he rinsed the cup, laid it on the counter, and headed again for his study ready to start another video.

Again sitting in front of the computer, he looked into the camera. The notes for this video, a little older than the previous ones, were hand printed on two sheets of paper. He had not yet had Susanna scan them into digital form into a computer document like she had most of the others. He laid the notes for the second video of the morning out of camera view and started recording.

As a rule, he kept his videos short. Instead of piling all his views into one long video, he decided to space them out over several short ones to avoid overburdening a potential viewer's attention span. He'd seen some prophecy related videos online that were three hours long or even more. He, in no way, wanted to do that. Who'd watch it? Also, he had noticed the long-winded speakers often tended to be a little obsessed—a bit crazy, in fact. He wanted to avoid that perception.

He began. "The question may be raised why God, in the coming Great Tribulation, is taking such terrible vengeance on the world. All the horror, pain, suffering, and death the world will endure is because the world has offended God and his holiness." He scratched his leg hoping the camera didn't pick up the movement. "The very essence of God's nature is absolute holiness. God is holy and he cannot be otherwise, nor can he tolerate the presence of sin. He cannot suspend his holiness or chose not to obey his holy nature. This is something that even God cannot do."

He continued his presentation and, as usual, didn't intend to spend a lot of time on just one video. He glanced at his watch. Time was running out. He reflected that this was true in more ways than one. There were things that bothered him—lots of things. But especially the general indifference to the present world condition, situations that to his biblically trained mind alerted him to the soon beginning of what Jesus called the Great Tribulation. This puzzled him. And the growing antipathy toward Christ and the Gospel deeply troubled him as well. In a way, he could get that some people just may not be interested in it, or didn't want to think about the end-time or the Gospel that can save them from its wrath. But for a growing number of people to be so outright against it alarmed him. It seemed surreal. However, he knew that this too was a sign of the end-time.

He continued. "So many people cannot seem to grasp this concept. It is as if there is some expectation for God to just let unrighteousness go unaddressed, to let things slide, as they say." He raised his right hand like a preacher in a pulpit might do. "Because of his absolute holiness, his wrath against sin and sinners is awesome. Just as now, in the Grace Dispensation of today, his love is so wonderful and mighty. In the Great Tribulation, his wrath will also be mighty. No half measures with God! Sin must be paid for. Either we let Jesus pay for our sins or we pay the price ourselves. *That*, we do not want." He shook his head. "God has given us so much – His Son, His Spirit, His Word and yet the world largely rejects them. And since the world rejects the salvation that pays for its sins, then it must pay for its sins itself."

He sat still for a moment looking solemnly into the camera, giving the recording some seconds he and Susanna would use to fade out. After that, he stopped the recording software and sat back. Deep down he knew he'd be viewed as another Internet crackpot, just another video poster who had an ax to grind. He couldn't let himself worry about that. He had a mission to let people know the coming Tribulation wasn't that far away.

He let out a long breath and looked at his watch. *Where's that girl!* He was curious what was holding up the pretty English major. Hiring her had been such a good decision. Years managing an office taught him how to make good hiring decisions. A half-year ago when he hired her, he did it in spite of the fact she was not a believer. That was okay. He had a job he wanted done and she was well qualified for it. Plus, she was a pleasure to have around. Also, he didn't want to hire someone who'd argue every little point with him.

He recalled the time, about a month after hiring her, he told her she radiated a sense of warm beauty that he found very endearing. After he said it, he felt a little embarrassed. He thought maybe in this PC day and age it was a questionable thing to say to a female employee. In the office, he had known better. But at that time he still had someone to come home to. But she had just smiled and didn't seem troubled by the remark. He was alone now, his wife gone for three years, his kids grown and moved out. Out of loneliness old guys sometimes say dumb things. He hoped she had understood.

He went to the kitchen and got out an ice-cold can of soda from the fridge; break time before making yet another short video. He sat at the table. This time, he planned to talk about the difference between knowledge and faith, how that often they were simply not compatible.

He realized he had forgotten and left the printed copy of the book manuscript along with a notebook he wanted upstairs. The notebook contained some comments he intended to use. They sat on the nightstand beside his bed. After his soda, he'd get them.

As he sipped the beverage, he blankly stared forward and thought back to when he started studying Bible prophecy. He was still a junior in high school at the time and had only been a Christian for a couple of years. He'd read the book of Revelation along with the rest of the Bible, but it seemed an enigma to him, something hopelessly beyond his comprehension. To this day some parts still challenged him. However, it was part of the Bible and he felt it was his duty to read the entire Bible whether he understood it or not. And as he continued to read Revelation time to time, and listen to sermons and teachings on various end-time subjects, along the way a pattern began to emerge and little by little he began to understand more and more. That was many, many years ago and that same process was still at work in him today. Through the years, he made notes and gathered materials until he came to a point he felt he was ready to add to the pool of knowledge about Revelation and the end-time. His biggest discovery, he felt, was that the day of the Rapture and the start of the Tribulation was far, far closer than he had ever imagined in his youth.

Cool against his fingers, the can moist with condensation, the soda was nearly done. He took a final sip and tossed the can into the blue recycle bin in the corner and headed upstairs to get the manuscript and notebook. Going up the stairs, the trip not nearly as brisk as coming down, he noticed again how the years were beginning to show. Inside the bedroom, he stepped across the plush carpet to the nightstand and picked up the book and notebook. Looking at the empty bed he and his wife had shared for so many years, he let go a long breath. *Won't be long now, Elisabeth. We'll be seeing each other soon.*

Elisabeth Lang and he had met in college, both still in their early twenties. She was the tall, slender blond who sat in the back of his business class. She was pretty—pretty in a way that, in his view, was special to women of German descent. A strong jawline supported a finely chiseled narrow face with clear, flawless skin radiating a pinkish hue at the cheeks. That magnificent face, decorated with crystal blue eyes, held an appealing feminine handsomeness that more and more occupied his mind. He found himself never being late for that class. Her lovely smile stayed with him all day.

He finally got the nerve to ask her out. After he got to know her better, he was more captivated by her keen mind and gentle spirit that even her beauty. She was everything he could have wished for in a woman. But most of all she loved God. He had always known that any woman he was going to share his life with would have to truly love God. He knew whoever he married would have to be a long-time Christian, a devout Christian, someone would was active in one or another kind of church ministry—benchwarmers need not apply. His mom had been like that; he knew that had influenced him greatly. His life was faith-centered; certainly, his marriage would have to be as well. He just didn't understand church people who married unbelievers. It puzzled him that people would go into a relationship with such a huge built-in conflict. In his heart, he thanked God for the many years of happiness he and Elisabeth had shared.

He opened the notebook to the page with the comments he jotted down last night. They dealt with how modern education has brainwashed western culture into a kind of pseudo-agnosticism and especially worked to convince the public not to believe the Bible using the vastly different views of science and the Bible concerning the creation of the world as a philosophical battleground. He drew in a deep breath and reflected on how hard it seemed for so many people to accept the fundamental truth that the Bible is right, that God created the heavens and the Earth and did it in six days.

He let out a breath. One day God would end it, too.

He carried the notebook and manuscript back to his study, sat down and opened the notebook again. He jotted down a few notes, put it to one side, and picked up the manuscript. It was still remarkable to him not just for its hefty weight—this being a big book—but the fact that, finally, it was actually done. He started reviewing some pages while he waited on Susanna to arrive, expecting her any time now.

Chapter Three

Susanna stepped into Albert's house and laid her shoulder bag on the red and white striped cushioned chair facing the center of the room. Quietly, she walked across the living room carpet and peeked through the archway opening into the study. There was the man himself.

Albert sat at his desk, an old office style mahogany monstrosity he'd gotten at a used furniture place back before she was born or the world began, she wasn't sure which. Later, after she learned the term *Gog and Magog* from the book of Revelation, she started calling the monstrous desk Mahog. She thought, hoped, Albert was amused. The desk sat just inside and to the right of the archway, the left side of the desk against the lower part of the of the arch. It was well kept by him and had been by whoever owned it before. It had not many scratches and the dark varnish still radiated a rich luster. He claimed it had character; she claimed it had termites—a joke he indulged with a faint smile.

His big, bald head was bent over the pages of the book manuscript. He was so engrossed in it, he didn't notice her. Probably didn't even know she was there, she figured, regardless of the tap at the door. He moved his head and the few straggling hairs on top, holding on for dear life, moved a bit.

Stepping into the study, she chirped, "Okay then!"

"That you, girl?" Finally, he looked up.

"Yeah. Like what you see?"

Albert held up the manuscript. "Hey, you did a great job with this! I would never have done it without you." He took off his glasses. "And I'm glad we finally worked out the title, too."

She smiled. "Just remember that when people contact you for a reference!"

"What do you mean?"

"You know," she replied, "when I start looking for my next job."

"Well, that won't be soon, I hope!" He laid the manuscript down. "We got a lot to do to get this published and soon we'll start on the next book."

"What!" The delight in her voice was unmistakable.

"Yes! Another subject I've been wanting to cover is the Babylonian era of Israel. The things that led to the captivity, the time in Babylon, then coming back to Judah and rebuilding everything. I'm gonna call it, 'To Babylon and Back'. That is, of course, until you kill that title and give it a new one."

On this prophecy book project, they had gone through so many titles they were a blur in Susanna's head. *Time of the End Times* was Albert's original choice. She blue-penciled that immediately. He had suggested *Days of the Apocalypse*. That one made her give him a mean stare; it sounded like some kind of supernatural soap opera. However, *The Revelations of Revelation* was the one she hated the most. A title of her own suggestion, *Eschatology:*

Truth and Reason sounded a little too formal for what Albert was hoping for: reaching average readers with his end-time viewpoints in a manner they could understand. After many more disasters, they finally settled on *Ancient Prophecy, Modern Truth*. Not great but they could both live with it.

"Oh no! *To Babylon and Back* is a great title!" She smiled and looked at him still trying to recover from the surprise, the shock, that she still had a job. She thought about Dora; she thought about Mrs. Mac; she thought about so many others she'd be able to continue to see. It made her smile even more.

"Oh my goodness!" She was careful not to let her excitement lead her into using language he wouldn't appreciate. Even though she didn't share Albert's Christian beliefs, she did respect them and him. "Oh, this is fantastic; thank you!"

"Don't thank me. You did such a fantastic job on this book it only makes sense to use your talents on the next one."

Looking at him, she smiled again and recalled the first time she entered this house and met him:

***

She parked in front of the house and got out of the car. For a moment she stood looking over the well-kept exterior of the domicile. Then, she bounded up the walkway to the door. As she stood before it, for a moment, she hesitated, giving herself a chance to gather herself and prepare mentally for the interview. She really wanted an editing job and hoped this might be it. After opening the storm door, she reached for the knocker and sounded her arrival. The door opened after only a moment. A man she assumed to be Albert invited her inside. Looking over each other, they shook hands and exchanged greetings—polite but non-committal. They were checking each other out.

Speaking with him on the phone a couple of times when they had talked about the job, he sounded nice enough. Standing here now in front of him, she had the opportunity to size him up a little more. He seemed affable. But she knew you couldn't always go by first impressions. The blue jeans and pullover, dark green shirt were clean and in good repair. He was clean shaved and his hair, what little still clung to the sides of his head, was combed neatly. He took care of himself even at home. She thought that spoke well of him.

Standing just inside the living room, she looked it over. Decorated in no particular style, cream-colored carpeting, and plush beige furniture, it was nice and easy on the eyes. To her right was a large archway leading to a room with several bookcases. On the other side of the living room was a staircase with mahogany balustrades going six steps up to a small landing that turned sharply left and continued upward. To the right of the stairs was a short hall ending in an open door, the kitchen visible through that. She liked what she saw; it looked like a nice work environment. She hoped her potential new employer turned out to be as nice as his house. She looked for a piano hoping for a chance to play once in a while. There was none; the only instrument in sight was a large acoustic guitar lying on the couch, a dreadnought, as she understood the body type.

The man gestured toward the archway. "Come on in the study and let's sit down." They stepped under the arch and into the small, cramped room she had noticed before; it evidently served as his study. He walked around the desk and sat behind it. A book lay in the first of two office chairs in front of it; she sat down in the farther of the two.

After a bit of small talk about the weather and her studies at school, they discussed what it was he wanted her to do. He explained the nature of his book, that it was religious and about Bible prophecy. At this point, Susanna felt some concern working on this type of book due to her own convictions, or rather lack of them on the subject. Albert said he wasn't looking for anyone to validate his points; he wanted someone to help him put them together into book form.

"I don't need somebody arguing viewpoints with me," he explained. "I've been working on this project for a long time and I know what I want to say."

She glanced over the small room that was really not much more than an alcove. A TV, its screen blank, sat on top of an old, cherry-stained bookcase that ran the length of the exterior wall to her left. It stood about four feet high. A similar bookcase ran the length of the wall behind her. The old bookcases held (what else) a lot of old books. Above the bookcase behind her, affixed to blue-painted wall, was a large, ornate chart of some type with a lot of images of trumpets, angels, strange animals and others images she didn't recognize. Except for the chart and the Bibles sitting on the shelves and lying on the dark, monstrous desk, the room was refreshing bare of religious paraphernalia. There were many Bibles of all sorts. Several English translations, Greek New Testaments, and she saw at least one Hebrew Bible; *Biblia Hebraica* the spine read. But there was none of the religious 'art deco' she'd encountered so often in Christian homes: religious pictures, angel figurines, that sort of thing. While growing up, she had friends whose families attended church. So many of their homes were filled with religious art and bric-a-brac. She recalled her Aunt Fran, also religious, also sans *religious deco*, who had told her she would rather display her faith in the way she lived rather than objects lying around the house. Susanna wondered if Albert felt the same way.

"Albert, I've told you my position on religion. May I ask, are you what people would consider a very devout Christian?"

"Devout? I try to be. I really want to be. I haven't walked on water or anything like that, but I'm working on it!"

She smiled. "You have a good sense of humor. I think that says a lot about a person."

Albert sat back in his chair, hands folded across his ample belly, the picture of relaxed informality. "Me too." He smiled. "To me, a good sense of humor indicates a person is emotionally well balanced and probably having regular bowel movements."

At that, she laughed out loud.

Albert smiled. "Why don't I bring us in some iced tea, then we can go over what it is I want done on the book." He got up, came around the desk, excusing himself as he passed so closely in front of her, and stepped out of the room. She could hear him moving toward the back of the house and in a moment the sound of glasses tinkling against each other as, she presumed, he got them down from a shelf.

Susanna looked to her right at the book she spotted earlier in the other chair—two chairs, all the cramp study would allow. The title on the cover read *Daniel With Commentary*. The author's name was not familiar to her. She picked it up and began thumbing through the pages; she stopped at a collection of black and white illustrations. They were very dramatic and striking pictures of various strange creatures similar to those on the chart behind her. One was a lion with wings like on a large bird. Another was a bear lying on its side holding something in its mouth. Another one looked like a leopard with four heads and it had four wings as well. The last one was a nondescript monster with lots of horns, giant teeth, and claws. She didn't understand this imagery or the meaning of these creatures. She heard Albert returning and quickly closed the book. But before she could place it back completely, he came in carrying a tray with two glasses of tea and a china plate brimming with what looked like cookies, oatmeal by the delightful aroma.

He glanced at the book. "What do you think of that?" He placed the tray on the desk within easy reach.

"I was looking over some of the drawings." She moved as he made his way back around the desk. "They're very—unusual."

He sat back down. "Yes. In prophetic literature a great use is made of imagery like that. Dispensational teachers use it because the Bible makes use of such imagery. That's one of the points I want to bring out in my book, the reason why such imagery is used." He picked up a cookie from the plate and began munching.

She raised an eyebrow and reached for a cookie. "Well, why *is* such imagery used?" She picked up the glass of tea; the coolness almost bit her fingers.

He took a sip of tea to wash down the bite of cookie. "It's like the saying goes: A picture is worth a thousand words. Seems the good Lord thought so too as he directed Daniel and John in writing their books. The use of strong imagery conveys a lot of information in a striking manner." He took another sip of tea. "And you've got to keep in mind the book of Revelation was written two thousand years ago. The book of Daniel," he pointed to the book in the chair, "long before that. These books had a job to do over thousands of years to many different cultures and generations. The use of this type of imagery made those books relevant to all of them. Each century, each culture could interpret them into a meaning that was relevant to them. It's a great testimony to the brilliance of God's wisdom."

"What about our time?"

Albert gave her a serious look, the most serious she'd seen from him.

"Our time most of all," he replied, his head nodding. "Because the message they convey is for *our* time." The first cookie gone, he reached for another. "It's information like this that I want to offer to the public. That's why I'm doing this book."

Unsure exactly how to take any of this, she just nodded and kept quiet. She wasn't that interested in the subject but she was interested in getting the job. And in an editing job it didn't require that she be interested in or even like the subject matter. It was important, at least to her, that she liked the person she'd be working with and she thought she'd like Albert. It wasn't official just yet but she knew he'd offer her the job and she knew she'd take it.

"A good example," Albert continued, "are the prophecy charts drawn by Reverend Clarence Larkin." He pointed to the chart on the wall. "That one is his *Book Of Revelation* chart. The entire book of Revelation is portrayed there. He was very talented and insightful to be able to do that. It required an intense understanding of the book."

"Really," Susanna said, more out of politeness than real interest.

"Yes. I don't agree with every point, and that's something I also want to deal with in the book. But it's a work of real brilliance." He nodded.

The phone rang. He excused himself and picked it up and listened to whoever it was. Susanna sat waiting, eating another of the oatmeal cookies, which she thought were really, really good, the cinnamon unmistakable.

***

Albert told her, "I've already been doing some video recording this morning." He nodded toward the camera and monitor, the large desktop computer set up on a computer stand at a right angle to the desk. "I still haven't uploaded anything yet. I'll need you to help me with that."

"Yeah, be glad to," she said absently, still taking in the good news. "Let me make us some tea and we'll get started."

She went into the kitchen, got the kettle, filled it halfway and put it on the stove. While she waited for the water to boil, she looked around for some of those little candy bars she knew he kept stashed. She found them in the drawer right of the sink and helped herself to one. Finished with that, the water starting to boil, she got down two cups from the cupboard and fished two teabags from the box.

Looking out the window, she loudly said, "It's such a beautiful day! I should have stood you up!" She placed the cups on the counter and the teabags in the cups. "But I'm glad I didn't now that I know I've still got a job!"

She started pouring the water and from the other room, she heard him saying, "Because knowledge is the enemy of faith," and realized he'd already begun recording again. She put down the kettle and grimaced, embarrassed that she'd been shouting while he was recording.

She carried the two cups into the living room and stood in the archway. She waited as Albert looked into the camera and continued speaking. She stood quietly, knowing he kept his videos short.

A noise came from across the street. The kids she'd seen playing when she came in had burst into a fit of gleeful laughter. Instinctively, she glanced over her shoulder out the large bay window. Suddenly, the laughter stopped—not died down, not faded but instantly stopped as if someone had flipped a switch. Through the window, she saw nothing unusual, but from this angle, she could not see the yard directly across the street. Turning back to Albert, her eyes widened and her mouth parted. He wasn't there! A second ago, he was sitting at the desk and now he was gone.

She stepped into the study and looked around. He wasn't there; he just wasn't there. She had glanced away only for a second; there was no other way out of the room and he couldn't have walked by without bumping into her. He was gone! Just plain gone! She stepped closer and looked at his chair. There on the floor lay some clothes. She put the cups down on the top of Mahog and leaned forward. Yes! These were the clothes he'd been wearing just a few seconds ago, shoes and all. Now they were on the floor, shoelaces still tied and the clothes, as far as she could tell, still all buttoned as if he had simply disappeared right out of them.

Chapter Four

Patrol Officer Tim Jordan looked at the distant horizon of the green, verdant forest beneath the blue sky. This town with its many homes and businesses was carved out of a vast woodland covering the central part of the state. However beautiful the landscape, it was the road that snaked from the center of that distant point that occupied his attention. The gap in the trees, the road cut through the forest, seemed to spew forth cars like a volcano expelling rocks.

He sat and watched, literally, as the world went by—mostly on four wheels. Happens a lot to a traffic officer. He sat behind the wheel of his patrol car—parked on the traffic island between the lanes—and kept an eye on the cars traversing east and west on the two-lane road. The few pedestrians walking toward the bus stop in front of the shopping center and around the shops were all behaving nicely; no jaywalking or skateboarding.

He wondered how many more years he'd be doing this, if maybe he'd move to another division of the department, maybe investigations. It was that kind of morning; the kind that made you think about your future. The kind of morning you have after you get a call announcing that a huge chunk of your future had just gone down the drain.

Sweet-tater. That's the term of endearment Candace used for him when they first got together, and for some time remained her pet name for him. But after only three months of engagement so much of the affection seemed to have evaporated under the strain of the upcoming responsibilities. They both thought about and discussed the non-stop flow of monthly bills, the constant burden of upkeep on a home, the conscious effort they would have to make to keep the relationship *fresh*. It all took its toll; all the planning, and it seemed to him overplanning, took so much of the joy out of the engagement. Over such a short time, the girl who had called him *Sweet-tater* had become little more than an acquaintance. And she came to never, ever call him *Sweet-tater* anymore—not for weeks. To Tim, the prospect of marriage to Candace came to seem like an investment that demanded more and more capital and offered less and less of a return. Marriage is a big responsibility and all that responsibility is a heavy price to pay for that *something* you hope to find in someone, that *something* that so many had informed both of them that is so fleeting.

A silver SUV rolled past him at a pretty good clip but not bad enough for him to give chase. It was followed by a sparkling blue small pickup keeping pace.

And the call he received yesterday from her brother—she couldn't even be bothered to call herself—letting him know she'd changed her mind and would send the ring back to him, was as impersonal as if they were canceling a pizza order. Maybe the idea of marrying a police officer didn't appeal to her after all. It was a pity he had to think about such bad news on a beautiful morning like this. *Well, it's not the end of the world*, he told himself and adjusted his sunglasses.

He had been parked on *station,* the traffic island in front of the shopping center, monitoring traffic for the last two hours. Traffic was flowing smoothly and thankfully there were no accidents yet. Usually, if there were going to be any they would have happened by now. By this time of the morning, most people were well on their way to work. He'd give it another few minutes and then start patrolling.

A yellow convertible, with some very nice mag wheels, rolled by. Narrowly, he eyed it. He was getting bored.

The car seat was getting a little warm against his back. The vinyl seats of the patrol car—the seats are made of vinyl so that the blood and vomit donated by some of its less *together* passengers wouldn't stain them—tended to get hot if you sat on them too long. The back of his black uniform was starting to get a little moist. He leaned forward to let a little air cool his back.

Traffic was thinning out now. It was time to start patrolling. He hesitated a moment and let a station wagon get out of the way. He whispered, "Okay, let's roll." His declaration was short lived. Just as he started the engine and was about to put the car into gear, suddenly, there was a crash directly ahead. He looked straight up the road and there he saw the station wagon that just past him about a hundred feet ahead. It had just collided with a utility pole. He hit the light array switch and pulled into traffic. After only a few seconds, he pulled behind the vehicle and parked, lights still swirling.

Out of the car, he walked to the driver's side window. He stopped dead in his tracks, stunned to see no one behind the wheel. He looked through the other window and saw no one in the backseat either. If anyone had gotten out of the car he would have seen it. He never lost eye contact with the vehicle since he pulled off the median and got there. He pulled on the handle of the driver's door to get a better look inside. The car was locked.

He walked around the car and tried the door handle there. It was locked, too. Through the passenger's side window, he could see the interior was clean and neat except for a bunch of clothes lying on the driver's side floorboard along with a pair of shoes. Some garments were also on the seat where the driver should have been sitting. No one was there—just clothes.

The station wagon was well off the road sitting on a grassy lawn alongside a convenience store; the damage to the car was not that bad. The pole it hit stood unharmed some feet away from the road. Traffic was passing the scene of the accident unimpeded and there was no immediate need for a tow-truck. He stood beside the vehicle dumbfounded wondering what had become of the driver. He stepped behind the wagon to call in the license plate and start a call-for-service with dispatch.

After stepping behind the vehicle, from this angle of view, he spotted yet another accident up ahead at a spot where the road curved to the left. A red sedan sat on an embankment to the right beside a small group of trees. It was obvious the car had run off the road and up the embankment. He wondered if anyone was hurt and drove over. Pulling off the road and behind the red sedan, he got out and went to the driver's side window. Like with the station wagon, no one was there. The driver's side window was rolled down. He opened the door. Again he found a bunch of empty clothes. He laid his hand on the seat. It was still warm. It was the kind of warmth that came from body heat—as if someone had been in this seat just seconds ago.

He looked further up the road. From his vantage point he could see at least seven vehicles strewn there, sitting in various positions to the side of the road or on the median. He wondered how many of them had missing drivers.

Needing help with this many cars, he reached for the radio handset clipped to his shoulder strap. He pressed the push-to-talk button. "Unit 709." He waited for an acknowledgment. Several long seconds passed. Again, he broadcast his unit number.

A harried voice came back. "Unit 709 standby." The familiar split-second radio hash that follows a hurried broadcast termination followed this.

He wondered what was going on that they couldn't attend to his call just now. Had there been a disaster somewhere and they were all handling emergency calls? If so, why had he not heard the calls on his radio?

None of the cars were causing any real traffic problems except for the rubbernecking of the passing motorists. He decided to give dispatch a few minutes to take care of whatever it was they were dealing with. In the meantime, he'd take a look at some of the other cars.

The closest, a black minivan, was near enough that he just walked to it. Except for the ninety-degree angle at which it sat, it seemed almost purposely pulled to the side of the road.

At the driver's side door, he repeated his procedure of the previous two cars and tried the door. It opened and he looked in. As he expected—and on some level dreaded—he saw clothes lying on the empty seat and floorboard.

"Did you see what happened to her!"

Startled by the voice, totally caught off guard at hearing it, he instinctively moved his right hand to his gun. He leaned down a little more and saw a teenage boy sitting in the passenger seat. He just simply had not noticed him there.

Angry with himself for not seeing him right away, he reminded himself that being distracted as he was by the strange circumstances may have been the reason for it, but it was not an excuse for bad police procedure. And bad police procedure was how active officers sometimes became permanently inactive officers.

"What's that you said?" He looked at the boy, mid-teens at the most.

His voice shook. "Did you see what happened to my mom?"

Tim shook his head. "Young man, tell me what happened here." He made himself speak calmly. Three years as a police officer had taught him to do that. But he was feeling anything but calm. He wanted an answer to this mystery and hoped this kid could provide it. But the boy's question did not promise answers.

The slim young man with thick, black curly hair was still buckled into his seat. To Tim, the kid looked about sixteen, the same age he was when he decided on a career in law enforcement eight years ago now. "Mom was taking me to the mall. We were just sitting here riding along when suddenly she just wasn't there anymore." He waved his hands like he was fanning a fire. "I mean one minute she was sitting there and then poof! She was gone, man!"

Tim cocked his head to one side and listened to the words the kid spoke. But they just didn't seem to register; it was as though his mind was incapable of accepting their implication.

"The van started to veer toward the median," the kid continued. "I was afraid it would jump over into the other lane. I grabbed the steering wheel and turned it hard to the right. It came back over and ran off the road." He rubbed his face. "It hit really hard and knocked the engine off."

The kid was in mild shock but not injured; he was just shaken up. Looking down the road at all the other stopped cars, presumably, with empty driver's seats, Tim Jordan was beginning to feel a little shaken up himself.

He turned again to the kid. "Young man, quite frankly, I don't know what's going on." He pointed down the road. "You don't seem to be injured and I need to check out these other cars." The kid stared at him with a look of mild panic.

"You got your license yet? Can you drive?" The kid shook his head. "Why don't you call someone to come get you and the car. As for your mom, go ahead and call that into the police station. I'll look around when I get the chance but I need to see what's going on with these other cars right now."

"Look around!" The kid blurted out the words as if the concept was absolutely brilliant. "Yes, I'm gonna get out and look around!" He undid his seat belt.

"Well...that's fine. Just stay out of the road and—"

Before he could finish his safety warning, the kid suddenly pulled on the door handle and sprang out, shouting, "Mom!" He drew a deep breath and yelled, *"Mommmm!"*

Tim left him to his search and, as the kid walked into the nearby trees calling for his mom, he, for some reason, thought of Don Quixote.

He reached for his radio handset to try again then stopped. Instead, he pulled his phone out of his shirt pocket and began punching numbers. In a moment, a lady's voice answered.

"Hey Rosa, what's going on down there?"

Rosa, a forty-something brunette, was one of the police records department clerks. She, like the other clerks, often helped in the dispatch room when someone was out for the day or gone to lunch.

"It's a madhouse in here right now."

The fact that she had answered the records department phone let Tim know she wasn't at this time helping out in dispatch.

"Why? What's going on?"

"They're getting calls from all over town about people disappearing. I don't mean missing person kind of thing but people literately disappearing into thin air. Calls keep coming in from all over town. We're all on standby while they try and figure out what's going on."

"Yeah, I got that kind of thing going on here. I couldn't get anybody to take my call for service."

"All the patrol officers are in the same situation; they're all dealing with a lot of sudden disappearances. With all the phone calls pouring in nobody's available to take radio calls except in a major incident; and even a lot of phone calls aren't getting answered right now with the high call volume. Maybe when things calm down a bit you guys can get through, but right now it's just too crazy in here to take traffic calls. They got people on the phone screaming and crying. Some of 'em babbling on about the Rapture."

At the mention of that word, his skin tingled.

"Jordan, I gotta go."

"Yeah, I'll see you later when I report in."

He put the phone back in his shirt pocket and stared straight ahead a moment. Shaking his head, he walked to his car, got in and drove away to check on the other stopped vehicles.

He parked behind a red sedan and repeated a procedure that had become all too familiar all too fast. This one was totally empty. Others he checked were all either empty or missing the driver. The abandoned passengers in the occupied vehicles sat in a state ranging from calm denial to outright hysteria. Also, there were other cars safely pulled to the side of the road whose drivers were screaming or yelling about passengers who had disappeared into thin air. And the more cars he checked the more cars he saw down the road. They were also sitting to the sides of the road, with one or two actually in the road. Finally, he just gave up checking on them altogether and drove away confused and worried—very, very worried.

Chapter Five

Albert's clothes were on the floor. That's all. Just some clothes lying on the floor. How could something so innocuous, if untidy, be so disturbing? That question might have been a puzzle to others, but to someone who had worked so long and so hard on a book about end-time prophecy, it held a portent of ominous speculation—like an omen.

A thought, a certain word, tried to form in her mind; it was an idea that made her skin crawl. She shook her head and refused to give it access. It was a word that had become an anthem to some and a joke to others, parodied on TV and in films. This *thought* was something she just wouldn't give in to.

Abandoning the cups of tea, Susanna turned away from the desk and faced the living room frantically looking around. She needed to find Albert and get him to explain this. She *had* to find him; she felt like maybe her sanity depended on it. Her search, she decided, would begin upstairs.

Out of the study, she left that unsettling pile of clothes behind—clothes removed but not undone or unbuttoned, belt still fastened and shoes still tied. She rushed across the living room, toward the stairs, in a flash, her small, sneaker-clad feet made a soft tattoo against the carpeted steps as she ran up. Who knows? Maybe he did slip past her and she had just zoned out for a moment and didn't notice—didn't notice a six-foot tall, two-hundred-pound man walking past her. It occurred to her that denial was setting in. She met that idea with more denial.

After knocking on the bedroom door, she waited for a reply. A few moments passed and she cracked the door open a bit and peeked in. She didn't see him there.

"Albert!"

There was no reply. Something told her there would never, ever be a reply. She ignored that thought, denial doing its job.

She came out of the bedroom and searched the rest of the upstairs including the other two bedrooms and hall closet. Nothing. She came back downstairs and thoroughly searched the rest of the house. Back in the study, she stood staring at nothing, hoping that Albert would crawl out from under the desk and yell, "Surprise!" But she knew that wasn't going to happen. Albert was a mature, intelligent man not given to childish pranks. She knew he wasn't under the desk and, no doubt, she would have heard him moving around anyway.

That *thought*, that impossible *thought* once again tried to insinuate itself upon her mind. She pressed her hands against her head and again denied it access; she denied its possibility. She'd been entrenched in this prophetic line of study for half a year now and had practically written the book for Albert, a book on the end-time and the Rapture. She knew the book like the back of her hand.

In light of that, not to give the implication of a man suddenly disappearing almost in front of her eyes its due recognition was, perhaps, an illogical thing to do, but still she did just that. She reminded herself, *People do not just disappear into thin air!*

She again looked at the clothes lying on the floor. To her, they seemed like a tangle of snakes ready to strike. Denial was still holding fast and she now gave it all the encouragement she could. Again, she turned from the desk.

There was no basement to search, so she went out the back door and frantically walked around the yard, not forgetting to check inside the brown and white, barn-shaped lawn shed. There were no trees on this property. If there had been, she would have climbed each one in her ever-growing desperation to find the missing man. She needed to see him; denial could only do so much. She wanted visible, tangible evidence that what she feared had happened had not actually happened. She walked around the side of the house; he wasn't there either.

She cut across the lawn and stepped onto the sidewalk and headed back in the direction in which she had earlier taken her walk. She looked to her left at the other side of Albert's house and lawn—no one there either.

The house next door to Albert's was a simple wood frame place stained in dark walnut. An old lady lived there alone. She looked past the empty side yard into the backyard. He wasn't there; only old Mrs. Kent sitting in a lawn chair fanning herself with a magazine.

"Hey, Mrs. Kent!" She tried to sound calm, tried really hard, but wasn't doing a very good job of it.

The old, white-haired lady wearing a simple blue dress looked over. As usual, her face was unsmiling; she was not the friendliest of neighbors.

"You seen Albert in the past few minutes?"

"Naw." She shook her head. T'aint seen him all mornin'."

Susanna stood still for a moment. "Okay, thanks. Uh.., if you *do* see him please tell him I'm looking for him."

The old lady nodded. "Wha' jor name, girl?"

"Susanna." She smiled but it took some effort.

Again, Mrs. Kent nodded. She fanned herself again even though it wasn't all that hot.

"Okay, bye Mrs. Kent."

No farewell was returned. The old lady looked away and stared toward the back of the yard, waiting for this girl to go away and leave her alone.

Susanna turned around and looked across the street at the blue split-level directly ahead and the side yard where the kids had been playing *Star Wars*. The Davidson house faced Tomato Lane that intersected with Cucumber Street, the street Albert's house faced. The Davidson house sat right at the corner of the T-bone intersection.

Mrs. Davidson was standing on the lawn looking down at the plastic lightsabers and empty clothes and shoes that lay abandoned over the yard and sidewalk in neat individual piles—including what looked like a white Princess Leia costume. Susanna's eyes widened. This further confirmation of what she thought may have happened, that which she so vigorously denied, was terrifying. *Didn't Albert say that innocent children would go in the Rap*—. She shut her eyes and stopped that word, that dreadful word, from sounding in her mind.

She turned left and again started down the street, her feet pounding against the sidewalk furiously. The terror creeping over her gave her small feet impetus. She continued down the block looking for someone her unconscious mind kept telling her she would never see again. Her blood ran cold. Denial was not doing its job.

Her phone rang. She drew it out of her pocket and saw her mother's ID on the screen.

"Yes, mother," she answered flatly.

Her mother's voice was a little shaky. "I've been looking all over for your Aunt Fran and I can't find her anywhere! And the strangest thing happened. I found a pile of clothes on the floor in the spare room; it was the clothes she'd been wearing when I saw her this morning."

Susanna's blood ran even colder. "What!"

"We were going out for lunch later and I wanted to ask her if she wanted to go to that new Thai place." Her mom's breath puffed against the phone speaker. "You know how she loves Asian food." She chuckled.

"Yeah, yeah." She heard the tension in her voice but reminded herself this was her mom. She tried to maintain what little patience, what little control, she had left. But the whole world, her whole life, had just suddenly taken a terrifying turn and Asian cuisine was not all that important at the moment.

"I just don't know where she could possibly be!"

Susanna took a deep breath. "Mom, I'm sure it's all right. I'm sure she's fine." She was sure of no such thing.

"You really think so?"

"Yeah. Listen, I'm gonna come over as soon as I can. I don't have much work here today and I'll finish up in a little while. We'll look for her together." Susanna's hand gripped the rectangular frame of her smartphone so tightly the plastic was crinkling under the pressure. "It's gonna be fine; it's gonna be just fine." Oh how desperately she wished she could actually believe that.

And of course, after the Rapture, the Tribulation immediately begins with—. She shut her eyes and audibly spat, *"No!"*

cutting off the thought, the recollection of something Albert had said, not allowing it completion.

Her mom's shocked voice came over the phone. "What!"

"Sorry, mom, sorry. Uh, a big dog was about to jump up on me, that's all."

"Oh."

"Mom, I've got something to do just now. But just wait till I get there and we'll see what's going on. Might take a little while but I'll be there as soon as I can. Okay?"

"Yes, dear."

"And don't worry about Aunt Fran; I'm sure she's fine and just stepped out for some reason." She and her mom exchanged farewells and she put the phone back in her pocket.

At the house past Mrs. Kent's, no one was in the yard. She had no definite plan of action but thought she'd just start her inquiries with people standing outside, maybe knock on doors later if necessary. She glanced back at the blue split-level and frowned. She wondered where the Davidson children were, wondered if they had gone in the Rap—. There was that word again! There was that thought she refused to entertain. In the pit of her stomach, a hard knot was forming.

She stood still and took a deep breath. *I wonder where he is?* She looked around hoping to spot him somewhere—anywhere. Perhaps, he was taking a walk of his own and went down one of the side streets that extended off this one. *He likes to take walks! He told me so himself. He just usually waits till evening around sundown so the sun doesn't shine down on his bald head too much.* She wondered what route he took. She wondered why she had never bothered to ask him which way he usually went. That kind of information could be important. So why hadn't she ever asked?

She resumed walking, her feet now coming down hard on the sidewalk, so hard that if she had not been so preoccupied she might have felt some real discomfort. But for now, she only felt the need to hurry. Hurry, hurry, hurry!

***

Sunshine poured through the open window and brightly illuminated Mrs. Mac's whole kitchen. The gentle breeze wafting in was comfortably warm. It was a good time to take Buddy for a walk. The fat beagle sitting beside her on the immaculate linoleum floor looked up at her and whined as if to confirm her astute conclusion. Mrs. Mac sat at the kitchen table staring at the bright screen of the laptop computer in front of her. The world's favorite social network displayed some all-important messages of who's feeling how and doing what and sharing pictures of dogs, cats, and grandkids in an overabundance of mendacity.

She read a post from her *friend*, Sally. A friend she had never laid eyes on: 'Ever had almond milk? Discovered it a couple of weeks ago at the market. I thought I'd try it as an alternative to regular milk and soy milk (which I don't really care for) to save on some carbs and sugar. I didn't know anything about it and a lady there, also shopping, helped me to understand what it was. The almond milk I got was the store brand, the sugar-free version. It has less than one gram of carbs and zero grams of sugar per one cup serving. That's pretty low. It tasted awful at first but after I put some artificial sweetener in it, it was actually not bad and works well on cereal. I still use regular two percent milk sometimes but I may use this almond milk more. We'll see.'

How people lived in the past without such valuable information was hard to understand. She smiled and was glad that most of the time she contained her sarcasm when around 'real' friends, people she actually knew and that actually knew and cared for her.

She looked over a post she had written the day before: 'Great morning yesterday! About 8 a.m. Buddy and I stepped out onto the steps to go walking. The day was just totally a pleasant surprise. It was sunny but not too hot; in fact, the temp was very comfortable. Humidity was up but not oppressive. And I could smell honeysuckle in the air. Oh, more like this please!' A few 'likes' were registered and in the comments were agreements and a happy-face icon or two.

The beagle whined again and she looked down into Buddy's big, beautiful brown eyes, mascara-like outlines adding color and depth to an already handsome face. She said to the fat beagle, "Okay, buddy, I know it's walking time; just give me a minute." She reached down and scratched the top of his velvety head. He leaned his head back to receive the full benefit of the nice massage. She cheerfully asked her beloved companion, "Did you like those bones last night? Huh?"

Last night she had fixed lamb chops. It was the first time in a long time, maybe a couple of years, she had done so. They were good but a little bonier than she liked. She wasn't all that experienced with lamb. Growing up in a small southern town it was ham, chicken, (especially chicken) and other favorites of the south she'd grown up cooking and eating. There wasn't much around in the way of lamb. The cuts she had, she prepared the same way she did large pork chops. She didn't know for sure if the bony chuck chops were a good cut of lamb or not. But Buddy had liked the bones just fine. However, she thought it might be awhile before doing lamb chops again. She cooked them to get more protein in her diet and reduce her carb intake a little. Oh, how she loved carbs! But not the effect they had on her blood sugar.

She scratched Buddy's head again. "You're a good puppy! I love you." She closed the computer lid, shutting off the World Wide Web. It was time to spend some quality time with her *real* friend. The world could wait.

She got up and Buddy followed her to the front door. She picked up a pair of sunglasses from the hall table and put them in her shirt pocket. Then, she got the leash from the table and hooked him up. The newspaper she had picked up when Susanna walked by lay beside it unopened. She opened the door and stepped out into the beautiful morning.

The first sensation was the pleasant breeze against her face that carried again that scent of honeysuckle. It was welcome as usual. Next was the bright sunlight striking her eyes as she stepped out from under the small roof over the step at her door. She pulled the sunglasses from her pocket and hurriedly put them on. She and Buddy stepped along the walkway leading to the sidewalk. Buddy's nose was already scanning the ground, his head swaying side to side as they walked.

Often, she walked Buddy at night when the heat wasn't so taxing on him. Plus, it's nice to walk at night and get a little solitude, just her and her Buddy. One night last week as she walked him at around nine, she noticed a very bright star about 20° above the horizon north-northwest. Later, after they had gotten home, she did a web search and found out it was Venus. She read a bit and then explained to Buddy, "It says here that it's the brightest object in the sky except for the sun and moon." She briskly rubbed his long ears. "Just FYI, don't call it in as a UFO. Says here that's already been done plenty of times."

Buddy stared at her lovingly.

Today, with the temperature so mild, she knew ambient heat wouldn't be a problem. However, she'd have to make sure to keep an eye on him in case the sun shining against the thick, black fur covering his back overheated him. That could happen even on a moderate day.

Before they reached the sidewalk, Buddy suddenly stepped to the right and tugged hard on the leash. Mrs. Mac looked at him and saw that he was trying to walk across the lawn and over to Susanna who was again coming down the sidewalk. She was a little surprised seeing her again so shortly after this morning's walk.

She smiled. "Hello! Didn't expect to see you out again so soon."

Without ceremony, Susanna stopped and almost demanded, "Mrs. Mac, have you seen Albert!"

Hearing young Susanna speak so abruptly, with such a harsh, unsmiling demeanor—all so uncharacteristic of her—Mrs. Mac didn't know what to think.

"Well, no, dear. Is anything the matter?"

"No. No. I'm just looking for him."

Without a word, she marched on without giving her a second look and ignoring Buddy altogether—something she had never done before, always having a kind word for him and time to kneel down and affectionately scratch the side of the beagle's big belly.

Puzzled, Mrs. Mac stared at her as she stormed away, moving with a determination she had never before seen in her.

She led Buddy to the sidewalk and they turned left and started walking toward Coffee Lane, the street Susanna had walked past just a little while earlier and now hurried past again. Her back was turned to her; it seemed, in more ways than one. She hoped Susanna was all right.

Mrs. Mac enjoyed these walks, and Buddy lived for them. His short beagle legs, the perfect length for allowing his highly sensitive nose easy access to the ground, moved quickly back and forth with a grace that rivaled ballet—at least in Mrs. Mac's humble opinion. His face bowed to the ground, his head quickly jutting back and forth maneuvering that long nose (a precision instrument) around, allowing it to scan the sidewalk and the edges of the lawns for anything of interest, he sniffed vigorously. His enthusiasm was unmistakable.

Chapter Six

Right before his eyes! It happened right before his eyes! The pile of clothes on the floor that his wife Lindsey wore a few seconds ago confirmed the reality of what he had just witnessed. Something she'd warned him about a thousand times had finally come to pass! He knew it as soon as it happened! He knew what it was! As he stood in the living room looking down at those empty clothes, those blasted empty clothes, dread filled his belly like a gut full of frigid ice.

The day had started out normally at the Doug and Lindsey Harper house. He got up at the usual time. Today, it really wasn't necessary for him to get up early; it was his morning off from the paint store where he was the assistant manager; Buckley Davidson was the manager, owner, and only other employee. But old habits die hard and his body was used to getting up at this time, trained to do it by so many years of practice. He was awake now and he knew he'd not be going back to sleep. Lying there, just staring up at the ceiling, was something he hated. So he got up, slipped a robe over his green pajamas and walked into the kitchen.

Lindsey had preceded him there by a good ten minutes and already had the coffee started, no doubt one of the gourmet blends she loved so well; she abhorred the taste of the profane brands sold to the masses. Those common coffee blends with familiar names and much lower prices. The coffee now percolating had been ordered over the Internet from some specialty coffee website and certainly did not come from some lowly supermarket. To Doug, it all just tasted like coffee no matter where it came from. However, that little opinion he kept to himself. Years of marriage had taught him well.

His plans for the morning were simple: surf the web for rare coin bargains (not coffee) and take his sweet time reading the morning paper. Soon they were sitting down to a breakfast of French toast and melon balls with some oatmeal on the side; it was the instant kind but still good.

She brought him a steaming cup of coffee; it smelled like that mocha something or other she liked so much. He picked it up careful not to let any spill onto his lap. Memories of past mishaps had also trained him well. He took his time sipping it. There was no rush, no need to hurry like the other mornings of the workweek. He didn't have to be at work until noon. He and Lindsey could take their time over breakfast and spend some time together, something they always enjoyed, even after all these years of marriage.

He picked up the knife and sliced off a bit of French toast and held it before him on his fork. She glanced at him as he brought the fork to his mouth and chewed on the bite slowly. After fifteen years of marriage, she was still amused at how he ate a piece of bread coated with egg, like it was sirloin steak. He even used a steak knife for the occasion. She said nothing. Years of marriage had trained her well, too.

And after fifteen years there was no need for a lot of conversation, no need for a lot of back and forth. They were comfortable—comfortable with each other and the life they pleasantly shared. Neither were romantics. Never had been even when they were dating. Like so many people do, they somehow just drifted together and, thankfully, managed to stay together. They were happy. What else is there?

The only sticking point between them was religion. She had it; he didn't. And she very much wanted him to have it so he'd be ready for the Rapture. She had found religion about seven years before. At that time she had gone out west to Texas to visit her sister, Nannette, whom everyone called Nana, for a couple of weeks. She made this trip alone while he stayed back and worked. Her sister was married to a fundamentalist pastor whose church was having a revival for one of the weeks she was there. To be polite to her brother-in-law, she went to the services. Toward the end of the revival, after five nights of sitting under the preaching of a young gifted speaker, the message had gotten through. One night when the evangelist gave the invitation to come forward, to her sister's delight, Lindsey stood up and walked down the aisle. Seven years passed and she had never looked back.

Over those years Lindsey developed an interest in Bible prophecy and, in fact, became fairly proficient in the subject. She started out by watching a few televangelists who specialized in end-time prophecy, then began reading a lot of books. Often, at one neighborhood event or another (similar to the upcoming cookout at Mrs. Mac's), she had spoken to Albert on the subject, asking questions and giving opinions on modern global events and social trends. Above all things she believed fervently in the closeness of the Rapture. "Any time now," she would often say.

***

House after house, yard after yard, there was no sign of Albert. After leaving Mrs. Mac and Buddy, Susanna had gone all the way down to the end of Cucumber Street and stood looking at the two-lane blacktop of Collins Road for the second time that morning. Undecided what to do, she stood still, trying to decide if she should walk up and down this road looking for him.

The land on the opposite side of Collins Road was not developed. It was bordered on one side by the houses of Cloverdale and on the other by forestland owned by the county and not open to development, one of the big attractions for living in Cloverdale. The last thing the people living in this planned housing development wanted was for someone to come along and build another planned housing development nearby. To their way of thinking when the forest land that preceded Cloverdale had been ripped up by bulldozers and backhoes, felling trees and evicting wildlife to make room for this neighborhood, that made *them* interlopers enough against nature and no more need apply, thanks and good day.

There was no sidewalk on either side of Collins road. It was essentially a lonely country lane running by a developed neighborhood, or at least half a country lane with houses on one side.

Susanna shook her head; searching this road was not a good investment of time and effort. Albert surely wouldn't take a walk on a road without sidewalks when street after street in the neighborhood had them. She crossed to the other side of the road and started working her way back up Cucumber Street.

***

Time after time Lindsey had warned Doug of the approaching event and the harsh judgments it represented to the world, the unspeakable horrors coming upon a doomed planet. Doug would listen politely for a minute and then change the subject. She didn't shove the subject down his throat; she didn't think that it should become a problem in their marriage. But she didn't let him forget about it either. "One day honey, I'm gonna be gone," she'd say. "I want you to be with me."

He would look at her with a solemn stare.

But this morning she really never got the chance to bring it up.

After breakfast, Doug headed for the computer in the small room just off the kitchen. It was a spare room that he had converted into a kind of den for himself. He was glad he had plenty of time to indulge his hobby of online coin shopping. Who knows, he might get lucky today and come across a real find!

Doug pulled the chair back from the small computer table and sat down. Switching on the desktop CPU, the monitor lit up and soon displayed a famous software manufacturer's logo as the machine booted up. While he waited, he glanced at the shelf holding the collection of thin, cardboard slats with small pockets cut into them. They held the coins he had stuffed into them over the years. He hoped he could add to that collection today.

After a long while of looking over several coin websites and typing responses to the comments left on his own website, Doug's Coin Page, he wanted some more coffee. He came out of the den and back into the kitchen and got a cup from the cupboard. The coffee maker had kept Lindsey's coffee hot and smelling good. As he filled the cup, he turned and looked out the open kitchen door into the living room. Lindsey stood beside the front door looking at a picture on the wall to the right. She reached out as if to straighten it.

He stepped into the living room and looked at her as he took a big sip of the mocha blend. She reached up and moved the picture a little to the left. Then, she disappeared into thin air. He stood there blinking, staring at the empty space his wife had occupied only a second before.

"Girl!" That's what he had always called her. Not 'babe' not 'honey' but simply *Girl*. He stood frozen and glared wide-eyed around the empty room, the coffee in his shaking hand splashing onto Lindsey's immaculate floor. Somewhere in the back of his mind, he thought, *I must remember to clean that up! She doesn't like it when I made spills on the new hardwood.* But he knew that was not going to be a problem now. His problem now was how he was going to live without her. Again he shouted, "Girl!" He drew in a ragged breath. "*Girl!*" this time screaming at the top of his lungs.

The cup fell from his hand and smashed against the new hardwood floor. He kept screaming for her—over and over and over. He put his hands on each side of his head and screamed and screamed until his throat was raw.

Then he stopped. He just stopped and stared and did nothing. He remained like that for a long time, standing, staring, eyes bulging, mouth gaping. Then, slowly, his eyes and mouth resumed normal shape; his face settled into a cold blankness. There was no look of terror, no look whatsoever. His face was as blank as his mind.

Somewhere in the dim recesses of his now ruined mind, his subconscious recalled something he saw in a documentary about mental disorders, a condition called dissociative state, something about how the mind was only able to take but so much before it broke down and gave up. Like when a mind is faced with a situation it simply cannot conceive of or accept, it could actually just stop working. It could just stop normal functions and a person could just continue on in a kind of automatic fashion—*automatism* was the word the TV program used.

He walked back into the kitchen and stepped over to the plastic basket beside the sink where the breakfast dishes Lindsey had washed earlier stood drying. She was always so fastidious about the washing up. She didn't leave them until later like Doug did sometimes. Oh, so much like a man. No, no, she'd make sure, blessed sure, they were clean like she made sure her house was clean. Lindsey was a great housekeeper, a great cook, a great companion and he was so very, very lucky to have her. In fact, he just wouldn't know what he'd do without her. *Where is she?* He wondered. *I don't know where she could be.*

He stood in front of the basket and looked down. There was the steak knife he ate breakfast with—the wonderful breakfast Lindsay had prepared for him. He wondered what she would fix for breakfast tomorrow. His eyes widened as a cruel memory seeped through the fog of his mind. There would be no breakfast from Lindsay tomorrow—there would be no Lindsey tomorrow. He reached out a trembling hand and picked up the steak knife, and brought the point close to his eyes. He stared at it a long time.

***

After having him for two years, walking Buddy was still the high point of Mrs. Mac's day. She was never tired of her beagle's antics: his constant sniffing of the ground even if it did slow their daily walks sometimes to a crawl, his sudden spurts to hurry and catch up to a scent or his sudden stops to take his sweet time sampling a spot of interest. He'd stand with his head bowed taking in deep breaths that made a clutching sound in his throat. Sometimes he would lick the spot to get an even better sample of the scent he followed. That's what a beagle is all about. And his firm determination that no rabbits would be safe on his watch was something she accepted and understood. He was a hundred percent beagle; he knew it and so did she. She looked down at him as he trotted and sniffed and smiled.

After passing several houses, Mrs. Mac and Buddy approached Doug and Lindsey's place. Mrs. Mac thought this was as good a time as any to tell them about the cookout she had planned for Saturday. They turned onto the walkway leading to the door. Mrs. Mac picked up the newspaper left, almost abandoned it seemed since it was this late in the morning, on the lawn to bring it in for them.

As they got closer to the door, Buddy raised his nose to a sharp angle; his head moved side to side sampling the air. His snout made that soft clucking sound she knew so well as he quickly and deeply drew in air. There was an unusual scent coming from inside the house, something rich and aromatic. He nearly dragged her to the door and barked softly.

Mrs. Mac looked down at him. Puzzled by his unusual behavior. "Buddy, what are you doing?" She knocked on the door. There was no reply. The car was still in the driveway and they only had the one vehicle. After a moment, she cried, "Hello!" She waited a moment. Buddy started to whine. She knocked on the door again. "You okay in there?" Still no answer. Buddy now began scratching at the white six-paneled door and Mrs. Mac decided to try the handle to just peek in. The knob turned freely and she opened the door just a crack.

She called out, "Yoo-hoo! Anybody home!" There was no answer. The silence was ominous.

Suddenly, Buddy bolted forward and pushed the door open. The knob slipped from her hand as did his leash.

"Buddy!" she admonished. "What do you think you're doing!"

He trotted briskly into the living room and made an immediate left turn into the hallway. Mrs. Mac had no recourse but to follow him into the silent house and retrieve her nosy two-year-old. She stepped over a pile of clothes on the floor and turned left into the hall spouting apologies until she heard Buddy whimpering. She followed the sound to an open bedroom door to the right. She saw Buddy sitting on the floor staring at the still figure on the bed. He whimpered loudly in that begging fashion that had gotten him so many dog biscuits.

Her mouth gaping, Mrs. Mac stepped over to the bed. She looked down at Doug's body and the steak knife sticking out of his throat, blood oozing from the wound.

Chapter Seven

What started out as such a beautiful morning, fresh air, glowing sunshine, people bustling about busy with their lives, now seemed *alien* somehow, something not normal. And it wasn't just the situation, the disappeared people, but it seemed like the world itself was just—*different*. The shops and fast-food places along Madison Street, places Tim had seen day after day, were still there and, indeed, still doing business. People came and went, coming out of them often with big plastic bags from the shops or small paper bags from the fast-food places, going on as usual.

Guess they haven't heard the news yet. His grip tightened on the wheel.

The streets, too, all looked the same—except for the dramatically increased number of abandoned cars sitting everywhere. Normally, it wasn't unusual to find one or two left along the side of the road but never this many. There had been a few sitting directly in the road, keys still in them, that had caused him to stop, put on his lights, get out and move them. But that was all he did. The tow trucks could come get them like scavengers gathering road kill. Since leaving all those other cars at the first scene to their fate, an act some might view as abandonment of duty, this is the policy he adopted to the cars left behind by those who went—wherever.

Now, he just drove around going nowhere trying to get his head together. He wasn't sure just what to do at the moment; he just knew he wanted to get away from those cars and the enigma, the weirdness, he now associated with them. BLET (Basic Law Enforcement Training) had not prepared him to deal with people mysteriously disappearing into thin air and it was messing with his head.

This confusion of duty bothered him. He was proud of being a law enforcement officer. It was what he had wanted to do since he was sixteen and had gone with some other kids from high school on a career day field trip to the police station. Some of the other kids came in with juvenile anti-cop attitudes, spouting smart aleck remarks to one another as they toured the station and met various police personnel, learning what they do, visiting different departments. But Tim liked what he saw and very much wanted to become a part of it. The adventure the job offered was exciting. No sitting all day in an office cubicle somewhere watching the clock and his life tick by. Police work allowed him to be out there on the streets where the action is, up close and personal. The sense of authority, and to some degree, power, the idea of being an *insider*, being someone in the know, not like the general public getting information spoon fed to them, filtered by the media, also appealed to him. So while he waited to reach twenty-one, the minimum age requirement to join the force, he immediately, one week after graduating high school, joined the military and spent two years in the army—training that later proved very invaluable in his law enforcement career.

But as for those cars, he just walked away from them. What could he do about those missing drivers and passengers or the people left sitting in the cars? He couldn't make missing people magically reappear like they had, seemingly, magically disappeared. And the others were physically okay; just a little shaken up, that's all. He knew they would make calls and make their way home. There was no sign of anyone in distress, no sign of an immediate emergency.

In no great hurry, he drove slowly along Madison Street looking through the windshield watching for any sign of trouble. His brow furrowed; he was worried he was going to find it. The traffic around him was sparse. He saw a lot of people on foot outside the businesses and homes lining the street. They all stumbled around looking here and there for something, or perhaps someone, lost. They looked a little lost themselves.

Since leaving that first strange scene, he had come across many more abandoned cars on other streets. It was a problem too big to deal with alone—and it was clear no help was immediately coming. What he was going through, he was sure every police officer in town was too. He glanced down at the radio; he was expecting a special call to come over it any second now.

He let out a long breath. He needed to pull over and close his eyes and try to get a better grip on himself. He saw the turn for Cloverdale. Normally, he patrolled this part of his assigned area only when things were really slow. Nothing ever happened here and he usually concentrated his patrols in areas more likely to see trouble, like around the bars, shopping centers or rough neighborhoods. But right now, he needed to just pull over somewhere quiet and collect himself.

***

For a neighborhood that at this time of day was usually very quiet, there was a lot of activity going on. Just on this street, there were a good number of people out walking, looking around, calling names over and over, asking questions to those they saw—just like Susanna was doing now—about someone missing. She didn't know what to think about all these people doing the same thing she was doing. Did it encourage her or only add to her growing uneasiness?

From one house to next, Susanna kept walking, keeping an eye open for any sign of Albert. She saw none and no one she asked had seen him.

Back up the street now, across from Mrs. Mac's, she saw Mr. Davies rambling around the freshly watered front yard of his brick ranch house. When he saw Susanna, he asked if she'd seen his wife anywhere. She was nowhere to be found.

"No, sorry, Mr. Davies. Have you seen Albert?"

"No, can't say that I have." He looked frazzled, worried. "I don't get it. We were in the kitchen talking about vacation plans and I stepped into the bedroom for a minute. When I came back she was gone. And the strangest thing is her clothes were lying on the kitchen floor. I mean, that doesn't even make sense!" Frantically, he looked around. "I mean, how can somebody change clothes that quickly? I was gone out of the kitchen less than ten seconds to get a magazine with an article about bass fishing in Virginia." He ran his fingers through his thin hair. "I wanted to show her a place we might go to later on this year!" His voice rose along with his panic. "And where did she go? She sure didn't cut out the back door naked, running 'round the neighborhood like *that!*" His eyes widened. Suddenly, he took off around the house. "Maggie! Maggie!"

Susanna turned and walked away. She could still hear him calling for his missing wife.

Next door to Mr. Davies she saw no one in the yard but heard a man shouting from inside the house. She couldn't make out the words but the tone was one of terror, total abject terror as if someone was pleading for their life. Was this someone praying? The shouts of Mr. Davies for his wife began fading as he, she assumed, cut across the backyards of the neighbors in the rear continuing his search. *His futile search*, her mind suggested. In an effort to dislodge the thought, she shook her head.

A bit earlier, she had seen Mrs. Mac and Buddy cut across the street and enter the house of Doug and Lindsey Harper. At this point, she was down the road walking back from the intersection with Collins Road. Only a few moments after they had gone in, she heard a woman, she assumed to be Mrs. Mac, screaming. She sped up to see what the problem was, but Mrs. Mac, pulling Buddy after her, came out of the house and ran away, heading, no doubt, for her own house, leaving the Harper's front door standing open.

Susanna decided not to pursue it anymore. Whatever had happened in the Harper's house was over and done; she was sure there was nothing she could do to help. And besides, she had her own situation to deal with: finding Albert.

Leaving the shouting behind, she continued up the street. Suddenly an idea occurred to her, an idea that stopped her dead in her tracks. *Albert's probably back by now. Yes, of course!* Somehow it was so obvious. How could she not have seen it! *He's back by now wondering where I am!*

She hurried and quickly passed a few more houses. In front of his white A-frame house, she saw Greg Carlson standing beside his gray sedan, a cell phone pressed to his ear. She slowed down to ask him about Albert and overheard him speaking. He was calm and spoke as if nothing unusual had happened.

"Thanks to Giorgio," he said, referring to his pit bull, "I got a new dent in my car. Last night after I got home from work, I stepped out of the car and Giorgio came up to greet me as usual. I stepped across his tie-down cable to go to the steps and instead of him following me as he usually does, he rushed toward the side of the house for some reason and pulled the cable tight around my ankles. Well, I tried to step out of it but it was too late. The cable pulled my feet out from under me." He paused as the person he spoke to said something. "Yeah," he chuckled. "So I began back-pedaling trying to regain my balance but it didn't work. I fell backwards and hit my back hard against the left front fender of the car. I landed on the ground sitting up. After a bit, I knew I was okay so I got up and looked at the fender. Now there's a big dent there about the size of a china saucer." He stopped a moment to shoo away a fly. "I'm looking over the dent again now." He bent down. "Thank goodness it was my upper back that hit the fender and not my head. It was a hard fall and might have been bad news if it was my head that hit it. Like they say, a head injury is nothing to play with."

Susanna thought, *If what I think has happened has really happened, a dent in your car is the least of your worries.* She realized she had actually let that thought into her mind. She gasped loudly. *It's not that! It's not that! Albert just walked away somewhere, that's all! I'm sure he's back home now.*

Greg Carlson looked at her for a moment and then resumed his phone conversation. She decided not to question him after all; she was sure he knew nothing that could help. Instead, she put her young, healthy feet into motion again and started once more back toward Albert's house. It was time to find him and settle this nonsense. She moved so fast it was more like power walking. Quickly putting one foot in front of the other, she hurried; she mustn't keep Albert waiting. It was then she started running.

She was making good time and, soon, Albert's house was just in sight. Sitting across the street, parked beside the Davidson place, was a police car. The children's clothes still lay in the yard but Mrs. Davidson was no longer there. The pickup marked *Davidson Paint And Tile* parked in front of the house let her know Mr. Davidson was home.

Susanna stopped and looked at the police car. The driver, from this distance, seemed like a young man. She started walking again, wondering if there was a problem with Albert. Closer to the car, she slowed down and stepped cautiously up to the open window. "Excuse me, officer. Is there a problem at this house?" She pointed to Albert's place. "There's nothing wrong with the man who lives there, is there?"

The officer looked her over and noted how frayed she seemed. "No, I haven't heard of any problem there. I'm just parked here keeping an eye on things."

"Well, I was a little worried. You see, I work for the man that lives there and he's missing. I've been out looking for him." When she said that a strange look flickered across the police officer's face.

"Yes," he said, nodding slightly. He repositioned his hands on the wheel and the movement made the front of his crisp uniform shirt move; the name tag reading *Tim Jordan* moved with it. "We've been getting those kinds of reports for a while now."

"Uh, do you know what's going on?"

Just then a loud squawk came from the radio under the dash. It was followed by, "All units, all units, Code Six, Code Six. Patrol and observe. Maintain order. All other priorities rescinded." At last, here was that special call he'd been expecting. "All units acknowledge."

Then from the radio came, "701 acknowledge." Then a different voice said, "702 acknowledge." And then, "703 acknowledge," this time a female voice.

As different police units called in their unit numbers, acknowledging the command, Susanna asked, "What does that mean?"

Tim held up a finger signaling her to wait a moment. He picked up the handset of the police radio mounted under the dash. After another unit acknowledged, he pushed the button on the side and said, "709 acknowledge." He put the handset back in its place and turned down the volume.

He looked at the girl. "It's just a radio check." There was no way he was going to tell this already frazzled girl that Code Six was the disaster code—that all officers were to be on alert, maintain high visibility while on patrols, and respond only to life-threatening situations.

With all these missing persons, panic was setting in and the usual minor calls: fender benders, public drunkenness and the other nickel-and-dime incidents that make up a police officer's day, could go unanswered for now. And that even went for serious incidents that were over and done and nothing could be done about them. Meaning, in a manner of speaking, '*Let the dead bury their dead.*'

When someone is dead they're dead, and it was no use tying up valuable manpower and resources needed in maintaining order to try and help them. All the cars with flashing blue lights parked around, and all the police officers with bright shining badges standing around, were not going to bring the dead back to life. For now, during the Code Six, the focus was on preventing riots and further deaths, not investigating those already dead and beyond help. And in the worst-case scenario, if things got too far out of hand and order just simply collapsed and the city became a war zone, the police would simply withdraw and let it burn itself out and, perhaps, let the National Guard take over. And even that was not guaranteed. The thin blue line only stretched so far.

Tim was sure if the city could just make it through the night things would be okay. People would have time to settle down and adjust to the new circumstances and be calmer though, perhaps, frightened.

Around ninety minutes ago he'd been monitoring traffic in front of the shopping mall. Now he was dealing with a Code Six alert. This was his first Code Six. The only other Code Six in the history of the department, as far as he knew, was when the 911 terrorist attack on the World Trade Center occurred. He didn't tell her that either. Right now, he knew all off-duty police officers were being contacted and told to report for duty. He wouldn't be surprised if another officer ended up riding with him before the night was over. There were only so many cars available.

To Tim, the young lady standing beside his car seemed like a nice girl and he was beginning to feel some concern for her. "Listen, miss, what's your name?"

"Susanna Kelly. But I don't have any identification on me right now."

Tim smiled. "That's okay, Susanna. My name is Tim Jordan. Why don't you go on inside and try to relax a little?"

As she listened to him, immediately her eyes and mouth flashed open. A simple thought had hit her like a slap in the face: *Albert's cell phone! Why didn't I think to just call Albert's cell phone?*

Instinctively, Tim leaned back a little not knowing what to think of this sudden change of manner. Quickly, she pulled her phone out and, as Tim looked on, she made a call. All she got was a message on the screen; she frowned as she read: Service Temporarily Unavailable. She pushed the stop button and tried again. This time it rang.

But that's all it did; ring after ring. There was no answer.

And there never will be! Don't you get it! Don't you know by now! She closed her eyes, clenched her teeth and stood there struggling, pushing away the awful thought, the awful truth: *The Rapture has happened! Two thousand years of warning, two thousand years of waiting, at last, are over!* In her mind, she pictured those clothes lying on the study floor with a cell phone among them ringing for someone who would never answer.

Tim got out of the car and took the phone from her. He held her by the arm and looked her in the face. Her eyes were unfocused; she just stared blankly at him. After a second, she blinked a few times and looked at him with recognition. He handed her the phone and told her to put it in her pocket. She, like a dutiful child, obeyed.

"C'mon, Susanna. Let's get you inside." He took her by the elbow; she was trembling. Gently, he led her across the street to the house she had pointed out. They walked slowly; her head bowed low, they took small steps. She seemed pretty off balance at the moment and he didn't want her to slip.

When they got to the front door, he tried it and found it unlocked. He kept the storm door back using his shoulder and held the front door open for the girl while still holding her elbow. She still seemed a little shaky. Inside the living room, he flipped the light switch on in case he needed extra light. He called out, "Hello! Hello! Anybody here!" There was no response. He looked into the small study to the right and led her there and sat her down.

She straightened herself in the chair and put her hand against her forehead. Staring at the desk, she watched it as if it were about to attack. Tim followed her gaze but saw nothing. He looked back at her.

She whispered, "Behind."

He leaned over the desk and saw the pile of clothes on the floor and understood what was bothering her.

Chapter Eight

The church wasn't far from Cloverdale. That's why Reverend Roland Jasper bought a house there so he wouldn't have so far to drive. He wanted a much bigger and more expensive place in a more exclusive (meaning rich) neighborhood but his finances at the time just couldn't swing it. He'd have to fleece the flock a little longer before making that move. Now after pastoring this church for seven years, luring in parishioners with promises of blessings of wealth, it was getting near the time that nice new house would be his. A lot of churchgoers talked about a mansion in heaven but he couldn't wait that long. He wanted it now. And his efforts were paying off far better than he at first planned. Not only could he now afford to buy the new place, he was also going to get the church to pay for it altogether. He'd adapted well the lesson he learned from 'get rich preachers' and politicians; he understood that the way to get people to do what you want is to tell them what they want to hear and make them believe it's the honest truth.

Usually, it took him under five minutes to drive from his house on Curtis Road, just three doors up from the big Curtis house, (Oh, how he wished he could have gotten that place when he moved to Cloverdale!) and pull his luxuriant German sedan into his reserved parking space at *Prosperity Tabernacle*, the name he'd chosen to replace the old, outdated name: *Faith Fellowship Tabernacle*. The church sign had the legend *Pray And Grow Rich!* added underneath the new church name. Much of the congregation didn't like it; he informed those time-bandits and deadbeats, without hesitation, to go elsewhere if that was the case. The sign was set in an attractive chocolate brown brick rectangular monument that matched the brick of the building and stood on the lush, well-trimmed lawn out in front.

The church was a beautiful blend of traditional and contemporary styling. The chocolate brown brick exterior was about the only thing he liked about the church when he arrived years ago to take over the pastorate. The beautiful brick walls had none of those old-fashioned stained glass windows. He had them removed along with the old name. The church now featured elegant cut glass windows each beautifully etched with tasteful designs of various flowers, sunflowers, roses, and buttercups. The glass was opaque enough not to let in too much sunlight to overheat the interior or shine in the eyes of the congregation, but the sunlight did illuminate the windows into glowing works of translucent art.

Impressive.

And Reverend Jasper wanted his congregants to be impressed; he believed this helped put them in a mood more conducive to respond to his impassioned encouragements for donations, those impassioned encouragements usually accompanied by scripture quotations, often out of context, that promised great financial returns on their investment. The bounty that appeared in the offering plates indicated this tactic was working quite well.

But the brick and cut glass windows were just two of the elegant appointments of the church. Now, there was a brand new one he very much wanted to get a look at, something he was sure would add to the prestige and perception of wealth he wanted this church to reflect. Jasper knew if he wanted his church to be a rich church, it first had to look the part.

Wilson Mattock, one of the older, and therefore less desirable, members he had offended into leaving the congregation, had said to him, "Mene Mene Tekel Upharsin. That should be the new name of this place after what you've done to it." The old man had stared at Jasper's unmoving, and decidedly uncaring, expression. "Yeah, Upharsin or should I say, 'You for sin' in your case?" Fortunately, the old man who had given sixty years of service to his beloved church stormed off after the confrontation and never bothered Reverend Jasper again.

He didn't like or use the term 'pastor'. He thought it was too personal, too committal, like he was somehow responsible for these people. Reverend Jasper was his preferred moniker. Whenever anyone called him Pastor Jasper, he corrected them immediately and asked them to call him Reverend, please, and not Pastor. He used the excuse it was an outdated term and he wanted his ministry and this church to be *fresh*. People, for the most part, seemed to buy it. And he didn't like the name Roland either. If some friend spoke to him on a personal level it was just as Jasper as if that was his first name.

As he strolled down the aisle left of the center of the sanctuary with three rows of pews, all now empty, he looked over them ensuring that the cleaning people had properly done their jobs, that the pews were nice and clean and there was no trash laying around the floor. He continued toward the podium holding the phone to his ear.

He loved being on the phone. The sound of his own voice was like music to his ears; he loved it almost as much as he loved the money he was raking in with the church. The chance to share that music with anyone was always a pleasure. His phone's ringtone was himself saying, "Opportunity calling."

To anyone else, his voice wasn't anything special. Not bad, not great; a light baritone like millions of others in the world. But if anyone had pointed that out to him he would not have believed it. His appearance, too, wasn't anything extraordinary. A man of forty-five, average build, an average face, close cut brown hair and brown eyes, he didn't turn heads when he went out anywhere in public, at least not for his looks. However, he did draw attention sometimes; he adored it whenever he got a little public recognition, when someone said to him, "Hey, ain't you that TV preacher?" His local religious TV program had been steadily building an audience the last couple of years. Many of his new congregants had started coming because of it.

Into the phone, he said, "Yeah man, I really preached Sunday. I mean, I preached like I was on fire, man." He grinned widely and paused a moment to allow Brother Bernie on the other end of the line a chance to laugh. Brother Bernie dutifully obliged.

"I mean I gave 'em a little bit of this, a little of that. Man! They ate it up." He paused and waited as Brother Bernie said something about how his own sermon went well too. It's not as if Jasper was listening; he never really listened to other people. He just waited until they'd shut up so he could talk some more. Mostly in this conversation, he and Brother Bernie had talked about business, church business. And by church Business Jasper did not mean the work of the ministry or the care of the congregation—not even the day to day operation of running a church facility. They literally meant pastoring a church as a business, the operation of it as a profit center in which to generate income and as much as possible. Sometimes he thought about when he first started preaching and had the fire in his belly to spread the Word of God. Often, he recriminated himself for having ever been that naive.

Jasper loved the ministry as long as it didn't involve any actual ministering to anyone, especially those 'needy people' as he thought of them—people not financially profitable, those in actual need of emotional or spiritual guidance, the kind of people that investing time in would not yield a good financial return. That's just sound business practice. He loved the attention he got while standing in the pulpit screaming platitudes at the top of his lungs, or making promises based on biblically shaky premises. But most of all he loved the money. All he had to do was tell the people what they wanted to hear, make them believe heaven was going to make them millionaires if they, of course, donated to the wonderful work he was doing. His congregation was only too glad to oblige. Those who wanted a more balanced and sound doctrine, he ignored—his way of pushing them out in favor of his growing number of greed-gospel followers. It was this kind of thinking that led to his wife's exit from his life, one of the reasons he moved here to take over this church and make a fresh start.

He often recalled how his wife, Esther use to chasten him so often because of his greed and how he had let it get away with him, how it had blinded him to the truth he once so passionately preached. She reminded him of a scripture they had both read in the Bible about 'the deceitfulness of riches'. And she brought up a statement they heard at the Bible college where they met, how one of the teachers had said, "One of the worst things that can happen to a preacher is to become successful." And he especially recalled that final confrontation with her, the shouting match that took place in the kitchen, and how he had told her if she didn't like the direction he was taking she was welcome to leave anytime she wanted. He had to admit he was a little surprised when she took him up on the offer right then and there and was packed up and gone in under an hour. They had no kids. After the divorce, he often thought maybe that was for the best. Besides, it meant no child support payments for her to bleed from him.

Midway down the aisle, he stopped in his tracks. His head raised, he stared gaped-mouthed at the new decorative feature he'd just had installed. That was the reason he was here, to inspect the new installation. It was fantastically beautiful! This was the first time he had a chance to see it since the installers came and hung it yesterday. It looked even better than he had imagined.

He took a breath and resumed. "So I told them, 'Hey, as minister of a church preaching prosperity, I can't be seen living in some low-class neighborhood anymore.'"

He allowed his fellow minister, the Reverend Brother Bernard Gracie, pastor of a church in Georgia, to ask a question.

Jasper caught himself staring again wide-eyed at the beauty. The way the light glinted off the ice blue surface was enthralling. It may have cost a fortune, money that could have been given to help a local food bank or something like that, but he wasn't into that sort of charity thing. He knew a good investment when he saw it. And he was looking at one now.

He replied, "Yeah, there were a couple of deacons that balked at the idea. But some of my faithful guys spoke up and argued for it." He gently scratched his belly as Bernie made a wise suggestion. "I know! I'm gonna hafta get rid of 'em somehow. I can't have dissenters on the church board." He switched the phone from left hand to right. "Church should be getting me the new house in the next month or two. I'm tired of living in a low-class place like Cloverdale."

Brother Bernie spoke and Jasper replied, "Yeah, I'm looking at it right now." He let out a long breath. "You should see it! Man! It's unbelievable—unbelievable."

He took his sweet time staring at it, the new blue crystal cross just installed, now hanging from the hardwood cathedral style ceiling. It had a wingspan of six feet and stood (or would have if it had been on the ground) twelve feet tall.

Jasper continued toward the front and turned left. He bounded up the steps of the podium and over to the door set discreetly in the corner angled not to draw much attention. He unlocked the door, stepped into his office and immediately stumbled forward, his foot caught on something.

He balanced himself and looked behind him at the offending impediment. His foot was hooked in a long, orange drop cord curled on the floor like a giant orange snake lying right next to the door. A loop of the rolled up cord stuck out in front of the door.

"Man! Somebody left a big monster drop cord in my office! I just nearly broke my neck tripping on it. Guess one of the installers put it in here for some reason and forgot it when they left. I'm gonna call 'em about it; you can believe that!"

He drew his oxford clad foot—the shoe custom made and costing more than a week's wages for most of the members of his congregation—out of the cord loop and stepped clear of the menace.

He saw a package resting on a chair. "Hold on, Bernie. I need to set the phone down a minute. He laid the phone on the top of the desk and picked up a large box from the chair beside the desk. He walked around the desk and put the box down. He sat down and read the label.

He picked up the phone. "I got that package I been waiting for." A buzzing emitted from the phone. "Yeah, it's that hunting jacket I ordered. Diana had sat it here in my office instead of the back pew like I told her."

For a man who loved extravagance, his office was quite ordinary. He didn't mind; he wasn't in here that much of the time. A simple metal desk and manager's chair, a couple of office chairs, one by the desk, the other by the wall was plenty for him. A TV sat on top of a short file cabinet in the corner to his right.

When he met with people it was usually in the auditorium where they'd sit on one of the beautifully carved pews, or in the office suite downstairs using an empty office or the conference room there. This office was for him alone, a little hideaway he resorted to occasionally to relax alone and out of sight.

A white multi-line phone sat on the corner of the desk, but he rarely used it. Like so many people, he mostly used his cell phone, even at home. He got around so much the church phone system was set up so that Diana could easily forward his calls directly to it.

Diana's office was on the basement level with the rest of the riffraff that comprised his staff. He refused to use any of the office space there and insisted that this old vacant room just off the podium be turned into his office. This way he wouldn't have to be around the others as they made small talk, told dumb jokes, or shared their petty concerns—he hated that most of all. And he wouldn't have to listen to some stupid phone ringing all day. Up here, near the sanctuary, he could be by himself where it was quiet and that's the way he liked it.

The phone in his hand made a clicking sound, another call coming in. He looked at the screen and saw it was just one of his lackeys from the basement. He ignored it and continued on with Bernie.

"Hey, let me tell you what happened last night. Me and Cecilia went out to that new steak place on Churton Avenue. It's called Mom and Pop's House of Steaks. We go in, sit down and order." More buzzing from the phone. Jasper chuckled. "Yeah, Bernie, I ordered a porterhouse like I always do." He smiled, broadly.

Again, he changed the phone from one hand to the other. "Well, I had to go to the bathroom really bad; I mean right then and there! The restrooms were down a hall to the side of the kitchen and I hurried as fast as I could without just outright trotting. More buzzing. "No! I didn't have the trots; I just needed to recycle some water, a lot of it, if you know what I mean." He leaned back. "Well, like I said, I was in a hurry and I saw a door with a three letter word that started with the letter M. 'Oh, this must be the Men's room,' I thought and rushed right on in. I looked around and didn't see a urinal so I went into one of the stalls and relieved myself." He puffed. "Man, that is one of sweetest sounds in the world when water hits water really hard and you feel all that relief." He chuckled. "Well, after I finished, I washed my hands and stood by the sink drying up. All of a sudden, the door opens and there's this lady standing there."

An excited buzzing came from the phone. "Yeah, some lady. And she just stood there looking at me. I looked right back and I said, 'Lady, what are you doing in the Men's room?' She said, 'This is the Ladies room!' and pointed to the sign on the door. I stepped to the door and looked real good; sure enough, the sign said Mom, not Men. I was in a hurry coming in and didn't notice." Buzzing. "Naw, I didn't say nothin'. I just walked right past her and got out. I passed the other restroom and the sign there read Pop. Guess they thought branding the restrooms after the restaurant would be cutesy.

Jasper stopped talking for a moment while Brother Bernie hooted with laughter on the other end of the line. Then came more buzzing.

Jasper raised his eyebrows. "Yeah, that would be a bad deal if she had called the police and made a big deal of it. Wouldn't that be something? Local pastor arrested for pandering?"

With the phone pressed firmly to his ear, he could clearly hear screaming in the background on Bernie's end.

Jasper quickly leaned forward. "Hey, man, what's going on?"

Bernie told him to hold on.

Jasper sat and held the phone hearing fragments of a disjointed, excited exchange going on in the background. He could make out Rachel, Bernie's wife, speaking in near screams, "She's gone!" repeating it over and over. The only other person living in Bernie and Rachel's house was their teenage daughter, Lola—a sweet girl very active in her church. Oddly enough, she did not attend her father's church.

Bernie came back on the line and told him he'd call back, his voice extremely tense.

Jasper set the phone on the desk and stared ahead blankly. He was curious to know what was going on at Bernie's. Not that he really cared. Bernie was a friend but a friendship, like any commodity, was only worth what it could do for you.

He sat back in his chair and pulled open the bottom drawer of his desk. He drew out a laptop computer and opened the lid. He clicked on his favorite game, Solitaire, and played for a while, winning three out of five games. He put the computer back up and put his feet on the desk to catch a nap. Up here by himself, he could do that. Downstairs with the others, he could not. Not wanting to be disturbed, he cut off his phone and scrunched deeper into his chair. Just before he drifted off, he again wondered what was up with Bernie and his wife and all the screaming.

Chapter Nine

Quietly, Tim sat beside Susanna keeping a close eye on her. His right arm rested on the desk near two cups of what looked like tea, now cold. She seemed to be recovering from the episode, the panic attack or whatever it was that left her standing in the street stunned as if from a blow. To him, it was very much like she had done a standing eight count. Now, she was breathing more normally and the trembling had stopped. Except for that one word, *Behind*, she had not spoken since she came inside. But it seemed the overall trauma was subsiding. She sat quietly, ashen-faced, looking at the floor—a more normal, if sadder, look than before.

She brought her hands up and covered her face. Softly, she began to sob. She lowered her head almost to her knees. He sat and waited. He knew the best thing to do was to let her get it out of her system, this despair or whatever it was. Maybe then she could talk.

After a minute, she sat up and reached into her back pocket and brought out a clean, folded-up paper towel. Carrying a paper towel in the hip pocket struck him as more of a *guy* kind of thing. She wiped her eyes and put it back.

Solemn, quiet, sad, she sat with her arms folded over her stomach and her head leaned back. It reminded him of a stabbing victim he once came across on a park bench. (Thankfully, Susanna didn't have a butcher's knife sticking out of her chest.) She brought her head down again and Tim saw her eyes grow very wide. He looked to his right. It seemed, she was looking at the computer. It was on and showing the study they now sat in.

"It's still on!" she whispered. Then louder, "Of course, it's still on."

She jumped out of the chair and sprang around the desk but came to a sudden, dead stop—the clothes, those horrible clothes were still lying on the floor.

She looked at the officer. "Excuse me, what is your name again?"

"Tim Jordan. Just call me Tim."

"Tim, could you do me a favor?"

"Yeah, sure," he mumbled; he didn't know for sure what to make of her right now.

"Could you take these out of the way?" She pointed to the pile of clothes.

He grimaced. Nodding, he started around the desk. He didn't have any more desire to touch them than she did, like they were abnormal, cursed, contaminated or just plain creepy. But he'd dealt with many unpleasant tasks in his job, many far worse. This was just another one.

He scooched by her and picked up the offending pile, shoes and all, with one quick effort and held them out from him. Again, there was that feeling that they held some contamination. Once done, it wasn't so bad. No worse than getting the dirty laundry out of the hamper and into the washer—a not unusual job for a man living alone. He worked his way with the load around the desk and carried the burden into the living room and dumped them on the sofa.

Susanna stepped behind Mahog and sat in the chair, the last place she had seen Albert. She turned to the computer as he came back and sat down.

"It's still recording!" She looked at him.

He stared at her, his face blank.

She held both hands out. "He was sitting here making one of his videos! The computer was still recording when … you know."

Now *his* eyes grew wide.

With the mouse, she clicked the stop button on the video software, some freeware that had come pre-installed on the computer. She looked at her image on the screen that the camera on top of the monitor picked up. He looked on and kept quiet, but wondered what was going through her mind. What he was going to see?

She moved the mouse and clicked the play button and the video began.

Albert's big, bald head came on the screen and he sat there a moment smiling into the camera. She had taught him to give the video a couple of seconds of pre-roll before speaking to prevent his opening words from getting cut off by a jerky start on playback. Although he'd only been gone a short while, seeing his image come into view was like watching an old home movie.

Before he began speaking, she heard her own voice faintly saying, "It's such a beautiful day! I should have stood you up!" And then, "But I'm glad I didn't, now that I know I've still got a job!" She felt her flesh tingle hearing the last words she had spoken to him. The last, she was beginning to accept, that she would ever speak to him. Her hands grew cold.

He waited another few moments before speaking. She could tell he'd remembered what she had said about mistakes and how she could easily edit them out. She was somehow flattered he remembered.

"Because knowledge is the enemy of faith," he began, "it is, therefore, imperative we understand that human knowledge only goes so far. There are things in God's word we must accept by faith and not rely on reason. In His great work, the Lord has done things contrary to man's science so that we are faced with an outright challenge to 'believe it or not' so to speak. Creation is a good example of—"

And he was gone. One second he was on the screen, the next second he was not. The clothes he was in held their shape as if still occupied for a millisecond before falling out of view. Susanna sat frozen, staring at the screen.

Tim jumped to his feet and brought his hands down hard on the desk almost knocking over one of the cups of cold tea. "What happened! Did the thing stop working!"

Susanna looked at him but didn't answer. She recalled it was at that moment she had glanced over her shoulder, distracted by the laughter of the children. That such a beautiful sound should be associated with such a terrifying circumstance was unsettling. For a long moment, she sat and watched as the video of a now empty office played. Then on the video they heard movement, and on the very edge of the picture, to the right, they saw her at the desk with the two cups in her hands. They watched as she sat the cups down, leaned over the desk and looked at the floor. She grabbed the mouse and hit the pause button.

Tim stood in front of the desk and pointed to the screen. "Susanna, what happened there?" He tried to keep his voice calm and patient; maintaining composure was part of his training and much needed in a job that more and more demanded patience or at least the appearance of it. But, as had been demonstrated on so many news reports, on occasion, a cop's patience only went so far. He was anxious for an answer.

For a while, she just sat and stared at the screen. Her denial had given up the ghost; she knew that. What was going on had become clear enough even if she couldn't admit it out loud yet.

Finally, she looked up at him. "The Rapture … that's what happened." They stared at each other for a long moment until Tim sat back down.

"You mean you believe in all that?"

She let out a breath. "I didn't … not for the whole time I worked on the book." She pointed to the manuscript still lying on top of Mahog. Slowly, she nodded. "But I think I do now."

He vigorously shook his head. "Play it again. Let's see if we saw what we think we saw."

She clicked on the start point of the video and it began again. And they watched it again. Then again and again. There was no doubt; they had seen a man vanish into thin air leaving behind his clothes. Susanna felt a little sick to her stomach. Tim sat still, stunned.

Again, they fell silent. Tim's throat had become so dry he had trouble swallowing. He picked up one of the cups of tepid tea and drank half of it in a gulp.

Suddenly, the computer screen went blank and they heard the hard drive power down. The light in the fixture above them flickered off then right back on again. It was a momentary power drop; it had knocked off the computer. They both looked around as if searching for an explanation.

"Oh please," he said, "don't let there be a power outage. Not now. Things are tense enough in this town already."

They waited a moment to see what would happen. The light above them continued to shine as if it had heard his plea.

Without a word, she got up and walked into the living room. Tim followed. She looked around and then at him. She glanced at the offending piles of clothes he had deposited on the sofa and then immediately looked away.

"Susanna, what's up?"

She shrugged. "I don't know. I thought I heard something out here. Did you?"

He shook his head. "What did it sound like?"

"Just a little pop, that's all."

He stood still a moment looking around and then stepped to the light switch and flipped it several times. The ceiling light did not come on.

"Blew a light bulb with that power drop. I remember I turned that light on when we came in."

She nodded and walked back inside the study. She stepped around Mahog again and resumed her seat at the computer. He stood at the desk looking at her.

She saw his expression. "I'm all right, Tim! Maybe a little hyper but I'm all right."

She pushed the power button on the computer and waited as the password dialog box came up on the center of the screen. She tapped away on the keyboard entering Albert's password.

"Give me a second to get this thing working again. I want to look over some things." She nodded at the tepid cups of tea still in the way. "Could you do me a favor and take those into the kitchen? It's just down that way." She pointed toward the back of the house.

"Yeah, no problem." He picked up the cups just as the computer screen displayed the operating system's logo. Then there was another password dialog box. He heard her clacking away on the keyboard as he carried the cups into the kitchen.

In a few moments, he was back with two cans of soda.

"Got these from the fridge." He sat one on the desk in front of her and sat down again in the chair below the Revelation chart on the wall behind him.

Susanna stared intently at the screen, her right hand moving the mouse around busily. She found what she'd been looking for. It was the very first video Albert had made, the one in which he began to explain some of his end-time viewpoints on the Seven Seals. She clicked on the icon and it began to play.

She pressed down on her heels and pushed the chair back a bit. From his seat, Tim could see fine. They both settled back and watched as Albert came on the screen again and began to speak. Like when she watched the video Albert made when he disappeared, she had an odd sensation. This time, it was as if she were listening to a ghost. Her mouth dry, she quickly popped open the can of soda.

"On this video," Albert said, his head bobbing up and down, "I'll try to explain the first five of the Seven Seals." He spoke more solemnly that Susanna was used to hearing him.

He glanced down, no doubt at some notes off camera. He continued. "The first four seals reveal the Four Horsemen of the Apocalypse. This ties in with Matthew twenty-four verses six through eight." He looked down and read, "'And ye shall hear of wars and rumors of wars: see that ye be not troubled: for all these things must come to pass, but the end is not yet. For nation shall rise against nation, and kingdom against kingdom: and there shall be famines, and pestilences, and earthquakes, in diverse places. All these are the beginning of sorrows.'" He looked again into the camera. "The first four seals are the fulfillment of what Jesus prophesied."

Looking down again, he resumed reading. "The Four Horsemen of the Apocalypse do not represent any persons as has been often taught; they represent events and conditions that precede the Tribulation. The events in the scriptures I read are happening in our world now. And the time of the first four seals is already in motion now before the actual start of the Tribulation. It is my position that the first five seals, as well as the Rapture, are all pre-trib, meaning they occur before the start of the seven-year Great Tribulation. This view may differ from that held by others, but it must be kept in mind that the Tribulation works on a definite, preset timetable and this timeline is set with the number of days for some key events actually counted out. It is important to get that timeline correct to better understand the course and chronology of the Tribulation events. And since the Rapture is the starting point of the Tribulation, and the first four seals are already being fulfilled, then the Rapture must be very close indeed."

Susanna took a large swallow of soda and wished Albert had been wrong.

"The book of Revelation is in chronological order and shows us that the Great Tribulation will be a continual global outpouring of God's wrath upon the entire earth and its people for mankind's sins and unbelief." He took a small breath. "Only one-fourth of the earth will be afflicted by the events represented by the first four seals. Therefore, it stands to reason the events represented by these seals are not part of the Tribulation itself but are a prelude to the seven-year Tribulation."

Tim exclaimed, "Do you really think he knew what he was talking about!"

Susanna kept her eyes on the screen and slowly nodded. She paused the video and looked at him. "He'd been studying this for many years and even more so in his retirement; he devoted himself full time to studying end-time Bible prophecy. He was very knowledgeable about it." Talking about him in the past tense made her both sad and frightened.

She resumed playing the video. "The fifth seal," Albert said, "is the prayer of the martyrs. This gives us further evidence that the Great Tribulation does not begin prior to the time of the first four seals." Indeed, it is a prayer for the global Tribulation to begin; it is a prayer for judgment on 'them that dwell on the earth' and not just part of the earth as with the first four seals." He nodded solemnly and then looked down, no doubt, to read from a different place in his notes. "It says in Revelation six verses nine and ten, 'And when he had opened the fifth seal, I saw under the altar the souls of them that were slain for the word of God, and for the testimony which they held: And they cried with a loud voice, saying, How long, O Lord, holy and true, dost thou not judge and avenge our blood on them that dwell on the earth?'" He looked again at the camera. To me, this means the first four seals are only the beginning of sorrows that Jesus talked about."

They listened as Albert explained each of the Four Horsemen of the Apocalypse and the circumstances they represented, things that were already taking place in so many places in the world. They leaned forward as Albert, on the video, talked about the first seal that represented conquest and how it was at work in the world and how the second seal meant war. The third seal, he explained, was about world hunger and suffering.

"Factors certainly at work right now," Albert added, his words spoken with an even more solemn tone. "The fourth seal represents death and Hell. He read, "'And I looked, and behold a pale horse: and his name that sat on him was Death, and Hell followed with him. And power was given unto them over the fourth part of the earth …'" He gently shook his head. "This fourth seal reveals human suffering over one-fourth of the planet. And as I said, this is suffering brought on by the consequences of the first three seals. Conquest is the driving force behind war. Food shortages, pestilence, suffering, and death are the result. Conquest leads to war; war leads to food shortages, rationing, and famine; without proper nutrition, clean water, access to medical facilities and medicine, pestilence and death follow, often by hundreds or thousands of deaths at a time. In these afflicted regions of the planet, there is also death by natural disasters, animal attacks, as well as war, disease, and pestilence. These mounting troubles cause astounding apprehension around the world as the Four Horsemen of the Apocalypse ride across our globe sowing death and havoc."

He stared stonily into the camera. "Hell follows death to those who do not know Jesus as Savior. This is a point of serious reflection because most people do not have the assurance of Salvation that comes through faith in Jesus Christ. These are not future events the first four seals are revealing to us; these things are happening now! We are in the prelude to the Tribulation. These are the latter days and the Rapture is imminent."

Susanna closed her eyes and held the cold can of soda to her forehead. *You were so right, Albert. You were so right.*

Chapter Ten

Jasper woke up feeling much refreshed. He removed his feet from the desk and sat up stretching and yawning. He enjoyed these *power naps* as he called them, a term he picked up from a football player on TV talking about his practice of napping before a game. He checked his watch and saw he'd been out a good while. From the center desk drawer, he pulled out a remote and turned on the TV to catch some cartoons before heading out. He hoped Deputy Dawg or Huckleberry Hound was on; he loved the classics.

As he flipped through the channels looking for the cartoon station—he never could remember the channel number—he noticed a lot of news reports were on, some of the anchor people he knew personally. He looked at his watch again; it wasn't time for the afternoon news programs. He wondered what was going on. For some reason, he thought about the phone conversation with Bernie that had ended so abruptly with his wife in the background screaming, "She's gone! She's gone!"

When he saw Georgette McMillan, co-anchor of the channel six news appear on the screen, he stopped channel surfing. She was one of the TV news personalities that he knew a little having met her on several occasions at local charity functions around the area. He liked her; he liked her a lot! He had wanted to ask her out but, in this, he was too diffident. Even his enormous ego couldn't delude him into thinking she'd be interested in *him*, not with his hangdog looks.

As she spoke, he leaned back and got comfortable.

"To recap some of the information we've been receiving so far, it is evident that some unusual occurrences transpired earlier. A definite starting time for these disappearances has not yet been clearly established."

His brow furrowed. *Disappearances? What does she mean disappearances?*

"We will keep you up to date as we get more information. For now we know that police and emergency services have been inundated with reports of missing persons, many making extraordinary claims of people vanishing right before their eyes."

At this, Jasper sat bolt upright and glared opened-mouth at the screen.

Georgette McMillan (Estell Wagstaff to her mom, dad, and siblings) sat at the highly polished TV newsroom desk, a model of posture and composure. She continued: "Police have no explanation yet to what has happened to all those missing. Many people have been calling the station, as well as the police, with possible explanations and theories."

Theories? Jasper wondered. *What theories! What's happened that people are calling the TV station with theories?*

"Some of these theories are extraordinary. However, interesting as they may be, they will not be commented upon until further review."

Jasper huffed, "You mean until the government gives you the okay; that's what you mean, ain't it?"

He listened a bit more and then picked up his phone. Diana and the New Girl were the only ones working today. He wanted to ask one of them if they knew what was going on. He turned it on and tried to call the office downstairs. The smartphone wouldn't connect the call. The screen displayed a message saying that a connection wasn't currently available.

"What's going on?" he whispered.

He picked up the desk phone and called. Even after ringing ten times there was still no answer. He stared at the phone in his hand, puzzled. *What's going on down there! They're not both supposed to leave the office at the same time, unattended, man! Diana knows better!* He tried again and again received no answer.

He didn't understand. Taking calls was a priority. People often made donations over the phone. For that reason, the church had a four-line system. That's a lot for even a good size church like this. Having several lines was intentional. It was to prevent anyone from getting a busy signal. But if they weren't picking up downstairs, what good was it?

He stood up, slipped his smartphone into his coat pocket, and hurried through the sanctuary. Quickly, he made his way to the office area downstairs and stood on the landing at the bottom of the stairwell. He looked around. The phone was ringing down the hall. He called, "Diana," but received no answer except a resonant echo from the hard walls, an effect the audio engineer who worked on his TV program had described as *wall reverb*.

The walls down here were concrete but attractively painted gloss white and decorated with posters here and there. One at Jasper's elbow read: *Give And It Shall Be*

Given To You. It featured a picture of two strong masculine hands cupped together and overflowing with golden wheat grain against a golden sunlit background. Jasper had bought it hoping the gold theme would work like subliminal suggestion encouraging people to give him their gold, their money.

"Diana!" he called out louder. Still no response. This was unusual. She was very attentive to his wants almost to the point of subservience. He often thought of her as a pet dog begging for attention. Too bad she wasn't better looking.

He looked down the hall listening to the phone that was still ringing. It was getting on his nerves. Suddenly, it stopped as if he had willed it, only to start again after just a few seconds reprieve. As he walked down the short hall, well lit by light fixtures recessed into the white ceiling, he looked into the two offices to his right; the doors were open and the rooms were empty. He figured the New Girl should have been in one of them. At the basement lobby, he looked to his left at the two glass entry doors. The brick staircase outside leading the short way down to the small landing in front of the doors, the handrail running down the middle, were easily visible through the sparkling clean glass. He stepped over and pushed one door open. *You mean they stepped away and left the doors unlocked!* He turned around and faced the door to Diana's office, the whole front of which consisted of plate glass with a glass door in the middle. At the center top of it, there was stenciled in white:

Church Office
Diana Pendergrass
Church Secretary

He stomped over to the door and pulled it hastily open, banging it hard against the side of his expensive shoe. He gritted his teeth as he shook his foot.

Again the phone stopped, rested, and started again as if it had paused a moment to catch its breath.

"Diana!" he yelled. *"Diana!"* even louder.

He looked at the offending phone sitting on her desk, reached behind it and pulled out the cord. Silence, sweet, sweet silence.

He looked around the empty office almost shaking with anger. *I'll teach 'em to leave the office unattended!* He noticed something lying on the floor. Seeing anything out of order here was very unusual; Diana was fastidious to a fault. He stepped closer and saw that it was a pile of clothes. He stared at them for a long moment. They seemed to be the clothes Diana had worn to work that morning.

He slowly stepped back into the small lobby, his head swaying side to side. "What's going on here!"

A faint noise like a distant hoot owl caught his attention. He stood still a moment and listened. It came again and seemed to emanate from the supply closet at the end of the hall. He stepped over and pulled the white door open and there stood a girl crying softly and hugging herself as if she were freezing. There were packs of post-it notes, pens, and rubber bands laying at her feet that she had knocked from the shelves while squeezing herself into the tight space. It was the New Girl as he thought of her, never remembering her name. It always took him time to learn the new people's names. With such a high employee turnover rate—once new hires got to know him most quit—he didn't make much of an effort to learn names. What's the point of learning the name of someone who's not going to be around for very long? As far as he was concerned, the New Girl wasn't important enough to remember her name. The New Girl looked at him without recognition, whimpering and making that owl sound.

"For Pete's sake, wha'cha doin' in there?"

She stood shivering, eyes wide open, fists clenched. In a moment, she focused on him and seemed to recognize him. "Reverend Jasper?"

"Yes!" he nearly shouted. "Now come on out of there." He offered her no assistance as she picked up her feet and worked her way out. "Now, what's goin' on?"

She stood in the hall rubbing her arms. "Going on? Don't *you* know?"

He slowly shook his head. "Now calm down and tell me what happened." It was a little cramped in this part of the hall; Jasper turned around and led her to the basement lobby. They stopped in front of Diana's office.

"I was in there," she said, pointing at the glass door, "and Diana was showing me how to use the accounting software." Her voice now was a little steadier and she wasn't rubbing her arms quite as much. "She had me sit at the computer and she stood behind me and told me what to do." She glanced through the plate glass at the desk and computer. "I turned around to ask her a question. She was looking at the screen just standing there with her hands on her hips…"

"Yeah, okay, then what!"

Looking away from Jasper, the New Girl whispered, "She disappeared." After a moment, she repeated, "She disappeared." She pointed at the office. "And her clothes fell to the floor in there." She began vigorously rubbing her arms again.

Jasper stared at her dumbfounded; he struggled to take in what the New Girl was saying. Slowly, he turned away and pulled open the door to Diana's office, walked inside and plopped down in the desk chair. The New Girl followed him in and took a seat in the chair by the wall, looking at him as if for guidance.

He wasn't even aware she was there. For a long time, he just sat there staring into space, expressionless.

"Reverend Jasper, what we gonna do?"

He looked at her and saw the fear and panic in her eyes. He now understood what had sent her to hiding in the supply closet. If he had witnessed something like someone suddenly disappearing maybe he would run and hide too. A scripture came to mind: 'Fall on us, and hide us from the face of him that sitteth on the throne, and from the wrath of the Lamb.' He recalled how once he had so passionately preached from that scripture in his youth. The sermon was titled *Can't Hide From Wrath*. It had gone over very well. He didn't preach like that anymore. He didn't believe that end-time stuff anymore—not until right now. Now, it was starting to sink in; he was beginning to believe again. He was remembering a subject he used to preach often and fervently: the Rapture.

He thought back to the time when he did preach such things, when he *believed* such things, before the whole prosperity gospel thing had gotten such a hold on him, when he and his young wife, Esther, traveled church to church holding revivals, winning souls, barely scraping by on the meager offerings they received and loving every moment of it.

Again, the New Girl asked, "What we gonna do?"

Guidance? Was this girl looking to him for guidance? He had none to give. He shook his head. "I don't know." Again, he shook his head.

Remembering the old days with his wife gave him an idea. He dug his phone from his pocket and punched out Esther's home number on the touchscreen keypad. Again the message appeared letting him know a connection wasn't currently available. "Still!" He struck the top of the desk and re-pocketed the phone. He glanced at the landline phone right in front of him and walked around the desk and plugged the phone line back in. It began ringing immediately. He sat down, found a line not busy, and made his call. It rang about fifteen times.

Finally, someone answered, "Hello." It was a faint voice, a woman's voice. The sadness in the voice, even with just that one word, was unmistakable.

"Hello, yes, I'm trying to reach Esther. Is she there?"

There was silence for a couple of seconds followed by gentle weeping.

"Hello, please," Jasper said, "tell me what's going on. Can I speak to Esther, please?"

The weeping changed to a throbbing beat of wracking sobs, a rhythm like someone beating on a small drum. She brought it under control long enough to say, "She's gone, Jasper. She's gone."

He stared at the glass door. "Darma? Is that you?" Darma was Esther's sister, no doubt in town for a visit. They often visited each other.

She spoke through the sobs as best she could. "We were in the kitchen ... getting breakfast together. I was getting something out of the fridge ... and turned to ask her where the mayo was. She was at the sink and was just beginning to turn toward me when she just—"

"She just what, Darma?" Jasper asked, already knowing the answer.

The sobbing subsided into a hard, hoarse breathing. "She just ... vanished."

Jasper continued to stare at the door—the door Diana would never traverse again, a door Esther had never, and now, would never walk through.

"Are you there alone?" he asked.

She let out a long breath into the handset; it brushed against the internal speaker loudly. "Don't pretend you care, Jasper." Loathing filled her voice. "This doesn't change anything between us. I'll never forgive you for what you did to my sister. She sacrificed the best years of her life and the comforts of home traveling with you, helping you build a name for yourself just for you to run her off when she got in the way!" She paused a moment and breathed heavily again into the phone handset. "Just because you sold your soul doesn't mean she sold hers. It's happened—the Rapture, it's finally happened." She sniffed harshly, the crying jag ending. "Me? I put it off too long. Mom and sis were always after me to get ready. After mom passed away, Esther kept at me and I kept promising that I would, but, like a fool, I kept putting if off." She sighed. "But you, Jasper, were ready at one time and you let go of it because of your greed. You are just so crazy for money. So, which of us is the bigger fool?"

"Darma, are you there alone now?"

"I already told you, Jasper, don't pretend you care." And the line went dead.

Immediately, Jasper looked up a number on Diana's computer as the office phone rang again and again. He ignored all the incoming calls. No doubt these were people looking for answers. He had none to give so there was no use talking to them. He called the home of Wilson Mattock, his former congregant that had given him the message: Mene, Mene, Tekel, Upharsin. He wondered if he would answer, if he were there or if he was—*gone*. He only got hold of a distraught brother who gave him a similar account to that his former sister-in-law had given him. He hung up and leaned back in the chair. The ringing started getting on his nerves again; he reached behind the phone and once more removed the cord.

During this whole time, the New Girl had sat there quietly listening, staring at him. He turned and looked at her, for the first time really looked at her, and noticed how pretty she was with her slight build and short, straight blond hair. One thing to be said about Jasper is that improper behavior with women had never been a problem with him. Even his ex-wife had said so on several occasions. It was money he loved and money he desired. Everything else, including Esther after a while, was secondary.

He looked at this kid, probably twenty-two, and asked, "What's your name again, young lady. I'm afraid I've forgotten." He sat back down.

"Julie Anderson, Reverend Jasper. It's okay; I only started last week. Diana said it took you a while to learn new people's names.

Jasper smiled and bowed his head. *Just like Diana ... protecting me then and, in a way, even now ... even now that she's ... gone.* He looked behind him at her clothes on the floor. *She's dressed in white, now. For white is the righteousness of the saints, the scripture says.* This was the first time in years he had thought about that passage of scripture.

Julie Anderson asked, "When's Diana coming back?"

His brow furrowed. He turned back to her—the office chair squeaked softly. He stared for a moment at her blank expression. It told him she was in a different place now, a place where her memory was rewriting what she had seen with her own eyes like a writer redoing a scene in a novel. He was about to remind her of what she had told him, of what she had seen, but instead, he told her,

"She'll be back … in seven years, Julie. She'll be back in seven long years." He shook his head. "Long after today; long after the Rapture."

He leaned back in the chair and stared at the ceiling. Then he looked again at Julie. "Julie, you don't have to stay around here. Go on home and be with your family."

However, she just sat there and looked at him. He realized she was looking to him for answers. It made him feel sorry for her.

"Seriously, Julie, just go on home. There's nothing you can do here." He breathed deeply. "There's nothing I can do here." He hoped she understood that he was telling her that there was nothing he could do for *her*, either. Still, she just sat there. "Julie, don't you want to at least call your family, see what's going on at home?"

Her eyes brightened. "Yes, I need to call my mom!" She reached for the handbag on top of the file cabinet and pulled out a cell phone. She tried her mom's number but the call did not connect. She looked at Jasper. "There a message on the screen that says 'service not available.'"

Jasper nodded. "I expect the cell towers are all overloaded just now." He thought about all the desperate and scared people out there that must be trying to reach someone for answers. "Come over here and use the landline phone like I did."

He got up and again retrieved the phone cord from the floor and plugged it back. Again, the phone instantly started ringing. Julie sat at the desk and reached for the handset.

"Julie, don't bother taking any calls from anybody. We can't help them. Just make your call and unplug the phone when you're finished."

She looked at the phone buttons and saw line four was free. She pushed the button and began dialing.

Jasper stepped out into the lobby. He stood there and put his hands in his coat pockets—a practice he usually never allowed himself. When you pay for a suit with what most working people made in a month, you didn't stretch out the lines by putting your hands in the coat pockets. Now? It really just didn't matter, did it? He stood there looking out the glass entry doors at the bright sunshine covering the parking lot. How could such a beautiful day go so wrong so quickly? He remembered a song he heard played on the oldies station a couple of times as he drove to church. It was the Neil Diamond tune, *Brother Love's Traveling Salvation Show*. He knew now that his little show was over and it bothered him. It bothered him that after all this time and effort, his plans for a luxuriant life had ended, and his whole prosperity scam was for nothing.

He walked back down the hall, climbed the stairs to the first floor and went back into the sanctuary and stood there, hands in his coat pockets, looking again at the new crystal cross. He looked at it for a long, long time.

Chapter Eleven

A slight cracking sounded in the tendons of her neck as she stretched her arms and turned her head slowly side to side. Her head tilted back, Susanna drained the can of the rest of the soda and put the empty on top of Mahog. Crossing her arms, she leaned back and closed her eyes.

Tim looked at her; she seemed a little overwhelmed. He remained quiet and gave her time to reflect or absorb or adjust or whatever it was she needed to do with what they had seen on the video. She needed a moment; he didn't blame her. After a minute, she opened her eyes and looked at him.

He said, "Tell me about this Great Tribulation Albert was talking about." He spoke softly, knowing she was still adjusting to whatever it was that was going on. But *he* needed to know what was going on, or at least understand it better than he did now.

"Well, it's all right there," she said, pointing to the Larkin Revelation Chart on the wall behind him. He turned around in his seat and looked at it, straining his neck in the process. "According to Albert's views on

Revelation and particularly the Great Tribulation, which is what he focused on the most, most of the events of the Seven Seals have already happened. And, obviously, the Rapture has happened. That means the cataclysm of the Sixth Seal is up next."

"What's that?"

She raised her brow. "Albert believed it to be a large asteroid strike."

He looked again at her and let out a long breath. *Oh, this just gets better and better.* He said, "What makes, rather, what made him think that?"

"He did a lot of study on asteroid strikes and found correlations between the details of a large strike and the details the Sixth Seal verses give about the event. He thought there were too many similarities to just be a coincidence."

"What do you mean details?"

"Chapter six of Revelation teaches that there will be a great earthquake, one so powerful the mountains and islands will be moved out of place; the sun will become black and the moon will turn blood red. It also says the stars of heaven will fall to earth and the heaven will depart like a scroll when it is rolled together, I guess, meaning the clouds will have a rolling effect, you know, like a mushroom cloud."

At that, his eyes grew very wide.

She sat up and reached for the manuscript, reluctantly picking it up. To her, it had acquired some of that creepiness she had associated with his vacated clothing. Easily, she found the section concerning the Sixth Seal. Having actually written the book for Albert, she knew it like the back of her hand. Under these circumstances, now that she actually believed, she understood the book so much better than before. And that understanding frightened her.

She read, "'Immense earthquakes will rock the globe; every island and the mountains will be moved—shaken. The meteor impact will create a mushroom cloud—the heavens departing as a scroll. The impact launches dust into the atmosphere and ejecta into space. The dust darkens the sky and entirely blots out the sun. Later, when it thins out, it makes the moon appear blood red. The ejecta, the rocks, and debris that is thrown out by the blast will be pulled back down by gravity and ignite in the atmosphere creating a fiery meteor storm—this is the stars falling from heaven. To ancient people, all the objects in the sky, except the sun and the moon, were stars.'" She looked up at him. He sat quietly, listening. "According to Albert, this crisis creates a global emergency, giving the Antichrist the opportunity to seize control over the entire world … the start of the one world government, the real New World Order."

Tim drew a deep breath and let it out slowly. After a moment, he nodded. "I think I see his point. The world is in such bad shape now with a shaky global economy, overpopulation, ecological disasters, world hunger, volatile relations between so many nations, and terrorism. All it takes for it all to come tumbling down is a serious global emergency … especially now with this mass disappearance thing going on."

"Yeah, and it was the first four seals, the Four Horsemen of the Apocalypse, that created those conditions; they paved the way for the Antichrist." She paused. "Albert knew his stuff, especially when it came to the Tribulation which, like I said, he mostly focused on." She glanced at the chart on the wall with all its absorbing images of monsters and disasters. "And now that the

Rapture has actually happened, it will only make things worse." She leaned forward a bit. "When the asteroid hits, the world will panic," she said, tapping the top of Mahog three times with her finger, "and it will be the perfect opportunity for one smart strongman to step up and seize power."

Tim sat up and threw his arms out. "How! How's he gonna do this!"

"At first by lies, claiming to have all the answers, and, indeed maybe he will have some answers. But later it will be by force. He'll have his army and his armaments. Once he gets into power, he will have no intention of letting it go." She looked at the manuscript, then back at Tim. "And of course, he'll have the very power of Satan to back him up."

Susanna felt funny talking this way. She reminded herself of Albert and how he had so often pontificated his views to her. Now, here she was doing it; she was the one speaking on the subject with an authoritative tone; she, who twenty-four hours ago, didn't believe a word of it. She rested her hand on top of the book, the red cardboard cover cool against her skin. She pulled away and clasped her hands together.

"Tim, may I ask what kind of religious background you have? Were your family church-goers?"

He shook his head. "Not really. We went every once in a while, like to a Christmas service or a family thing like a wedding or funeral, but we didn't attend much other than that. I mean, we believed in the Bible, I guess, but none of us knew it very well. You know, just some basic stuff everybody knows about."

"Did you know anything about Bible prophecy?"

"Just what I catch here and there. You know, like the end-time stuff on TV. And I've heard of the Rapture, but I didn't give it much thought."

"You mean until now?"

"Yeah, I guess," he replied. But the truth was he didn't totally believe it now; he wasn't sure what was going on. He knew something odd had occurred but he wasn't at the point he was ready to believe it was this Rapture thing, not like she, evidently, now did.

She leaned forward and laid her arms on top of Mahog. "I was an absolute unbeliever. The only reason I believe now is because I've spent the past half-year studying Albert's years of research in depth, in a way preparing for this day. If not for that, I would be totally denying it, using every scrap of logic and argument against it."

He realized that she would have understood his reticence to accept this Rapture thing if he had come out and said so. Still, he kept it to himself; he didn't feel like an argument or lecture.

"My family," she continued, "was agnostic while I was growing up. There was only the three of us: me, my mom and dad. None of us believed the Bible was much relevant anymore; same with church going. But like I said, the last six months has prepared me to accept what's happened." She shook her head. "And that was not immediate. In fact, it didn't really sink in completely until I was standing beside your police car and it just hit me."

"So that's what that was all about," he said softly.

"Don't get me wrong. We respected people and their deeply held beliefs. We recognized that there seemed to be instilled in people a need to believe in a power greater than themselves. I mean, you see it in all cultures throughout history. But as far as sharing those beliefs, we just didn't."

"I guess I believed in the social system as a greater power. Who knows, maybe deep down that's the reason I became a police officer."

She reflected a moment. "I think I had a fatalistic point of view, but in a kind of positive way, ya know, like whatever will be, will be. But now that I think about it, I did have a kind of faith that somehow things would just work out, that there was a positive force of some kind at work to bring about good although I had no idea of what it was."

He paused a moment. "Do you believe in God, now?"

"She raised her brow. "I guess I have to. I mean, if I'm going to accept the Rapture as real, and I'm afraid I do, then I'll have to accept a lot of other things too, won't I? Since it seems the Bible was right about this, to me at least, it seems it must be right about the rest."

Just then a vacant expression covered her face. He got a little concerned because it was the same expression she had when she blanked out while standing beside his patrol car.

"You okay?"

She focused and looked him in the eye. With a touch of awe, she said, "It just hit me! If the Bible is right about this, then that means that Jesus Christ is coming back to earth in seven years." She stared at him, mouth agape. "You and I may be among the few people on earth that know that, at least for now. You and I may actually see Jesus Christ on earth in person!"

It was his turn to stare at her for a moment. "Man, this is getting deep. I mean really, really deep." He slowly shook his head. "I'm still trying to catch up on all this, so help me out. Tell me about the Beast, the Antichrist. What's his motive in all this, anyway?"

"Power!" she replied. "He will be power mad, so power-hungry it will push everything else aside: love, desire, wealth, everything. He wants total power over the entire world. That, and he wants to be God—the ultimate power."

"What!"

She slowly nodded and tapped her fingers on the book. "All that is happening now is only the beginning." Again, she pointed to the chart. He looked back again but this time turned the chair a bit to save his neck from straining. "All those things are going to happen."

Tim got up and stepped closer to the prophecy chart. He carefully looked over the big rectangular graphic totally covered with intricate drawings and notations. It was a fascinating piece of work with it depictions of angels and trumpets, beasts, and dragons, along with so many other intricately drawn designs. As visually striking as it was, he thought it would have made an intriguing work of art on that alone.

"Look at it, Tim. Look at it and see what's coming." She spoke with a hard edge in her tone, which seemed out of character for such a sweet, pretty girl. "There'll be volcanic eruptions, massive deforestation, air pollution, water pollution, water shortages, meteor strikes, stinging locusts, billions dying in warfare, the mark of the Beast and the agony it brings." She closed her eyes and opened them again. "There'll be rivers and seas turning to blood, a global heatwave, political turmoil, the cities of the world collapsing, islands sinking, mountains crumbling, giant hailstones falling, and other things too." She slowly nodded. "That's the Great Tribulation for you. That's what's coming."

He plopped down in the chair. "Huh! This Great Tribulation doesn't sound so great to me, I can tell ya."

Susanna actually smiled. She couldn't believe it, but she did. Gallows humor, she supposed.

She stood up and walked around Mahog. "I'm going to the bathroom for a minute. I'm getting another soda, too. Want one?"

"Yes, thanks. Getting the life scared out of you is thirsty work."

She stepped out of the study, her footfalls following her as she headed for the half-bath beside the kitchen.

He looked at the manuscript on the desk and picked it up. Absently, he thumbed through the pages. He was willing to admit that, obviously, something strange had happened, but this Tribulation thing, he just wasn't sure. As he patrolled the streets, he had listened to the radio and heard the news reports that millions of people had gone missing around the world. Maybe it was the Rapture; he didn't know. It wasn't his job to know—just to help maintain order. He glanced at his watch; he'd have to be getting back on patrol soon. But all this other stuff Susanna talked about—he wasn't convinced. However, in his training and experience, he'd learned that there's a physiological tendency for people to just not believe that which they just simply can't handle. Some called it denial. He wondered if that was happening to him, and he wondered who in the world *could* accept this!

A heading on one of the pages caught his eye: World of the Tribulation. He read a passage: 'Imagine a global nightmare; the world devoid of God's presence and constantly pressing against your spirit is the dark, evil presence of demonic spirits. The air you breath is dirty, dense and hazy; the water you drink is tainted with blood. You're cursed with a mark that shows your allegiance to the Beast and his government; it is infected causing sores and agonizing pain. The sun beats down on you with intense burning heat and radiation. Its rays are like fire against your infected skin. No clear day or night; the world just languishes in a hazy kind of twilight. There is no peace; civil unrest is rampant; confidence in the government is gone; all hope is gone and the world languishes in spiritual darkness. Now a call to battle goes forth and the armies of the world again prepare for devastating war—this time against Christ himself. This is the world of the Tribulation. You learn all the promises made by the Beast for a better world were just lies and there is nothing you can do about it. And then things get worse …'

He snapped closed the manuscript and dropped it back to the desk. Again, he wondered, *Who in the world could handle this!* He put both hands on the desk and bowed his head.

Susanna walked back into the study carrying a tray with two cans of soda and a plate of oatmeal cookies. Albert always kept some around.

"You okay?" she asked, her tone sweet and gentle as more befitted her. He leaned back in the seat and let her get by. She walked around Mahog, put the tray down and resumed her seat.

"Yeah, I was doing a little light reading." He tapped the manuscript. "Lovely stuff you got there."

She smiled—an actual, real lovely smile and he felt immediately better, far better than he would have thought possible under the circumstances.

"C'mon, have a cookie! They're really good." With that she picked one up and took half of it in one bite; the other half soon followed. She popped open the can of soda and washed it down in a gulp. "I didn't realize how hungry I was," and she grabbed another one; a barely audible burp preceded the next bite she took.

Tim picked one up and took a bite. Taking his time, he opened his soda looking at her the whole while.

Chapter Twelve

She started on her third cookie and thought about what Tim had said about his church background. It prompted her to think about her own. There was little to speak of. She had been to church on some occasions, mainly, like Tim, for family functions and holidays. She recalled a service she went to when she and her mom had visited Aunt Fran last year in Dunlap Ridge, the small town in western North Carolina where her aunt lived:

They took dad's old car—Susanna's now that dad was gone these two months. Her mom had her own car but both of them wanted to use this one. It was in this vehicle that he took so many long drives with them—but not necessarily to see Aunt Fran. Riding together in his old car helped them recall some of the good times they had spent with him riding to one vacation spot or another, often to the North Carolina coast. Susanna recalled the time they stopped on the way to tour the USS North Carolina docked in Wilmington.

His reluctance to visit Fran was not because he disliked her. He just wasn't into all the religious ideology she embraced. Around her, he often felt like he was on guard. He was an open and honest man; being guarded was not natural to him. He had not grown up around her like his wife. He had not built up a resistance to her religiosity like she had, able to just tune it all out. Still, when Aunt Fran came to visit, he treated her kindly and made an effort to make her feel at home. Besides, on his own turf, he felt more in control.

All during the drive, neither Susanna or her mom speculated on where he was now in regards to the afterlife; neither thought about where the dead spend eternity much less discuss it. They knew Aunt Fran probably did, but she would, of course, say nothing—especially now that it was too late to do anything about it.

The ride was pleasant; the morning warm and bright. The two of them rode along chatting in spurts followed by comfortable silences special to those very familiar with each other. At those times, the quiet was filled by the radio.

Mom liked talk radio. Susanna tolerated it for her mother's sake. But in reality, she didn't necessarily relish the advice of idiots. It was funny about her mom. In a way, she was like some people of the political left in that she had no religious leanings. Otherwise, she was a card-carrying conservative. An American flag bumper sticker adorned her car bumper with the legend, *Long May It Wave*.

At Aunt Fran's, they knew they would have to share a room. Aunt Fran's house was small—only two bedrooms. The whole house consisted only of four rooms and a bath. An enclosed back porch almost counted as a room but not quite to Aunt Fran's point of view. It sat on a small plot of land on a back street that was unpaved until three years ago when the town finally got around to it—twenty years after annexing this small rural community. No one knew why it took so long. The house wasn't much, but as Aunt Fran liked to point out, it was all hers; the mortgage had been paid off years ago.

To Susanna, the relationship between her mom and Aunt Fran was a little odd. They were the closest of sisters and dearly loved each other and loved to be together, but in one big way, they were polar opposites. Aunt Fran was religious to the bone while her mom remained a devout agnostic if such a creature existed.

Years ago, her mom told her how she and her sister went there separate religious ways. They both had grown up as 'nominal Christians', meaning they thought of themselves as Christians by tradition but not necessarily by actual faith. They went to church with the family on Sundays, a church comprised of others who thought like them—social Christians, as some would call them—and sang the hymns and tolerated the sermons. Over time their parents began to go to church less and less and by the time the girls were in their early teens, they pretty much only went to church on special occasions. There was no definite point when Susanna's mom became unsure of it all. And if she had lost her faith there wasn't much there to lose in the first place. It was just a growing skepticism that over the years became agnosticism, having neither faith nor outright disbelief in spiritual matters.

As for Fran, after high school, she got a job working in the library of a Christian academy. She did not move into the outright agnosticism of her sister; she just wasn't interested one way or the other. An avid reader, she would look through some of the theology books in the library and became interested in faith matters but only in an academic sense. The school had a chapel service on Sundays. Fran, at the invitation of some new friends she'd made at the school, would attend and they would go out and do things together on Sunday afternoons. This went on for a time and somewhere along the way the messages, delivered so eloquently by the school chaplain, took root and she found herself coming to actually believe the Bible and not just paying it lip service as her family had once done. Her devotion grew from that to becoming a very devout Christian over time.

They pulled into the driveway and saw Aunt Fran standing on the front porch beaming a delighted smile at them. Inside and unpacked, they sat down to lunch and then relaxed in the living room, the two sisters chatting away while Susanna listened, putting in a comment now and then.

After the sisters went into the kitchen to make some coffee, Susanna, declining to join them, moved to the bench in front of the old, beautiful gloss black upright grand in the corner. Such an elegant artifact in such a humble home seemed a little out of place, but it was a very welcome sight all the same.

"Susanna!" Aunt Fran called through the archway to the kitchen; there was no door. "Go ahead and play something for us. I just had it tuned." She sat at the kitchen table waiting for the coffee to boil.

"Oh, yes!" her mom exclaimed. Across the table from Aunt Fran, she reached over and patted her sister's hand. "With her at college now, I never get to hear her play anymore."

Susanna lifted the lid of the keyboard and, like she had done on other occasions, admired the gleaming pearly white keys and the gloss black keys that perfectly matched the piano's immaculate black finish—all the keys in perfect shape, not a scratch or chip anywhere. Aunt Fran was not a great pianist, not the fine musician her niece was, but still, she appreciated this instrument and took very good care of it. Susanna had always loved it and was very thankful to her aunt for the promise she'd leave it to her someday. Aunt Fran had no kids of her own to bestow it upon.

She brought her hands up and hovered them over the keyboard a moment waiting for a song to come to her. She nodded once and started Bach's *Jesu, Joy of Man's Desiring*. The song flowed from her hands as if inspired. She wasn't religious but she couldn't deny the beauty in so much of the music wrought in the name of the Lord. As she played, she admired the genius that could come up with such a beautiful melody so cleverly juxtaposed with dramatic, richly chorded passages, the variations telling a story of their own. As she played, she recalled that before starting college she had seriously considered majoring in music. Instead, she chose to major in English, choosing words as her work. She reserved music as her joy.

After about twenty minutes, she excused herself and went to the bedroom to lay down a while. She pulled off her shoes and stretched across the old-fashioned bed like an old cat settling in for a good nap. The long drive, the nice lunch, a relaxing time at the piano, she was out in under a minute.

She heard voices—mom and Aunt Fran.

"Fran," her mom said emphatically, "I wasn't interested in church before I got here and that hasn't changed since I got here."

As Aunt Fran remonstrated, Susanna opened her eyes. The wall clock read six o'clock; she'd been out about two hours. She sat up and stretched, again resembling a cat. It was Sunday; she knew Aunt Fran was trying to talk her mom into going to the Sunday night church service. She rubbed her face knowing she was next.

***

Loudly and clearly, the preacher's voice rang out with an authoritative but affectionate tone. "Sometimes we can get very discouraged about wanting to help people. Sometimes it gets thrown back in our faces."

Susanna had to assent to this view. As she sat on the cushioned pew beside her aunt, she wished she could have stayed home with her mom. But she didn't have the same relationship with Fran that she did; Aunt Fran had asked her to come. At first, she demurred, but when she saw how much it meant to her, she gave in. After all, she was a guest in her house and very much didn't want to hurt her feelings.

The preacher chuckled and smiled broadly. "Let me tell you a little story of something that happened when I was pastoring in Hillsborough. One Wednesday, after I finished preparing my sermon notes for that evening's service, I had enough time before church to go walk my dog, Sammy Davis, and give myself some time to reflect on the message." He looked side to side at the congregation. "By the way, the reason I called him Sammy Davis was the family I adopted him from said he was multi-talented. I found out later that his talents consisted of eating, sleeping and staring at me whenever I had dinner."

The crowd gave him a pretty good laugh. If this had been a comedy club, he'd be rated perhaps not as hot but pleasantly warm.

She and her aunt sat about midway back of the sanctuary. The crowd was sparse; Aunt Fran told her it would be. Attendance on Sunday nights was far less than Sunday mornings. Susanna looked around. The congregation was attentive to the preacher. She wondered if it was out of true interest or, like her, politeness.

"When Sammy Davis and I made it to the corner of Murray Avenue and West King Street, I heard a lady calling out, "Gretchen! Gretchen!" and saw her standing about a hundred yards up West King in the direction of West Hill Avenue. She stood in a yard with a small dog. But on the road, there was a good-sized boxer-looking dog that was off the leash and walking in my direction. I stood still hoping Gretchen would come up to play with Sammy Davis so I could grab her by the collar and give her back to the lady.

"Well, Gretchen did come up to Sammy Davis. But when I tried to grab her by the collar she ran away and headed up West King Street toward Barracks Road. Sammy Davis and I headed off in that direction to complete our walk. Well, all along the way, all the way down Barracks Road, Gretchen kept coming and getting around Sammy Davis keeping him in a state of excitement; he loves other dogs. I didn't have a whole lot of time before I had to leave for church, so I wasn't crazy about Gretchen slowing us down. But I wanted to help catch and return her if I could. Other people had been so kind to help me and return Sammy Davis the times he got away from me."

Susanna didn't know if this story had a point or if Pastor Gray was just filling up space in the sermon like a writer putting in some extraneous material in a novel to pad the word count to please a publisher. However, she looked on politely as he continued.

"Finally, by the time we got back down to Eno Street, Gretchen came up to Sammy Davis again, but by this time Sammy Davis had lost interest in Gretchen and he wanted to investigate the wooded area along the railroad tracks. So Sammy Davis worked his way into a thicket of small bushes and the leash immediately became entangled around a small bush."

In a story, I guess this would be the element of conflict, Susanna thought. *Gotta have conflict.*

"Just then, Gretchen came up to me and this time, I successfully grabbed her collar which immediately came off in my hand. It had not been adjusted tight enough around her neck, so it slipped right off. Fortunately, she crouched to the ground and I was able to hold her in place, semi-wrestling Sammy Davis all the while stuck in the bush, and worked the collar back on Gretchen's neck. After that, I hooked her up to the leash. Actually, it was a tie-down cable I used as a leash with fasteners on each end. Now, here I was standing on the side of the road struggling with two dogs ... Gretchen pulling one way and Sammy Davis, or rather the cable, still tangled in the thicket, pulling the other way."

The congregation laughed gently.

"I kept calling to Sammy Davis until he finally worked his way out of the thicket. I pulled and pulled on the cable but it simply would not come loose. So I put my foot on Gretchen's end of the cable, unhooked Sammy Davis and, one handed, pulled the cable free from its entanglement as I held Sammy Davis with the other, and then hooked him up again. After some unquiet reflection, and a test of my sanctification, I decided to just take both of them to my home, get the car and take Gretchen back to where I saw the lady standing."

Susanna glanced over at Aunt Fran. She sat listening intently to the humorous antidote, her gaze steady, her expression somber and attentive, as if she were hearing the Sermon on the Mount.

"When Sammy Davis, Gretchen and I got to my place, I was frustrated to discover I had left the car keys in the house. I was getting ready to go inside and get the keys when I heard the lady's voice again calling to Gretchen. I was glad because I realized it meant I wouldn't have to put Gretchen and Sammy Davis in my car and spend a lot of time driving around looking for Gretchen's owner. I was preaching that night and time was getting short. Also, I'd had hoped to get some rest before going to church."

Let's hope you get there soon, Susanna thought.

"I turned around and there on the opposite street stood the lady by her car. I called to her, but she paid me no mind and just kept calling to her dog to come to her. By this time I was already a little aggravated and I wanted to bring this episode to a close and get on with my life!" Soft chuckles from the crowd. "I looked at her and wondered why she just didn't pull around to my house and get her blessed dog!"

More chuckles.

"This good deed of mine had turned into one long, aggravating affair. I went out to walk Sammy Davis hoping to reflect on my sermon but instead I was dealing with all this dog business." He took a step back and shrugged. "Now, I was very happy to help recover the dog. Like I said, many people have helped me recover my escape artist of a dog many times and I'm always glad to return the favor and indeed have done so many times. However, I had come to the point that I wanted this situation to end."

He grabbed the ends of the podium with both hands. "Evidently, the lady expected me to just let go of Gretchen so she could just come to her on her own. I didn't understand this logic. How was it that this rambunctious, free-wheeling, off-the-leash-and-I-don't-care kind of dog was suddenly going to become 'little miss obedient?" Some good hard laughs here. "I'd gone to a lot of trouble securing this dog and I wasn't about to throw that all away now. I spoke up and told the lady to pull around and she asked if her car could get through. This let me know that she probably wasn't familiar with the neighborhood. I told her yes and she pulled around. She rolled down the passenger side window and, if I understood the lady correctly, she wanted me to just let the dog go and allow her to just jump through the window all by herself. It was at this point that I wondered what kind of dream world the lady was living in." He shook his head and the crowd laughed again. "Gretchen had made her intentions clear: she wanted to run loose and just be fancy-free, at least for a while. I told the lady to open the car door. She got out, came around, and, Hallelujah! At long last, she put Gretchen in the back seat. Both Sammy Davis and I were now free to get on with our lives."

The crowd applauded the story. Susanna joined in but it was more out of politeness than actual enjoyment. She didn't get church humor.

The sermon continued another ten minutes and steered away from things like the humorous dog-walking stories and became more serious, more evangelistic. Toward the end, the church pianist, a gray-haired middle-aged lady, returned to the walnut baby grand on the podium, a nice piano for any church especially one no larger than this. She had played for the congregation as they sang and had done quite well. She began playing a slow heartfelt tune that Susanna didn't recognize and provided 'mood music', as Susanna thought of it, for the altar service.

"Let's all stand and bow our heads." The congregation responded to the preacher's request. Susanna stood; her head bowed, she was glad she'd gotten a nap in before she came. She would have hated falling asleep during the sermon and maybe wouldn't have had the energy to do a lot of standing.

"Is there one," the preacher inquired, "here tonight who'd like to come forward and receive salvation?" Looking over the congregation, he paused a moment. Then he added, "Is there somebody?"

Again she was glad for the sleep she'd gotten. With her head bowed like this, it might have been an invitation to a standing nap. She'd heard of such things.

"Is there one? We don't have any guarantee for another chance. But we have the opportunity now. The scripture says, 'Now is the accepted time; behold, now is the day of salvation.' Is there one? Don't put it off; we have no promise of tomorrow."

As the music played, many of the congregants prayed softly. The pastor stopped speaking for a while and waited for a response while looking over the people.

In the solemn atmosphere that now pervaded the sanctuary, her mood began to change. It seemed almost as if some external force was working upon her. She felt somehow nervous and didn't understand why. It seemed like there was something pressing against her heart; not some kind of physical force, but a weight she didn't understand made by something unseen.

"Is there someone feeling that conviction of the Spirit? I believe there is; I can sense it in my heart."

The thought of stepping out of the pew and going down the aisle to where the preacher waited worked upon her. But she resisted—she resisted with all her willpower. She kept her head down and avoided eye contact with the preacher at all costs. He kept calling for someone to come down and she didn't want to do it. She didn't really quite understand why she didn't want to do it. She just knew that it was something alien to her experience and it frightened her like she had never been frightened before. She fought. She fought with all her might. Her very essence seemed to want to go to the altar but another part of her would not allow it.

The struggle continued until at last the preacher said, "Very well, then. Let's be dismissed in order. Susanna felt the pressure easing off her. She felt herself quickly becoming more herself.

As the congregation kept standing, the preacher began, at some length, to repeat points from the sermon he'd just preached. Feeling more normal now, she realized they had all been standing a good little while. She wondered how Aunt Fran's arches were holding up. She glanced to her right; her aunt showed no signs of complaint.

After church, on the way back, Aunt Fran asked, "Well, what did you think of it?"

Susanna replied, "Well, he went a little long for my taste."

Aunt Fran smiled. "At least you didn't get the entire dose of what I call the 'three-time sermon'. That's when you get the sermon before the sermon where the preacher reads the scripture text and makes comments as he goes along, the same comments he's going to make in the main body of the sermon. And, of course, this is done while the congregation is standing all the while. Then comes the sermon itself, often several minutes longer than it needs to be, followed by the sermon after the sermon while just before the dismissal prayer, he recaps his sermon, repeating the things he's already said, also while the congregation is standing, like tonight." She chuckled. "At least you missed the sermon before the sermon part!"

Susanna smiled. "He must've forgot."

She gripped the wheel of the car and thought about the strange way she'd felt during that altar call—the weight upon her heart, that sense of urgency that had seemed to overwhelm her, and how she wanted more than anything to get out of there ...

Now, as she looked across Mahog at Tim starting another cookie, she finishing up the one she held, she realized that if she had accepted the invitation and gone down to the altar that Sunday night last year, then perhaps she too would have been among the missing—gone, safe in the Rapture from what was coming upon the world.

She stopped chewing for a moment and remained very still.

Chapter Thirteen

Buckley and Connie Davidson were much admired among the residents of Cloverdale. The attractive couple seemed to be very happy together as in fact they were. Their marriage fulfilled the state motto: *Esse Quam Videri* very nicely. Whenever friends were around—and the friendly, honest and open pair made friends easily—they could see how attached they were to each other, so easy together. It was an ease born of love and mutual fellowship, not a show put on for the neighbors. There was no doubt that they were the real deal.

Two years earlier, the Davidsons, a thirtyish couple with three kids, had moved into the house across the street from Albert's. The outgoing, friendly couple quickly settled into the neighborhood and became staples at backyard barbecues, yard sales, and other community gatherings. And to have an event without the Davidsons was unthinkable. The pretty, five-foot-seven brunette and handsome, clean-shaven hunk with the thick, black hair gave as good as they got and often had neighbors over for a Saturday cookout or midweek meal. The kids became popular with the other neighborhood kids and always had playmates over for one game or other in the yard.

Connie Davidson saw to it that the kids went to church every Sunday. It was a vestige of the faith she once knew, and a holdover of the influence, the example set by her mother, that compelled her to do this. It was as much out of social custom as it was an expression of faith—like with the large ornate family Bible sitting on the center of the coffee table. A book that seldom was opened.

A local church had a van service for kids—kids whose parents didn't themselves attend—that would stop by the house and pick them up. The driver would toot the horn three times, the Trinity Toot as Miss Clara, the forty-year-old driver, called it, and alert everyone the van was there. She always had a big smile for the kids as they clambered on board. On the side panels and back door of the pale blue and white van, those being the church colors, *Faith Chapel* was emblazoned in gold lettering. It was not like the full gospel church she had grown up in but an independent evangelical church. Still, they had a good solid message with good solid people—and, perhaps most of all, they had a van service.

The Davidsons had considered letting the kids go to *Prosperity Tabernacle*, a church just five minutes away, but after running into Reverend Jasper while taking a stroll near his house a few streets over, and talking to him for only a few minutes, they decided they didn't want their kids to have anything to with that phony. Neither of them were church-goers nor practicing Christians, (though Connie might have bucked at that classification) but they could still tell a hypocrite when they saw one.

When she was a kid, Connie used to go to church with her mom. It was at her mom's insistence; her attendance was not voluntary. She made Connie go at least on Sunday morning for Sunday school and worship service. The Sunday night and Wednesday night services were optional. Over time Connie got more and more involved with church and really came to believe its message. At a service one Sunday, the thirteen-year-old responded to the invitation given at the end of the sermon to accept salvation and she walked up to the altar and made a confession of faith, all to her mother's delight. After that, she started to attend church more often, now on Sunday and Wednesday nights as well. And all without having to be forced by her mother.

Connie joined the choir and, with some training and practice, became a good alto singer. When she was fourteen, she and two other church girls, the McAdams sisters, formed a trio and became pretty good. The choir training had helped Connie to understand harmony parts and she was able to teach the McAdams girls reasonably fast. They became very popular with the congregation of the small church that comfortably sat about 250. When revivals were held—those one or two week campaigns for souls and spiritual renewal of the congregation—she willingly attended every night and her trio would sing nearly every service. They sang with such force, such anointing, that many came forward to the altar to accept salvation without the necessity of the sermon or invitation. The visiting evangelists, as a rule, had no objections to this. They would say something like, "As long as the good work gets done and people came to salvation, that's all that matters." Anyway, they knew they would get paid just the same simply for showing up.

But in only a short time, as she got a little older, Connie's interest began to wane. This was a trend that so many pastors and godly parents have witnessed too many times before. Young people who once were on fire for their faith somehow let the fire burn out. By the time Connie reached the age when she was taking more and more notice of boys and also the music, fads and fashions that teenagers, no matter what the era, fall prey to, she again was getting reluctant to even go to church. To make matters worse, as far as her devout mother was concerned, the boys who attracted her attention were not those who attended church. The religious types just didn't seem to interest her very much. Perhaps, it was a case of Bad Boy Syndrome—a condition she understood all too well.

As a young woman, she too was attracted to a young man not in her church or any church. His name was Todd. He was not a mean guy or really a bad boy but a manly, fit youth who was not all consumed with religion like the guys in her church were. He appealed to a very different aspect of her nature. She and Todd eventually got married with her harboring the delusion that one day he would suddenly become interested in church and start attending with her—a delusion shared by a lot of church women in similar situations. He never did.

Later in life, Connie's mom came to marvel how often devout, church-going women, like herself, who truly loved their faith and church, would, in a way, betray it and become 'unequally yoked together with unbelievers,' as scripture might describe it.

It happens a lot—a whole lot.

And now, Connie seemed to be on a similar path but even more, and alarmingly, divergent. As her interest in spiritual things dimmed, her church attendance became sporadic and her priorities became slowly readjusted to other things like education, career, and dating with a view to marriage. Worthy and important things, her mother agreed, but as her mother often told her, she could pursue them and *still* be in church. But to her mother's sorrow, by the time she indeed did get married at nineteen, to a nice looking, fit, and definitely unchurched young man named Buckley Davidson, her interest in church was gone completely. Connie still believed but not enough to do anything about it. Not anymore. *Esse Quam Videri* may have applied to her marriage but no longer to her faith.

During her church days, Connie had learned about the Rapture. Her fundamentalist evangelical full-gospel church had educated her to the doctrine that the day was near. Every so often, the church would have prophecy teaching on Wednesday nights. The pastor would talk about devastating calamities coming upon the earth, earthquakes, fiery hail falling to the ground, and also hailstones weighing maybe seventy-five pounds. He would talk about great air and water pollution, a plague of stinging locusts, and other judgments to be brought upon humankind. He explained the symbolic meaning of various creatures—beasts and dragons—mentioned in the Book of Revelation and Daniel. But the Mark of the Beast was, most of all, what really left a mark on her imagination.

But she had lost interest in that, too.

Now standing on the lawn, the warm sunshine falling gently against her bare arms, she looked down at the piles of clothes on the ground with a faint memory of those old teachings coming to mind.

She had been looking through the kitchen window over the sink, where she stood putting the breakfast dishes into the running water, and watched as the kids laughed and played with such happy abandon. *To feel joy like that again!* she thought. The only time she had felt that kind of joy was when she was still in church. Just as she stared at Lucinda, in her Princess Leia outfit, waving around the long, plastic tube serving as a lightsaber, her daughter disappeared, the toy and outfit falling to the ground. The other kids were gone too. Motionlessly, she stood behind the sink and stared out the window, her mouth and eyes wide open. A plastic plate fell from her wet hand and bounced on the floor.

Barefoot, wearing a sleeveless blouse and knee-length white cotton shorts, she ran across the kitchen floor and out the back door. Her long, thick black hair, pulled back in a ponytail, danced recklessly against the back of her neck. She flew around the corner of the house and stood looking down at the—remains.

Something from scripture came to mind. It was from the book of Daniel and it was about an angelic messenger who gave a wicked king a sobering message that his time was up and he had been judged and found wanting. It was also a phrase the pastor often quoted in regards to those who had tried the Lord's patience too much, those who had refused his call too often: Mene, Mene, Tekel, Upharsin.

The neatly trimmed grass beneath her feet suddenly seemed a little cooler. In fact, the day felt cooler despite the warm sunshine. She looked down not moving or speaking for several minutes. Then she knelt down before the empty clothes of her children and whispered softly, "No ... no-no-no-no-no ..."

And that was all. A blank stare replaced the expression of barely contained hysteria on her face. After a minute of staring quietly at the ground, she calmly got up and went back inside.

When she entered the kitchen, her feet splashed against the thin film of water overflowing the sink and spilling across the linoleum floor. She paid no notice but walked straight to the phone mounted on the wall beside the refrigerator.

***

Sunlight spilled through the large front window of the shop. It cast the shadow of the name, *Davidson Paint And Tile* onto the floor. Buckley Davidson had been here since opening time. He was working solo this morning since this was Doug Harper's usual morning off. So far it had been a normal busy morning with customers consisting almost exclusively of paint contractors coming in to get a head start on the day. Buckley stood behind the register and rang up the five-gallon bucket of semi-gloss sandstone latex for Joe Winton who stood beside it.

"Thanks, Joe," he said and handed him a receipt. Joe Winston smiled and tipped his cap, the one with the Jesus fish on it. He rolled the huge, heavy plastic bucket out the door. Buckley watched as Joe and his helper hefted the thing into the back of a pickup with Winston Painting stenciled on the side. A phone number was under the name.

For the first time that long morning, he was alone in the store. He knew the bulk of his business was done for the day. Now it would be mostly homeowners coming in and getting a gallon of this or that to do some sprucing up around the house. His wasn't a large shop; there were other paint stores in town twice as big with a more elegant decor designed to attract the non-professional, but he did good business with much less overhead than some of the other shops—meaning he could give professionals a bit better discount. That was mainly why his shop was so popular with contractors.

He looked around the compact shop, cans of paint stacked along the walls, and down the center aisle, and let out a breath. With things quieter, he thought about Doug and wondered what he was up to.

The sound of a crash made him step over to the front door and look out. Just across and down the street, a few doors from his shop, sat Joe's truck against the brick wall of the post office. The wall was bashed in a bit. The truck had crossed the street, come over the sidewalk and ran into the building. People stood on the short brick stairway leading up to the post office entry staring down at it. It didn't look too serious.

Buckley came out and trotted down the street. When he reached the truck, he looked through the driver's side window. No one was in the driver's seat.

"Where's Joe?" He looked at Joe's helper sitting in the passenger seat.

The young man—dark hair, about nineteen—sat very still, staring through the windshield. Jeff, he believed was the young man's name.

"Jeff!" Jeff looked at him. "Where's Joe? Is he hurt?"

"He's gone!" Jeff said, breathlessly. "We were coming down the street, he was talking about the job we were heading for across town and he just wasn't there anymore."

Buckley looked down and saw Joe's coveralls on the driver's seat—on top was his Jesus fish cap tangled in the still fastened seatbelt. The Sign of the Fish, the Ichthys, seemed to be looking up at him. He didn't know what to make of it.

He looked over the front of the truck. The bumper and left front fender were smashed up pretty bad and both would have to be replaced. Far as the grill and radiator, he couldn't tell. Looking around, there was no sign of Joe, a valued customer he'd hate to lose. He wondered where he went to and what the kid, Jeff, was talking about when he said he disappeared.

Just then a police car pulled up and he backed out of the way. Except for being a little shook up, Jeff seemed all right. With nothing more he could do here, he decided to head back to his shop. He turned to go but stopped. Since he was already here, he decided to buy a book of stamps; there were not many left in the store's office desk.

He walked around the truck and stepped away from the police and spectators gathering near the scene of the accident and headed up the steps. To his right, he noticed what looked like a pile of clothes lying on the brick steps. He looked over and saw two more of such piles. He didn't know what to make of them.

After returning to the shop, he put the mystery out of his mind and busied himself on the computer updating inventory. He placed a few orders online. Just as he began totaling receipts the phone rang. It was his wife talking something about the kids being gone. The way she talked, she sounded crazy.

Chapter Fourteen

Susanna brushed her hands together and knocked away cookie dust from her fingers. After picking up the remote from the desk, she pressed the power button and the TV on top of the short bookcase blinked into life. She wanted to see what was going on, how the media was responding to the sudden disappearance of so many people.

The TV was turned to a local affiliate, not one of the big cable news channels. She recognized the fortyish lady newscaster, Georgette McMillan, having seen her on TV so often in this very study. Albert usually turned on the four o'clock news; it would drone in the background as they worked. Why this newscast, she didn't know. The lady didn't seem to have any particular insight into anything. She was good-looking, smiled a lot, proficient at the phony, banal on-screen repartee with the other newscasters and read a teleprompter well enough, qualities Susanna pretty much assumed were all local affiliates demanded of their on-air personalities. (Brains not required.) She sometimes wondered if Albert had a little crush on the TV news lady. It was nowhere near four, so this had to be a special report.

"...and the police have not reported," Georgette McMillan said as they caught her in mid-sentence, "any real increase in incidents of violence, just a general sense of shock and dismay around the Triangle." She looked to her co-anchor, Bob McIntyre. "And of course, Bob, that is true all around the country, right now."

Bob McIntyre said, "As we've already reported, the number of missing person reports has dramatically increased as one caller after another has contacted law enforcement agencies all around the Triangle concerning the mysterious, unexplained disappearance of a friend or loved one. And in this time of anxiety, it's no surprise reports are coming in of churches being overrun with people trying to get in. But at many of them, no one is there."

Georgette's lovely, immaculately made-up brown eyes slightly shifted as she, no doubt, saw a change in the text on the teleprompter. "We have a special report from our network news department. It brings what might seem like startling information into an already incredible situation. Here's Jim Dillon in New York."

The TV screen switched to a handsome middle-aged man seated behind a large circular news desk in the network's news studio. Jim Dillon, the famous network news anchor, was looking into the camera. "In another bizarre twist of the amazing events of today, we have some startling video that reportedly depicts people standing on clouds. We take you to Philip Cary, our digital media correspondent."

Susanna sprang from the seat behind the desk and knelt in front of the TV. She became very still; one hand gripped the end of the bookcase beside her and she stared unblinkingly at the screen.

The picture changed to another studio. A young man sat behind an office desk. The name, Philip Cary, was displayed on the bottom of the screen. On top of the desk and to his left sat a laptop computer.

"On this, an already strange day, some remarkable videos have been popping up on social media and popular video sharing sites." He spoke in a chipper tone and held out his hands almost in supplication. "These strange videos purport to show people standing on clouds in the sky." He put his hands on the desk. "One of the amazing things about them is that they were all taken, it seems, at the same time the unexplained disappearances are believed to have taken place. And they come from all over the world. People using smartphones took several such videos as the one you're about to see. Let's watch this one taken from a plane flying over Atlanta. Look closely and you'll see humanoid figures all in white garments standing on the clouds.

The TV screen changed to a scene of the interior of an airplane. The small window in the middle of the shot had soft curved edges and was unmistakably an airplane window. The video, taken with a smartphone that the owner held remarkably still, had no audio. It was probably turned off by the news studio to silence the screaming in the background, Susanna surmised. Outside the window, the sky was filled with fluffy white clouds floating beside the high-flying plane.

And then she saw them. Tim did too and stood up. People were standing on the clouds. It was hard to recognize just exactly what kind of people, but definitely humanoid figures. And there were so many of them, all with their backs to the camera, all of them looking up as if staring at something. Susanna wondered if Albert was one of them. Their clothes were so white they shone even beyond the brilliant sunlight around them. It looked as though they were illuminated from the inside out.

"This is just one of many similar videos that have been posted on the Internet since earlier this morning."

The video ran for several seconds and suddenly the clouds were completely empty, all occupants gone. The remaining few seconds showed the clouds drifting silently by, unoccupied.

"Here's another video; this one was taken on a flight while it was approaching Tokyo." The next video began to play.

She sat down on the floor and watched, as on TV, Bible prophecy had been captured on camera. She looked at her unblemished right hand and wondered how long before someone demanded a 666 go there. A little bit of cookie dust still stuck to her palm as her hand trembled.

She got to her knees and leaned a bit closer to the TV. Her face was now only a foot away from the screen. She had not forgotten Tim standing to her left. She was careful to angle herself so that he could still see.

This time, whoever had taken the Japan video held the phone lens right up to the glass of the airplane window; no window edges were visible. The scene was one of a completely dark background, it being night in Japan when the video was taken, still night there now Susanna realized. Despite the dark, the scene was filled with countless points of brilliant light, lights dazzling against the dark background that stood perfectly still and radiated with a supernal beauty.

Some of the bodies of light closer to the camera could be made out as human shaped, having, like in the other video, torsos, arms, heads and presumably legs underneath the shining robes. Neither video was detailed enough to show the feet of these figures of light, but Susanna was sure the feet were like unto fine brass as she recalled the description of Christ's feet in Revelation.

Tim stared at the screen in utter fascination.

"I never, before today, thought it could be real." She glanced at Tim. "Never. Not once did it occur to me it could really happen," she said, her voice shaking. "And I guess if I accept this," she nodded toward the screen, "I'll have to accept the rest."

She thought about what this meant, all the horrors that the Tribulation would now bring to the world. For a moment, she felt a little lightheaded. Silently, she stared at the flickering images on the TV. The Great Tribulation Albert taught her, the seven-year period of judgment began, according to what she learned from him, the moment the Rapture occurred. She thought about all the horrors to be unleashed upon the world. All of the judgments coming upon Earth. It was like something out of a scary movie. *This is real!* she thought in dismay. *This is really happening!*

Tim tore his eyes from the screen and looked at her. "What do you mean the rest!"

The TV reporter continued. "But now let's take a look at some pictures you may find equally startling."

Susanna held up a finger and pointed at the screen.

Once more Philip Cary was on the screen. He was replaced by the photo that popped up. "This is a satellite image taken over West Germany at the same time of the videos you just saw. Look closely and you'll see people again standing on the clouds. They, too, appear to be looking up."

Susanna leaned a little back from the screen and stared at the picture. It was hard to make out exactly what she was looking at, but there were clouds and figures were standing on them. The picture was not zoomed in enough to give great detail, and the figures were very tiny. There appeared to be a huge number of them, all looking up as if waiting for someone to meet them.

The studio camera came back onto Philip Cary. "To see other startling video and pictures, go online to our website."

The screen again showed the anchorman; he was looking to his left presumably at a monitor.

Tim reached for the side of the TV and turned it off. "What did you mean, *the rest?* I'd like to know."

She looked at him almost with pity. "I meant the Tribulation like I explained before. Remember? That's what's next."

"You mean like the Apocalypse!"

"Actually, the word Apocalypse just means Revelation." She shook her head. "Listen to me; I'm starting to sound like Albert. No, I'm talking about the Great Tribulation like I told you about." She paused a moment, then said, more quietly, "Actually, it's already started. It started the moment the Raptured happened. And we'll need to remember that. I mean, today's date."

"Why?"

"There are things listed in the books of Daniel and Revelation that are on set timetables in reference to the seven years of the Tribulation, and the Rapture started the Tribulation." She paused again and reflected on the fact that she was now living in the Tribulation. She felt her stomach tighten—the cookies and cola near to coming back up.

He shrugged. "Well, that I didn't know. But I've heard of the Tribulation, you know, before you even told me about it. I had heard this and that." Again, he shrugged.

"I know that it's, you know, bad." He paused a second and said almost sheepishly, "I saw a Simpsons episode about it." His eyes widened. "Man! At the time I actually thought it was funny!"

She sat back down behind Mahog to steady herself; she felt herself coming back under control. "I can tell you more about it; go into at least a little more detail."

"Yeah, sure. I'd like to know what's going on."

Suddenly, his radio, which had been quiet an unusually long while, squawked giving a call to another unit. That brought him back to the immediate reality of what he had to do.

"Listen, on second thought, I've got to get back to patrol duty." He took a large gulp of soda and looked at her a moment. "Susanna, this is highly unusual to ask. But these are unusual circumstances. Would you like to come along with me on my patrol? I really want you to come with me." He wanted her near. She seemed to actually have some idea of what was going on. Plus, the idea of leaving her here all alone did not appeal to him. But mostly he just wanted her near. "You could explain the Tribulation to me while we ride."

Right now, being alone was the last thing she wanted. "Let me get a few things together and we'll go. She stepped into the front room and got her shoulder bag from the red and white striped chair where she'd left it earlier. She carried it over to Mahog and dug out a thumb drive that she plugged it into one of the USB ports. After she sat down in front of the computer, she downloaded all of Albert's videos and a digital copy of the manuscript. She saw on the computer the file folder she knew contained a collection of Bibles in various translations along with several commentaries. She copied that folder too. The Bibles and commentaries might come in handy later. She took the thumb drive from the computer and dropped it back into her shoulder bag.

She looked up at the Larkin Revelation chart on the wall and thought she'd like to have something like that as well. But she recalled how some of Albert's views differed with some points on that chart: chiefly the placing of the Rapture just before the First Seal. Albert's view was that it should be placed just before the Sixth Seal, making the first Five Seals as well as the Rapture all pre-trib, set just before the seven-year Great Tribulation. The Rapture itself, Albert had taught her, was the Tribulation start point. In light of the circumstances, she had no reason to doubt his views. Then it hit her again like it did while she watched the Raptured saints standing on the clouds to meet the Lord in the air, as it says in scripture. She looked away from the chart. *This is it! We're actually in the Tribulation. This is it!* She felt her skin cool.

Tim noticed her staring into space. "You okay?"

She focused on him. "Yeah." She shook her head. "Just had a bit of a reality check, that's all." Her eyes suddenly brightened. "I remember now! Albert made his own simplified timeline!" She opened the middle drawer of Mahog and pulled out a one-foot by two-foot white, glossy cardboard placard. The large poster was covered with simpler and more accessible lines and notations; it looked to him they had been drawn with a felt-tip pen. The wrinkles and discolored edges of the chart were evidence of constant consulting. She rolled it up and put a rubber band around it. "I'm taking this too," she said and put it in her handbag, the end sticking out like a French baguette just purchased from a bakery.

She glanced at the bookcase against the exterior wall and something caught her eye. She saw the new black hardbound, giant print New Testament Albert had ordered online that had arrived last week. The digital Bibles she'd copied were okay, but there is still a certain something about holding a real book in your hands that digital devices just couldn't match. She stepped over to the bookcase and pulled it out. As she held it, she felt the finely textured surface of the hardcover against her fingertips. The handsomeness of the trim, high-quality book, smartly accented with gold lettering on the front and spine, was something to be admired. It even smelled good. She dropped it in her shoulder bag with the rest of the things she was taking. She had gotten to know Albert very well and knew he wouldn't have minded.

She returned to the computer and pressed the power button on the top and watched as it began its boot-down routine. As she watched, the screen blinked off and she caught her reflection in the blank screen. To her, it was very much like saying goodbye to something.

"Oh!" she exclaimed as if she had just received an electric shock. "I need to call my mom. I promised I'd come over and stay with her." She tried her cell and got no connection. After several tries, still no luck.

Tim said, "The cell towers are all probably jammed up right now. Happens in a crisis." *Is this a crisis?* he asked himself. "Try a regular landline."

She looked at the phone beside the computer; Albert was one of the few people she knew who still had one of these as well as a cell phone. She picked it up and got through to her mom.

"Mom, I'll be over soon as I can, but I'm a little tied up now. How 'bout going over to Mrs. Danner's and you two keep each other company till I get there? I'll be with you in a little while, I promise." Her mom agreed and they hung up.

She stepped around Mahog and stood under the archway. Sure this would be the last time she would see the monstrous old desk and this cozy study, she took a moment and looked around, her face a little sad. She turned around and she and Tim headed for the front door.

Chapter Fifteen

As he approached his house on Tomato Lane, he noticed a lot of people milling around the streets and lawns and wondered what was going on. He parked in his usual spot in front of the house and noticed a police car parked just around the corner on Cucumber Street next to the side yard. The thought entered Buckley's mind that maybe the police were after him. After that crazy call from his wife, something about the kids disappearing, he'd closed the shop, got in the truck and rushed home. He got here in ten minutes. Maybe he moved a little too fast and the police had taken notice.

As he hurried up the walkway toward the front door, he looked at the police car. It was empty. He glanced around but didn't see a police officer anywhere. He looked at the house across the street. *Something up with Albert?* he wondered. Is that why all these people are milling around? He looked over the scattered crowd. Whatever it was, it would have to wait. He had his own mystery to solve. His all-consuming urgency to speak with

Connie made him hurry. Quickly, he opened the front door and went inside.

He stepped into the kitchen and saw water all over the floor. Connie was not there. He stepped over to the sink and turned the water off. Still, he heard the sound of water faintly singing in the faucet and knew water was running somewhere else in the house.

"Connie!" he shouted. From somewhere in the back of the house he heard her call his name. He walked down the short hall, bedrooms doors left and right, and saw her in the bathroom at the end of the hall, its door standing open. She was washing her hands in the bathroom sink. She turned the water off and picked up a towel.

"Oh, hi!" she said, smiling broadly, wiping her hands. "What in the world are you doing home this time of day?"

For a moment, he stood gaping at her. "What do you mean? You called me saying the kids are gone!"

She looked at him with a quizzical expression. "Gone? Of course, they're gone. It's a school day, isn't it?" She walked out of the bath and headed for the boy's room.

He shook his head. "No, Connie, it isn't." Following her into the boy's room, he added, "It's spring break; you know good and well they've been home all week." Now closer to her, he carefully examined her face. She seemed chipper, happy, unconcerned—a big difference from the monotone, barely restrained frantic tone she spoke in when she called him just a little while ago. Something was wrong. What it was, he couldn't tell, but something was very wrong. "Are you okay?" There was a glazed look in her eye he'd never seen before.

"Yes, I'm fine. Why shouldn't I be?" She turned to the twin beds and started to make them up.

He stared at her and spoke slowly, emphatically. "Connie, where are the kids?"

She kept busy and said, "I told you; they're at school." She moved around the beds quickly and was nearly done with one.

"No, they're not!" he shouted. "There is no blasted school this week!" He hated it when he shouted. He wasn't a loud man and it took a lot to get him angry enough to raise his voice—especially to the woman he adored and who was the mother of his three kids. And a great mother at that.

Without responding, she finished the bed and started on the other one. He stared at her in amazement. The kids were not here, and if she knew where they were, she wasn't saying.

"Have you let them go over to the Conroy's place and you don't want to tell me? You know how I feel about them."

A couple of weeks earlier the Conroy's two rambunctious nine-year-old boys had swiped a few of their dad's cigarettes and tried to get the kids to smoke with them. Buckley hit the roof when Connie told him and forbade the kids from being around them until their parents had straightened them out on smoking.

Connie glanced at him. "No, they're not with the Conroy boy unless …"

He gave his head a quick shake. "Yeah, unless what?"

Connie moved to the other side of the bed and quickly finished up. She headed out the door and started to her daughter's room.

He followed her and demanded, "Unless what!"

"Unless the Conroy boys went too," she said calmly, matter-of-factly and stepped over to the single bed and started making it.

Again, he quickly shook his head. "Went where, Connie? That's what I'm trying to figure out."

She said nothing; she was immersed in this simple task that obviously occupied her entire attention.

He stepped over and took her by the arm and gently turned her around to face him. "I'm tired of this. You tell me right now what's going on."

She smiled broadly. "It's the Rapture!" She giggled. "It actually happened." She started laughing. "The Rapture happened and the kids are gone and we're here!" She snickered a bit. "Ain't it wonderful? The kids made it. We didn't but the kids did." She smiled so widely her mouth gaped wide open and her brow rose to a high arch. She looked insane. "It's like Homer Simpson would say, and she spoke in a faux dramatic tone, "We done been left below," and she started howling with laughter.

Stunned, his mouth parted, he stared at her for a long moment. This woman he had loved since they were both teenagers, the woman who was one of the most level-headed women he'd had ever met, the woman he knew he was so very lucky to have as a wife ... this woman was—mad.

The insane smile faded and she looked him square in the eye. Taking a slight breath, she whispered, "And I looked, and behold a pale horse!" She held up a finger like a preacher in the pulpit emphasizing an important point. "And his name that sat on him was death, and hell followed with him!" She pointed the finger at Buckley and laughed again. "Don't you remember? I use to go to church! I use to know about all that stuff." Another broad smile. "I haven't tried calling my mom yet." A short giggle. "What's the use? I'm sure she went." She nodded vigorously. "She and the kids all stepping on the clouds!" She danced around a bit then burst into a fit of strident laughter.

He stepped back from her as if horrified. The kids missing and a wife gone mad, how much more could he take?

After several seconds, she calmed down and her face resumed that blankness she had while she did the boys' beds. Finished here, she walked to the kitchen and stood in front of the sink. She started on the remaining dishes, the water stone cold now.

Buckley came back into the living room and watched her through the arch leading into the kitchen. There was no door. Connie liked an open airy environment for her home. Growing up in her parent's house, everybody always ended up around the kitchen table, talking, drinking freshly brewed coffee, snacking on cookies or made-from-scratch biscuits. Connie loved that and carried on the tradition in her home. It was very informal and, like at her parent's house, most of their guests ended up in the kitchen. Connie thought that since they were going to see it anyway, why hide it?

As he watched her, he was still anxious to know where the kids really were. Hopefully, at one of the neighbors safe and sound. They often visited their friends as their friends visited them. Even if they were with the Conroy boys, at the moment, he wouldn't mind. At least that would make sense—not like this insane babbling.

He wondered what had happened to her, what had caused this, hopefully temporary, loss of reason. She didn't drink, a holdover from her church days, and she didn't do drugs; that was for sure. Maybe a product she used for some cleaning purpose had an adverse effect on her. He'd heard of such things. And now that he thought about it, it seemed very possible. She was fastidious to a fault and vigorous in her cleaning. That's why it was so odd she ignored the water on the floor. Yes, she could easily have spilled something on her skin that got absorbed into her bloodstream and caused some kind of psychotic reaction making her behave like this. He'd take her to the hospital as soon as he located the kids.

But as he watched her wash the dishes, he thought about Joe just a while earlier tipping his Jesus fish cap. Was Joe a Christian? He never heard him use bad language or tell off-colored jokes like so many of his customers did. Never saw him smoke or hungover. Maybe he was a believer. Maybe that's why he wasn't in the truck when he looked inside. Maybe that was why his clothes were lying on the seat and floorboard. Maybe he was—gone.

He looked around the living room at the windows. A movement outside caught his eye. Looking out, he saw that now even more people were milling about. He thought that things were getting very strange out there as well as in here and it made him feel uneasy, nervous and ... vulnerable.

Quickly, he went to the bedroom and opened the closet. He pulled down the black case on the top shelf and sat it on the bed. He worked the combination lock and then pulled back the lid. There lay his nickel-plated thirty-eight snub-nose revolver. In this day of nine-millimeter automatics, this weapon might have seemed a little old fashioned. But autos have been known to jam and they were a pain in the neck to clean, at least so it seemed to Buckley, admittedly no gun expert or even enthusiast. The simplicity of the revolver, such as no safety to disengage in a hurried emergency like a home invasion, appealed to him. Just point and pull the trigger, that's all. And it was a good quality gun too. Just looking at it, anyone could tell. Even a gun novice like him could see it when he bought it from Fred Wilkins at his gun shop over on the next street from Buckley's paint store.

He would never admit it to anyone, but having the gun, holding it in his hand, gave him a feeling of power. It was a secret indulgence of his that when alone sometimes in the room, he'd take it down and hold it, examine it and point it as if he was about to fire. It gave him a slight rush—it gave him power. He liked that feeling and he needed that feeling now.

He slipped the gun into his hip pocket. He didn't know what was going on. Having the gun countered that feeling of uncertainty. He walked back into the kitchen. Connie had finished the dishes and was wiping the sink, her bare feet squishing against the wet floor.

"Connie, I'm going to take you to see a doctor. First, I've got to know where the kids are."

Now wiping down the sink counter, she replied in a calm even tone, "I told you where they are; they're gone in the Rapture. Ain't that wonderful?"

He shouted, "I'm tired of all this nonsense!" He put his hands on his hips, his breath coming now in quick gasps. "I want to know where the kids are! What have you done with them!" Now he was scared. Has some chemical reaction that caused this state of mind caused her to do something with the kids? He's heard of that sort of thing, too. The thought was horrible.

She turned toward him and picked up a kitchen towel. "I told you already what happened to the kids," she said, wiping her hands.

As she stood there performing this simple, ordinary and normal act, she seemed more normal and rational than she'd been since he'd come home. The wild look had gone from her eyes and she seemed herself again.

Yet, the kids were missing.

There are moments in life when even a good man or woman can come to a point of no return. His wife was freaking him out. He was scared to death thinking of what she may have done to his kids in her present mental state. He wanted answers and he wanted them immediately. Now, he didn't care how he got them.

"One more time, Connie, where are the kids?"

She gave him a look of exasperation. "I've told you and told you. They're gone in the Rapture. I saw them disappear myself." She put the towel down. "I know it takes a little time to absorb but ..."

He yanked the gun from his hip pocket and pointed it at her head. *"Shut up! Shut up! Shut up!"*

She stood looking at her husband pointing a pistol in her face. Her last words were, "At least the kids made it. Thank heaven for that. Lord, forgive me. Lord, save me!"

That was it. That was the point when reason took a momentary leave of absence and he pulled the trigger and the woman he loved more than life itself flew backward and crumbled to the wet kitchen floor.

He didn't mean it. He really didn't. It was a reflex action. He only pulled the gun in the first place as a crazy attempt to bring her back to coherence, so she could tell him where the kids really were. That's what he told himself.

He stood looking down at her and heard a banging at the front door. A man's voice was barking orders. His dazed mind thought he heard the name Jordan. He'd had irate customers in the past that had been dissatisfied with the color blend he'd made for them. Some of them came back to the store and demanded refunds. Once, he actually had one come to the house seeking satisfaction. He wondered if it were one of them outside now making demands. He couldn't recall any customers named Jordan.

He continued to stare at the lonely figure on the kitchen floor, the woman he loved as much as he was capable of loving another human being. As the person named Jordan continued to bang on the front door, teardrops began streaming down his face. *What have I done! What have I done!* He wanted to scream; he wanted to yell his lungs out but he couldn't. The wracking sobs now bursting from his mouth prevented him from speaking. *What have I done!* His body shook so hard he almost dropped the gun, but instinctively, he held onto to it. He knew he wasn't through with it.

Now perfectly still, he stared forward for a moment. Then, quickly, he turned to his right and marched down the hall and into his and Connie's bedroom. After sitting down on the bed, he put the gun's muzzle to his temple and pulled the trigger.

Chapter Sixteen

Once outside, Susanna and Tim noticed things had become much more active out here. There was distant shouting coming from all directions, and a scream came from just down the street. More people were out milling around, craning their necks, searching for something or someone. Some seemed to be just onlookers puzzled by what was going on; others looked frantic as if afraid they knew all too well what was going on.

From across the street, they heard a gunshot. To Susanna, it seemed to come from inside the Davidson house.

Tim immediately drew his weapon and told Susanna to go back inside the house. She obeyed and shut the door behind her. Tim rushed across the street to the front door and stood to one side. He banged on the door and yelled, "My name is Jordan; I'm a police officer. Open this door!"

He banged on the door again and again. After a few moments, there came another gunshot. He crouched down. Normally, he would call for other units to assist but he knew, under these Code Six circumstances, every single unit was busy with its own problems and none would probably arrive, at least not soon enough to do him any good.

Loudly, he yelled, "Police!" Many of those milling around, shambling about almost like zombies, became more alert at hearing the gunshots and seeing a police officer respond. They looked on, curiously. Through the window of Albert's living room, Susanna watched as Tim stood at the door. She hoped he'd be very careful.

Tim yelled, *"Open the door! Now!"*

There was no response. There was no sound at all. He was afraid he knew what that meant.

His right hand held the police-issue nine-millimeter automatic in front of him—a hollow point just a finger squeeze away from discharge. With his left hand, he tried the door handle and found it unlocked. He turned the knob, pushed the door open and moved to the side standing clear of the entry. He leaned to his right, glanced inside and immediately pulled back. He'd seen no one moving, especially the poor woman on the kitchen floor. Still, there was no sound. He stepped right and sprang inside the room, his gun pointed forward. Again, he listened very carefully. Nothing. There was only the smell of gunpowder.

Susanna watched him go in, but he stayed inside for only a few moments. He came out, his head bowed low and his pistol now holstered.

She stepped out of Albert's front door and ran across the street and joined him on the front step of what used to be the Davidson's house. She could see partly into the kitchen. The floor was glistening with water … and something else, something redder, darker that was still spreading.

He looked up. "Don't go in there."

This time, she did not obey. She didn't know the Davidsons that well but she wanted to know what had happened. As for Mrs. Davidson, the answer was immediate. After stepping just inside the house, she could now see her lying on her back on the kitchen floor—a gaping wound where her face had been, an apron still neatly tied about her waist and soaked with blood. Susanna gasped and threw her hands to her mouth.

Tim reached inside, took her by the arm and gently pulled her out. On the step with him, her hands still clasped to her mouth, she stared wide-eyed at him. Looking her over for a moment, he reached inside and pulled the door shut.

He spoke softly. "There's a man in the bedroom … he's gone." Tim shook his head.

Feeling suddenly cold, she hugged herself, her hands trembling. Mrs. Davidson must have been at the sink doing something when … She clasped her eyes shut. Mrs. Davidson's denial, she thought, must have been even greater than her own; it seems she had just kept going about her daily routine before she was—interrupted. Then she thought about the little Davidson girl she'd seen in the Princess Leia outfit; she wondered if she were now in a galaxy far, far away—or even further.

He looked over the onlookers making sure they posed no threat. They simply turned away and resumed wondering about, looking around, calling names. It was as if somebody had flipped a switch and turned off their interest in what had just happened. If this was the reaction so far to this—phenomenon, he wondered what was to come.

He put his hand on her arm. "C'mon, there's nothing we can do here." He eyed her carefully again. She'd nearly lost it just a little while ago. How would she handle this?

Was she adjusting somehow to this outbreak of madness? He hoped so. He knew he was trying to.

They got into the police cruiser. She was quiet and sat sad-faced but seemed to be holding up okay. He reached for the radio handset on his shoulder and reported the murder-suicide and added that there was no need for any medical response.

The lady dispatcher responded, "Ten-four," with a touch of despair, a tone in her voice that suggested she'd heard that kind of thing a lot this morning.

He started the engine and, suddenly, Susanna blurted out, "Dora! I want to see Dora! Can we do that?"

He didn't know who Dora was. He simply nodded. "Which way?"

She pointed forward. "Just straight ahead." They drove the short distance to Dora's house and Susanna jumped out of the car. She bounded up the walkway and pounded on the front door. Tim came up behind her and glanced at the car in the drive. No one was in it.

"When's the last time you saw her?"

"Just earlier this morning." She pounded on the door again.

He tried the door handle. Like at the Davidson house, it too was unlocked. He sincerely hoped this was not going to be a repeat of that scene.

He cautiously led the way inside. She followed and they saw nothing unusual and heard nothing at all—no voices, no movements. They looked in the kitchen; no one was there. The dog dish was filled with dry dog food that seemed untouched. They went through the entire house and found nothing out of place. And they found no mysterious piles of unoccupied clothes.

Outside again, Tim asked, "Was that the only car here when you were here earlier?"

She nodded. "Her husband has a car but it was gone when I was here."

Tim looked around. "Must've walked somewhere." With a raised brow, he looked Susanna in the eye. "If they can do that it means they're probably all right." He wasn't at all sure that's what it meant, but he wanted her not to be frightened.

She nodded; the action conveyed more conviction than she actually felt. Looking across the street, she saw Buddy sitting alone in Mrs. Mac's front yard. Before leaving, she wanted to check on them both. "Tim, wait a little bit. I need to check on someone else."

"Sure, but not too long, okay?"

She nodded and headed across the street and knelt down beside Buddy. She put her hand on the back of his head and rubbed his long velvet ears. He looked her in the eyes and his forlorn expression made her heart break. This close, she could see he still had the leash attached to his collar as if Mrs. Mac had simply let go and walked inside and left him. She leaned over and hugged him gently; his body was tense.

"Buddy, I'm sorry I ignored you earlier." She gently began pulling her nails across his side knowing how he loved having his big belly scratched. "You know we're buddies, don't ya?" She patted his lower back and then scratched his head. She knew he really loved that and felt him relaxing. His wagging tail made her smile. Since all this insanity started earlier today, seeing Buddy was something to be treasured. She hugged him close, putting her cheek against the top of his head and caressed a long, velvety ear in one hand. Holding him like this reminded her of what love, pure and simple, was like. She thought, *And where will love fit in the New World Order?* She knew what was coming; she thought she probably knew it as well as anyone alive. She wanted to explain it to Tim better than she had with the quick summary she gave him in Albert's study, but would he be willing to listen? She thought maybe she shouldn't overload him with too much information just yet.

She scratched Buddy's belly again and felt it quiver as his stomach rumbled. "Oh, I bet you're hungry, fella, ain't ya?" His tail wagged a little more. "C'mon, let's go inside and find mommy and get you something to eat!" She rubbed the top of his head again and he yelped softly, the two-year-old's stomach now audibly growling.

Picking up the leash, she led him into the house and to the kitchen. She saw his green combination water and food doggie dish sitting by the refrigerator. Using a large glass sitting on the counter by the sink, she got water from the tap and filled one side of his bowl. He lapped it up.

Looking around, she saw a large bag of dog food leaning against the wall on the other side of the fridge. She uncurled the top of the bag and was about to scoop up two handfuls of food when she saw a white plastic scoop inside the bag, the kind used for scooping ice. She took that and filled the food side of Buddy's bowl. He dug right in.

While Buddy ate, she looked around for Mrs. Mac. Back in the empty living room, she saw a closed door to the right. She approached and knocked. There was no answer but she heard movement from inside. "Mrs. Mac!" she called. "You in there?"

"Yes," came a muffled response.

Susanna turned the handle and pushed the door open. At first, it was hard to see anything in the dark room. Her eyes were adjusted to the brighter light of outdoors and, now, the brightly lit interior of the house. She stepped inside and her eyes adjusted enough so that she could see this was a bedroom and that the shades were drawn. The light was out and the only illumination came from the open door.

Mrs. Mac sat on the side of the bed. She held a pair of scissors and was, evidently, clipping coupons from a circular, the kind that comes in the mail. How she could have done it in the near blackness of the room, Susanna didn't know. There was a tiny bit of light seeping through the edges of the blinds. Perhaps sitting in the dark, Mrs. Mac's eyes had adjusted enough she could get by with just that little bit of light. The scissors Mrs. Mac held concerned her. She wanted to get them away from her.

"Hey, Mrs. Mac!" Susanna said, feigning enthusiasm. "Wha'cha doin'!"

Mrs. Mac looked up and squinted. "Susanna, is that you?"

Without asking, Susanna turned on the light. With the added illumination, the scene before her was still very odd. Usually, people who clipped coupons did it at the kitchen table, and they didn't do it in near dark.

"Yeah, wha'cha up to back here all on your lonesome?" She hoped the fake cheerfulness would make her more welcomed.

Mrs. Mac smiled. "Oh, just cutting a few coupons for our cookout. I think it's going to be really nice." She was now carefully cutting around the edges of a coupon for hot dog buns.

Susanna added, "I brought in Buddy and fed him; I hope that's all right."

"Oh, yes," Mrs. Mac said, smiling. "Thank you for doing that; I'm afraid I forgot." Her eyes wandered a bit and then came back to Susanna. "Where was he, by the way?"

"He was in the front yard waiting to get in."

Mrs. Mac nodded. "Well, thank you for that." She returned to her task.

Just then, Buddy wandered in and laid down at his mistress' feet. He was full and ready for a nap. But that didn't mean he wanted to be alone; he loved people, especially these two people.

Susanna smiled at him. "Well, looky here, Mrs. Mac, it's good old Buddy!"

Mrs. Mac didn't respond at all.

Something Albert had talked about came to mind. She recalled a scripture he quoted about 'men's hearts failing them for fear'. Albert had explained it wasn't about heart failure although extreme fear could cause that, but minds giving way, failing, due to sheer terror. Was that what was going on with Mrs. Mac? Susanna wanted to test her a bit to see how her state of mind was. What she saw so far wasn't encouraging.

"So, what do you think about all this business going on?"

Without looking up, Mrs. Mac continued cutting. This coupon was for twenty percent off mustard. "What business?"

She tried to sound cheerful. "Ya know, this thing about all these missing people."

Now she did look up. "What missing people?"

It struck Susanna that she probably didn't know yet about the disappearances. Earlier, she had seen her walking Buddy like nothing had happened, cheerful as ever. It was just a little later that she saw her running out of the Harper's house screaming. So it must have been there that she saw something that did this to her. After she got back here, she might not have heard anything. There was no TV or radio on and cooped up in this room, which Susanna guessed was a guest room and not her own bedroom, not near nice enough, she seemed to be hiding. But from what? If not the shock of the Rapture, then what had sent her, and her mind, as Susanna was now sure of, into retreat?

"Mrs. Mac, did something happen to upset you?" Carefully, she added, "Something at the Harper's house?"

"Oh, you mean about Doug?"

Susanna nodded.

"Oh, he's dead," she said calmly. "Had a knife sticking out of his throat." She started cutting out a coupon for napkins.

Susanna looked at her, gaped-mouth and thought, *No wonder, no wonder.*

There was a knock at the front door. Susanna hurried to answer it knowing who it was. She opened the door to let Tim in.

"Susanna, we've got to go."

She glanced over her shoulder. "You'll have to go on without me. I need to help Mrs. Mac."

Tim tried to mask his disappointment and nodded. "Sure, I understand."

"I am going to try and reach her daughter and tell her to come over."

Again, he nodded. "In that case, why don't I swing by in about an hour and pick you up?" His expression was more hopeful now.

"That'll be fine," Susanna said. "I'll just leave my things in your car then."

Tim started toward the car and waved goodbye. He got in and drove off.

Susanna hurried back and found Mrs. Mac and Buddy just as she'd left them. "Mrs. Mac, what's your daughter's phone number?"

Mrs. Mac thought for a moment. "She has a new one; I can't quite remember. It's written on the first page of the phone book in there." She pointed to the living room. "Why do you want that?"

"I'm going to call her to come get you," Susanna said, smiling. "Wouldn't you like to spend some time with your daughter?"

She thought for a moment. "Why, yes, that would be nice!" She smiled broadly. "Maybe that's who's been trying to call. The phone's been ringing off and on for a good while now but I've been too busy to answer." She looked down at the coupons in her lap.

Susanna suspected her daughter had already been trying to get in touch. She went into the living room, found the number for her daughter's cell phone and tried her luck. She used Mrs. Mac's landline phone and got her on the third try. She learned she was right; the daughter had been trying to call and was, at that moment, getting in her car to start on her way over. Susanna explained Mrs. Mac's condition and what she had seen in the Harper's house. The daughter said she would be there in thirty minutes.

***

It was a little more than an hour before Tim returned. He'd gotten caught up in a couple of minor altercations he'd spotted while patrolling; it had taken him some time to break things up. It was early afternoon before he got back. As he approached the house, he saw Susanna sitting on the front step with that dog at her feet and a big bag of dog food to the side. She waved as he pulled up.

He stepped out of the car. "Don't tell me you're a dog mommy now!"

She stood up. In one hand she held the leash to the dog and in the other, a dog dish. "Mrs. Mac asked me take him and take care of him." She recalled the way she had said it; to Susanna, it sounded like Mrs. Mac wouldn't see Buddy again. She knew Buddy was hers now—her burden and her blessing. "Mrs. Mac's son-in-law and one of the kids are allergic to dogs so he couldn't go with them." She looked over her shoulder at the house. "I don't think she'll ever be back. Her daughter was very concerned. She seemed like a nice lady."

He looked at the giant bag of dog food. "You sure you got enough?"

"It'll do till I can get supplies," she said, ignoring his sarcasm.

"C'mon Susanna, I can't take a dog with me." He thought for a moment. "Why don't you leave him at Albert's; he'll be all right there and you can pick him up later."

She shook her head. "I can't leave him alone. He's not used to being alone. And besides, I don't know when or if I'll be getting back to Albert's. I may have to leave my car there for a few days before I get back; I don't know."

He put his hands on his hips and blew out his cheeks.

"Sorry to be stubborn, Tim, but if Buddy can't come then I can't either. I promised Mrs. Mac I'd take care of him." She leaned down and hugged his neck, her soft cheek against his furry face.

He rolled his eyes. "Okay, get in … both of you. Guess the department doesn't care if I have a dog in the car. Right now they got other things to worry about." He put Buddy and his bag of food in the back seat along with the dog dish. Susanna, again, got in the front passenger seat smiling.

Chapter Seventeen

Slowly, the car moved along as Tim conducted a drive-through of Cloverdale, Susanna and Buddy along for the ride. This neighborhood that before had been so familiar to her now seemed so—*alien*. She had never done a police ride-along before. Under different circumstances, patrolling with a police officer might have been interesting and fun. But now, seeing so many people wandering around, searching for loved ones she was sure they would never find, made her uneasy. Back at Albert's, she had been in familiar territory, somewhat shielded from the harsh reality of what was going on. And on a certain level, she had blocked out, at least to some degree, the dreadful terror of the situation as if it was just an academic point and not real. Now, back out here, the dreadful reality of it started to sink in again.

Not wanting to distract Tim, she quietly looked out the window at the people who were, more or less, walking around in a state of shock like she had done. She had recovered a good deal. At first, the Rapture portended to her an omen of doom—which, of course, it was. But accepting the truth of the situation was a breakthrough. Despite her renewed anxiety, she felt able now to handle it better. The Rapture has happened. She closed her eyes. She knew the first thing she'd have to do was learn how to take things a day at a time, even an hour at a time, if necessary. As shocking as events were today, the missing, the dead, seeing those enigmatic figures on TV standing on the clouds, she thought she could manage to deal with it all this way.

After about fifteen minutes of moving from one neighborhood street to another, Tim spoke up. "This is what's called a ride-along."

She looked over at him.

"That's what it's called when a civilian rides on a patrol with a police officer." He smiled. "The other kind of ride civilians participate in is called an arrest."

She smiled back. "Which one am I, again?"

He looked into her soft, brown eyes and smiled even bigger. "Just glad you're here." He spoke very plainly, without reservation, without looking away.

Susanna smiled and began to better understand why she was here.

A whine came from the backseat. She turned around and looked through the protective cage behind the front seat. Buddy was looking up at her in that forlorn way she'd seen before when he wanted something.

"He all right back there?"

She grinned. "Yeah, he just feels a little left out, the big baby. Pull over a second."

He pulled the car to the far right side of the lane and stopped. Susanna hopped out, opened the back door and pulled Buddy out. She guided him into the floorboard of the front and got back in. He sat looking up at her as she sat with her legs to one side, like riding sidesaddle, making room for him.

"You gotta understand," she said, "Buddy's a big spoiled baby." She looked down into his big brown eyes surrounded by his natural mascara. "And I love him." She rubbed his head. "Yes, I do." She was so very glad to have Buddy with her. Seeing the unconditional love beaming from his eyes made the current insanity so much more bearable.

Tim chuckled. "Maybe we should get him some diapers."

Happy to be so near her, the beagle lay down at her feet filling the floor of the right side of the car. Like this, she was able to stretch her legs over him and get into a more comfortable sitting position.

They resumed patrolling and saw more people. Susanna knew some of them at least by sight. There was the man she saw mowing his yard this morning as she drove to Albert's. There was Miss Jensen! She was still in her blue jeans and short-sleeve checkered shirt.

Susanna started to roll down the window and call to her and inquire how she was doing but stopped herself. The expression on Miss Jensen's face was very different from that of this morning; the world was a different place from that of this morning. Miss Jensen looked—angry, scared, bitter—dangerous. It was hard to figure out exactly just how she looked. But she didn't look like Miss Jensen; not anymore. She pulled her hand away from the window button and put her arm back on the rest. Aside from her expression, Miss Jensen seemed physically okay, so she left her alone.

Of all the people they saw, so far no one was causing any real problems. They were like she had been: stunned, frightened and confused, not knowing really what to do.

Once in a while, Tim would stop if he saw people quarreling. He'd roll down the window and ask if there was a problem and they'd all say, "No, officer." It was good to see that, so far, there was still some respect, some fear, for law enforcement. Because if that was gone—.

After a while, Tim turned the car back in the direction of Cucumber Street and passed Albert's house again. Susanna looked at her car sitting parked innocently like nothing had happened, as if, since she parked it, the world hadn't completely changed. She wondered when she would see it again. She intended on asking Tim to take her directly to her mom's place when it was time to go home. She didn't want to drive under these circumstances. She knew he'd be okay with it; his glances hadn't gone unnoticed. She could just get her car in a couple of days when things had, hopefully, calmed down. They headed down Cucumber toward Collins Road, the back way out of Cloverdale.

Tim glanced over at his charge. To him, that's what she was now. She had again become quiet. Seeing the almost zombie-like state of the stragglers, he knew, had affected her. He thought it might be a good idea to keep her talking, keep her mind occupied.

"I was thinking about something you said. You mentioned you're the one who actually wrote that prophecy book."

"Yes. I was doing some editing work for Albert about, well, this." She held her hands out. "Fact is, I ended up pretty much writing the book for him based on his notes and verbal instructions." She shook her head. "I wonder if he knew how right he was?"

The car made a right onto Collins Road and headed toward the intersection a half-mile ahead with Phyllis Blvd, one of the town's main avenues.

"Isn't it kind of strange he'd hire a non-believer to help him on this kind of book?"

Susanna looked at him, this time taking a real look. He was nice looking with a clean-shaven face, a firm, square jaw and honest eyes. Very trim as well. "He didn't want someone around who would constantly be interjecting their own views into the project. In this field of study, everybody has their own little opinion. Or should I say *had* an opinion now that it's started?"

He nodded. "Go ahead and tell me more about the Tribulation; you know, now that you're the world's leading authority." He smiled.

"There's a lot in the book of Revelation about the Great Tribulation. To a large degree, it deals with three groups each with seven disclosures that are somewhat shrouded in symbolism, some more than others. There's the Seven Seals, which are now pretty much accomplished, the Sixth Seal prophecy that is soon to be fulfilled. The Seventh Seal brings in the Seven Trumpets which introduce the first set of plagues and judgments that cover the first half of the Tribulation." She held up her hand and stretched it forward like a lecturer in a classroom might do. "Then there are the Seven Vials, or bowls, which are the seven last plagues. It works like this: The Seven Seals are bad; the Seven Trumpets are terrible; the Seven Vials are horrifying." Talking about the things to come made her blood run cold. Now it all seemed too real, too true, and not academic like when she was writing the book. She looked down at the sleeping beagle. Seeing him so relaxed calmed her a bit.

It wasn't a very detailed explanation. He thought maybe she didn't really want to talk about it—didn't really want to think about it. He didn't blame her. He didn't push it but he did have one question.

He glanced over at her and asked, "Why?"

She looked up. "What?"

"Why is this happening? Why is God doing this if he loves us so much?"

At the intersection, they turned left onto Phyllis Blvd and began patrolling along the important city business district with its many shops and office buildings lining both sides of the street. To Susanna, it seemed they were going nowhere in particular.

"Judgment," she said. "That's the reason."

He braked for a jaywalker crossing his path. He glared at the offender but let it go. "Yeah, I've heard of Judgment Day, but I thought that was like way later on in the Bible."

"Yes, there will be a Judgment Day when each individual is tried." She listened to herself speaking in such definite terms, as if these things were indeed going to happen, like she was a person of—faith. Was that what she was becoming? She believed now the Rapture was for real. Was it now, 'In for a penny, in for a pound' with her and Bible prophecy? "The Great Tribulation is the judgment of mankind as a whole. Humanity and the physical world are to be punished—now."

She spoke the last word so softly Tim had trouble picking it up. He let out a long sigh. "Glad I asked!"

"That's something else Albert use to talk about, especially since I asked him the very same question. He talked about how we live in a day when people dismiss the Bible, dismiss Jesus as being just a good teacher and not God's own son. It's like with this whole Da Vinci Code thing, a book with a heretical idea that sold sixty million copies. He talked about how so much of this generation of humanity had rejected God and the Bible and how the world would have to be punished for that."

Tim didn't respond and they rode in silence for a minute. Then he said, "You know, I remember some of the images on the chart I looked at. It reminded me that I've heard of some of this before about the beasts and creatures and things. But ... I just don't get what's up with all the symbolism. If the Almighty had something to say, why didn't he just come out and say it?"

"Albert and I talked about that too. He pointed out how much symbolism is used in life. The subconscious mind speaks to us in dream images all the time. Psychiatry to a large extent is built on figuring out what these images, these symbols, mean." She raised her brow. "Is it so unusual then that the Almighty should speak to us in symbols?"

"I guess not."

"And Albert also pointed out that the use of symbolism, like in Daniel and Revelation, kept those books relevant to all generations over the past two thousand years. Each generation interpreted them to their own time and circumstances."

"Yeah, I can see that."

A right at the next intersection brought them onto a side street that had only a few older buildings, some of them large warehouses, and not much else. Not many people were around here at the moment. They cut through this small area quickly, the street being short.

They came out on George Ave, freshly paved, the white lines still fresh and clean. The street and neighborhood were a bit more upscale than the one they had just left. Here and there were wooded grounds with lots of tall trees; they blocked from view the utilitarian buildings they had just passed on the other street and hid them like they were some dirty little secret.

They drove quietly for a while, Susanna sunk in her seat with her head resting on her fist. Suddenly, she pointed to the left. "Look!"

A slim, pretty blond stood in the parking lot of a church, *Prosperity Tabernacle* the sign read. She was waving at them furiously with both arms raised high above her head. He pulled into the parking lot and up to her.

"Everything okay?" Tim asked after he rolled the window down.

"It's Reverend Jasper!" the pretty blond said. "He's acting so funny; he scares me saying the things he's saying!"

"Okay, miss. Just tell me what's going on."

To Susanna it seemed funny for Tim to call her miss as if he were an old man; he wasn't much older than she was.

"But first," he said, "tell me your name."

"I'm Julie Anderson; I'm the new girl here at the church working in the office." She paused and stood looking unfocused for a moment."

He looked closely at her. "Julie, you okay?"

"I-I was just thinking, now that Diana's gone, I'm the only girl working in the office now."

Tim didn't react. His training had taught him not to exacerbate a situation by interjecting personal judgments or unnecessary observations. He simply waited a moment. "Julie, how can I help?"

She focused on him again. "Come inside and talk to him. He's talking so funny about people just disappearing, 'bout Diana coming back in seven years."

Susanna realized she meant the pastor of this church, the man who lived on Curtis Street not far from the Curtis house. She'd seen him a few times going out to his expensive German car. Miss Jensen had told her who he was.

"He didn't go," Susanna whispered softly to herself. Tim turned toward her. She looked back at him. "He didn't go in the Rapture!"

Julie leaned down and looked into the car. "Yeah, Rapture! That's something he said!"

Seeing it was useless trying to get information out of this near hysterical woman, he decided to just go in and see what was going on. "Julie, let's just go inside and talk to him."

"Okay. He's upstairs in the sanctuary just standing there looking up at the new cross they put in. I mean, that's all he's doing!"

Entering through the basement door, Tim and Susanna made their way upstairs. Tim had wanted Susanna to stay in the basement with Julie, but she refused. She wanted to know why a preacher, a supposed man of God, didn't go in the Rapture.

He looked Julie over. He felt confident she was okay; and indeed, she had calmed down since they came in with her and she wasn't alone anymore.

"Julie, just wait in the office until we get back, okay?"

She nodded and went into the office and sat down.

Upstairs, they found Reverend Jasper as Julie described, just staring at a beautiful cross hanging from the vaulted ceiling. At his feet lay an orange drop cord.

"Hello," Tim said. "You doing okay?"

Jasper looked at him. "Yes, why wouldn't I be?" He seemed genuinely puzzled by the question.

Susanna stepped closer to Tim. "Reverend Jasper, do you know what's going on out there?" She hooked her thumb sideways indicating the outside.

"Yes, I know what's happening," he replied softly. "I spent many an hour in the old days studying the Bible, studying Revelation, in fact. I use to know it quite well."

Like a Shakespearean actor hamming it up on stage, he threw his chest out, lifted his arm and shouted, "The first angel sounded!" Then more subduedly, "And there followed hail and fire mingled with blood, and they were cast upon the earth, and the third part of trees was burnt up, and all green grass was burnt up." He stepped back assuming another dramatic pose using the other arm. "And the second angel sounded!" Again bringing it down, drawing his audience in, "And as it were a great mountain burning with fire was cast into the sea, and the third part of the sea became blood!" He looked over his audience of two and saw he was having a decided effect on them. He was glad that after all these years he could still move his listeners. He was, in fact, a pretty good speaker; he knew how to preach. "And the third part of the creatures which were in the sea, and had life, died. And the third part of the ships were destroyed." A touch of sadness came to his face and he held both arms out. "And the third angel sounded, and there fell a great star from heaven, burning as if it were a lamp, and it fell upon the third part of the rivers, and upon the fountains of waters. And the name of the star is called," this he whispered, "Wormwood." He took a dramatic pause and closed his eyes. When he opened them, he said, solemnly, "And the third part of the waters became wormwood, and many men died of the waters because they were made bitter."

Now Jasper suddenly stepped forward and Susanna and Tim stepped back. Tim kept a close eye on the clearly disturbed man. She tightly gripped his arm.

"And the fourth angel sounded." Jasper lifted his eyes as if he were looking into the heavens. "And the third part of the sun was smitten!" He waved his hand in a wide arch. "And the third part of the moon, and the third part of the stars, so as the third part of them was darkened, and the day shone not for a third part of it and the night likewise. And I beheld, and heard an angel flying through the midst of heaven, saying with a loud voice," here he screamed, *"Woe! Woe! Woe!"* then bringing it back down again, "to the inhabiters of the earth by reason of the other voices of the trumpet of the three angels which are yet to sound." He bowed his head and put his arms down.

Again, he looked at them; he smiled broadly. "See, I remember!"

They stared at him silently not knowing what to say or even if they should speak, anxious of setting him off again.

After an awkward moment, Susanna finally asked, "Pastor, you know the Rapture has happened, don't you?"

He nodded slowly. "Oh yes, it has happened. And please don't call me pastor."

Ignoring his last remark, she asked, "Then why are you here?" She shrugged. "Why didn't you go?"

His eyes widened. "Because it is written." His eyes relaxed and, to them, he seemed normal now. "'Not everyone that saith unto me, Lord, Lord, shall enter into the kingdom of heaven, but he that doeth the will of my Father which is in heaven." He smiled. "The good Lord wasn't kidding around."

Tim, wanting to get Susanna away from this man, leaned over to her. "Please, go check on Julie. I'm kinda worried about her."

She looked at him.

"Now ... please."

She nodded a goodbye to Jasper and quietly left.

He turned back to the Reverend. He again was standing still, staring up at the cross.

Jasper said, "He hung on the cross to pay the price of Salvation."

Tim said, "Right," and stared at him, wondering what he was up to.

"Officer, do you think that's the way, you know, hanging on a cross?"

Tim sighed. "I'm afraid I don't know much about the Bible, but I've always heard that was the price." He, too, looked up the cross.

Jasper glanced sideways at him and smiled; he knew he didn't understand what he meant.

Suddenly, a scream came from downstairs. Tim, fearing for Susanna, rushed down the aisle heading for the foyer. As he ran, he shouted, "I'll be right back!" and shot through the open doors toward the stairs leading down.

Jasper picked up the long orange power cord lying at his feet, walked to the podium and set his plan into motion. Quickly, he tied the end of the cord into a hoop, a lasso of sorts.

When he first came up from the basement, after staring at the cross for about ten minutes, he went to his office and dragged out the orange drop cord. He went back to the aisle and dropped the cord at his feet and resumed staring at the cross. He had stood there a long time when the New Girl, Julie Anderson, came up and tried to speak to him, her voice quivering. He did not respond. He stared at the cross. He worked out his plan. He knew what he had to do. She left after several vain attempts to get his attention.

With the power cord lasso in his right hand, he looked up at the top post of the cross. He knew that if he took his time he could catch it probably on the first try. He used to be pretty good at this when he was a kid playing cowboy. If the cord caught the top post from the back, the side facing the podium, it should cantilever the weight enough so that the cross wouldn't tip over and let it slip off; the cord should stay firmly on the top of the cross and not fall off when his weight pressed down on it. He threw it up and just missed the top post. He tried again and got it.

Firmly pulling the cord, keeping it taunt, he worked his way up to the top of the pulpit and stood there, balancing himself on the slanted top. He shortened the length of the cord and tied a crude but workable noose into it just at his neck. He slipped it over his head and tightened it good and snug. He looked up and double-checked the length of the cord, making sure he wouldn't hit the floor.

He leaned forward, came off the pulpit and swung right under the cross. His body weight tightened the noose even more, so tightly that it dug into the flesh of his neck.

Immediately, with both hands, he grabbed at the cord around his neck and tried to pull free, his feet kicking wildly. But with the noose so tight, there was no way he could get it off now. The cross groaned under his weight but the supporting cables held firm—the installers had done a very good job. He hung there, legs flailing, as the life choked out of him. Quickly, his body motions slowed and then came to a total stop. He dangled a foot off the floor. If he had possessed the presence of mind, and if he weren't dead, maybe he would have been gratified to know that his plan had worked.

Chapter Eighteen

Tim and Susanna, with Buddy lying on the right front floorboard, pulled out of the church parking lot and quickly drove away. To Susanna, he seemed in a hurry to get going, to get away from this place. Julie, in her red hatchback, pulled out and went the other way. Susanna glanced at him suspiciously but said nothing.

After going downstairs to see what the scream was about, he found Susanna standing beside Julie; the pretty blond was clutching her arm. Susanna explained she had startled her. Julie had been standing at the basement exit looking out when Susanna came up behind her and spoke. She hadn't heard her approaching, and with her nerves already on edge, it didn't take much to spook her. Despite his gentle efforts to pull her away from Susanna, she held on to her arm and yammered on about how frightened she had been. Out of courtesy, he let her speak—Susanna standing by patiently listening—and get it out of her system.

By the time he'd gotten back upstairs, Jasper was dead and hanging. He dropped his head and put his hands on his hips. He had been gone for only a couple of minutes, but, regrettably, that was more than enough time for the preacher to—finish. Tim surmised he must have moved very quickly to get the drop cord up and over the top post of the cross. Evidently, he had choked to death in under a minute—panic and terror, no doubt, accelerating his demise.

Tim took his utility knife from the narrow pouch on his garrison belt and cut him down. There was nothing else he could do for him and he decided to just leave him there on the floor, his eyes bulging, staring up at that cross he seemed to have loved so much.

He turned and briskly made his way downstairs. He didn't tell Susanna and Julie about the Reverend. What good would it do? He hinted that he just wanted to be alone and that they should respect his wishes. Tim told her he had work to do and it was time to go. He told Julie to get her personal things from there and leave now. She was calm enough now to drive safely home. She'd told them she only lived a few blocks away. Tim told her not to come back. The preacher had made it clear the office was shutting down and her job there was ended. She nodded and didn't seem at all upset at the loss of her job. He thought she wanted to get away from there as much as he did.

They exited through the basement door. Julie locked up and put her church keys through the delivery slot at the side of the door, not needing them now. Quickly, she walked to her car.

After a minute of silent riding, the radio hissed a millisecond as a broadcast started: "All units stand by for radio check." For a long time, radio traffic had been at a minimum. That was to be expected during a Code Six when only very high priority calls would be dispatched. However, now, dispatch wanted to do radio checks and check up on the units. "All units begin radio check."

One by one, like before, the officers began calling out their unit numbers. As a voice answered for unit 708, Tim reached for his radio handset and immediately followed with, "709, loud and clear."

The calls kept coming from the other units giving the dispatch call center confirmation that all the unit's radios were working, and more importantly, that all the officers were still unharmed and able to respond—the real reason for the radio check.

As they rode, Tim and Susanna listened to the radio checks until all units were done. At the end, the dispatcher called, "1402 hours; all units reported. Radio check complete. All units continue Code Six."

Susanna said, "Does that mean everybody is okay?"

"Yes," he said, "let's hope it stays that way."

"Guess you got a long day ahead of you."

He grinned. "Long day and night. Everybody stays on duty until the Code Six is over. I'll be working at least until tomorrow morning; I'm sure of that, maybe more."

"You know, I think the public, including me, doesn't quite appreciate what you guys have to go through."

He nodded. "One of the first things you learn in law enforcement is that it's a tough and pretty much thankless job. But it's important; society couldn't exist without it." He nodded. "That's what keeps me on it, I guess. Gives me a sense of purpose ... that what I do is important. Since I was in high school, I always wanted to be a police officer. I still feel that way."

"Well, this citizen thinks you're doing a great job."

There was that smile again. For Tim, that smile, that beautiful smile, made working day and night worthwhile.

He shouldn't be doing this; he knew it. There was no real reason to have her along on this patrol; in fact, during a Code Six, it was a little out of order. But he liked having her around. He may have been a law officer but he was still a human being with feelings. Having her around made him feel better, better than he had felt in a long time. Plus, the world had gone a little crazy today and she helped him cope with that. For those reasons, he felt justified having her in the car. He knew he was rationalizing but so what? He would make every effort to keep her out of harm's way.

On the corner, they spotted a young black man, a kid really, standing on the street. He seemed to be preaching. Couldn't have been more than nineteen by the looks of him. Tim slowed down to listen a bit.

At the top of his lungs, he shouted, "You need some word-loaf, people, the bread of life!" He stood tall extending himself to his full six-foot height, bobbing back and forth like a charismatic preacher in a pulpit. "You need some Bible on the brain, people! It's done happen'd. I missed it 'cause I was lax and not living like I ought."

On the side of the brick wall behind him was written, *God's Grace Is Still In Place*, in red neon spray paint. Tim wondered if the young preacher had done a little gospel tagging before the police car showed up.

"I done repented now and got myself right with the Lord. You better get right with the Lord, too! You gonna need his help for what's coming', that's for sure. All the trials and troubles of the Great Tribulation brought on by the Lord Jesus Christ, you gonna need the power of his might to say no to the Beast and to the number of his name—yeah!"

Street preaching was no problem; he just wanted to make sure he wasn't making any inflammatory statements that might cause those milling past him to get upset. He noticed there wasn't much chance of that happening. The disoriented people, preoccupied with their own thoughts, walked past him paying his words no attention.

"You ain't on some black list," the kid continued, "you on the hell-on-earth list! And you gonna be on the Lake of Fire list lest you get right with God and stay right with God!"

Susanna sat silently and listened. She didn't react. She was a little numb from what she heard, afraid the kid was right.

Tim decided the kid was no problem and was about to drive away when a woman's voice came over the police radio. "709."

His left hand on the wheel, he reached right-handed to his left shoulder and took hold of the handset clipped to his uniform shoulder strap—the walkie-talkie itself rested in its holster on his garrison belt. "Go ahead."

"10-51 in progress. 2221 Garry Street."

"Ten-four. Ten-seventeen." He let go of the handset. He looked into the rearview to make sure no one was behind him and made a quick U-turn. "I gotta respond to this call, but first I'll drop you and Buddy off at a safe place." He glanced at Susanna as she looked at him with those big, brown eyes. "Okay?"

"Yes," she nodded, "but my Mom's house is just on the next street over from that one. You could let us out on Garry and we'll just walk over to my mom's."

"Okay, that's even better."

"Can you tell me what's going on?"

"Fire in progress. They want me to help with crowd and traffic control. By the sound of her voice, I'm guessin' it's not too serious."

She exhaled softly. "I hope not."

He hit the lights and the car sped away.

***

Slowly, Susanna's eyes struggled open and she looked around the room. She was in her mom's living room nestled into the big easy chair near the bay window. She stretched and then settled right back into the comfort of the chair. She was not yet willing to give up the restful security of being, and feeling, at home again. She glanced at the wall clock. She'd been out for about two hours.

As she got out of Tim's police car, she had felt dead tired. The day was catching up with her and the idea of just sitting down and resting was very appealing. She got Buddy and his bowl out of the vehicle. Tim had told her to just leave the big bag of dog food and he would bring it over later. She gave him the address.

She cut across a neighbor's yard, she knew Mr. Kent wouldn't mind, and led Buddy to the other street, over to her mom's house. Her mom had been keeping watch and saw her coming up the street. She came out of Mrs. Danner's and went with her into the house. Inside, Susanna stood still a moment and looked over the familiar home; she was glad to be in it again. Even though she'd been there for dinner just a few days before, after today, it seemed like a long, long time.

Beside the chair, Buddy was lying on the floor—a pose that was becoming very familiar to her now. The house was quiet; no TV, no radio. At the moment, they were not interested, not ready for any more news from the outside.

"Mom?" she inquired, her eyes closed again.

"In the kitchen!" Her mom's voice was distant. "I'm making us something to eat."

"Good. Need help?"

"No, dear, I've got it covered."

"Good," she replied and snuggled up in the depth of the chair, her father's old chair.

Her mom came into the living room and sat on the couch. "I've got some nice vegetable soup heating up and I'm going to make some fresh biscuits."

"Good." Eyes closed, she rested, her shoeless feet curled up under her. Buddy's tail beat against the floor twice. "How's Mrs. Danner holding up?"

"Oh, she's fine. Some of the neighbor menfolk came over and sat with us. Said they'd stay with her until her son got here from his place somewhere over past Raleigh." She leaned back on the couch. "He's going to pick her up and take her with him. She's all packed and ready." She looked at her daughter resting in the chair. "And how are you doing?"

Susanna thought about this bizarre day: Albert's empty clothes, the man with a knife sticking out of his throat that Mrs. Mac had told her about, the wonderful couple whose lives ended in a murder-suicide, the mystery of Dora. She said to her mother, "Fine," in a whispery, reed-thin voice.

Her mom looked down at the fat beagle lying on her carpet. In a chipper tone, she inquired, "And how are you doing, ol' doggie?"

Buddy replied with two more beats of his tail—the same spot Aunt Fran's clothes had landed, clothes Mrs. Kelly had cleared away when she knew her daughter was headed over.

Just then there was a knock at the door. Susanna opened her eyes and watched as her mother went to answer it. She pulled back the curtain that covered the glass to see who it was.

"Why, it's a police officer!"

She opened the door and a familiar voice said, "You must be Mrs. Kelly."

"Yes, I'm Eloise Kelly. Come on in."

Tim came inside carrying the big bag of dog food.

Susanna put her feet on the floor and sat up.

"I brought you this." He sat the bag on the floor.

Buddy got up and greeted the bag like an old friend, one that he sniffed repeatedly.

To Susanna, it seemed that Tim's voice had acquired an air of artificial pleasantness; it had a 'taking care of business' tone to it. Except for the episode at the church, this was the first time they had been together with a third party. And at the church, it had been business. Then, he had been on the job performing his duty. Now here he was in her mom's house seeing her—and meeting her mom—under a different kind of circumstance, another atmosphere. At the moment, he wasn't the one solely in charge.

"Hey, Tim. Thanks for bringing it by."

Her mom said in a tone much too chipper, "Oh, I'm glad we've got something to feed our new family member. Susanna told me the wonderful news." She smiled as she looked down at the fat beagle.

Tim smiled at her feigned joy at having a dog coming unexpectedly into her life.

Susanna chuckled. "Mom, of course, was thrilled. Can't you tell?"

Mrs. Kelly asked, "So, they don't let you keep dogs in your dorm room at school, do they?"

"Ah, no, mom. They don't." And it didn't matter. Susanna knew she wouldn't be going back to school except maybe to get her things. She hadn't told her mom yet. "Don't worry, I'll take care of him, the big baby."

Buddy looked up at her and wagged his tail. He loved attention.

Tim smiled at the beautiful beagle. This time a good smile. Not a 'just to be polite' smile, but a genuine 'glad to hear it' smile.

Susanna saw her chance. "Now sit down and take a break. I'm sure you could use it."

He hesitated a moment and then sat on the couch. Buddy came over and he scratched his long ears. "Fire wasn't that bad; just a grease fire on the stove. Traffic wasn't much. They really didn't need me but it's procedure to have law enforcement present at the scene of a fire. You never know how things will go." He patted the dog's back dismissively and Buddy walked over to Susanna and laid down again. He loved his new mommy.

"Now you gotta stay and eat with us," Susanna demanded. "After today, I'm sure you could use a hot meal."

"No, no, really. I don't want to get in the way." He shook his head.

"Nonsense," Mrs. Kelly said. "We've got plenty."

He smiled and nodded and she left for the kitchen.

They sat silently—no attempt at small talk. With all they'd been through together this day, they both felt it was unnecessary. They'd had a crash course in getting to know each other; a comfortable silence was welcome.

Tired from a long day of duty and anxiety, he knew there was so much more to come. She was still in the big easy chair using it like a hiding place from the insanity taking place in the world just outside the door. He got into a comfortable position in the corner of the couch and crossed his legs. He closed his eyes just to rest them;

she did the same. In a moment, she heard his breathing become sonorous and realized he'd fallen asleep. That was fine with her. She understood the need and was glad for the couple of hours she had managed to catch. She lifted her feet from the floor and snuggled up again in the chair. Despite being a little hungry, she became very still. Immediately, it seemed, her mom was standing in front of her shaking her shoulder. She realized she'd fallen back asleep. She looked up at her mom.

"Time to eat," Mrs. Kelly softly said and walked back into the kitchen.

The wonderful aroma of her mom's veggie soup and freshly made biscuits filled the house. She felt even hungrier. She looked at the clock; it was 5 p.m. Tim was stirring, no doubt aroused by the movements in the room.

He rubbed his face. "Sorry, didn't mean to nod off like that." He took a deep breath and checked his watch. "Wow, I was out for a while. You should have woken me."

"Naw, you needed it, deserved it. Besides, I clonked out again myself." She put her feet back on the floor. "Is this the kind of thing you get in trouble for, you know?"

"Sleeping on the job?" His brow rose. "Ordinarily, yes, but under these circumstances when we're working a twenty-four-hour shift, as I'm sure we will be, they turn a blind eye to us catching naps or taking a break so long as we don't do it in front of the public. They'd rather have us rested and functional than burnt-out and useless. And we'll need to be rested, and to be ready. The night is still to come."

He said that with such an ominous air it caused her skin to tingle. Slowly, she rubbed her forearms. "Well, that means you're gonna need some really good nutrition.

Let me tell you, my mom makes some of the best dadgum veggie soup and homemade biscuits around." She stood up and stretched. "C'mon, let's eat."

Buddy struggled to his feet. Pushing his front paws forward, he slowly stretched his back, a wide yawn accompanying the act. He assumed the dinner invitation was for him as well and hoped that nothing as ridiculous as a 'don't feed the dog from the table' policy was in effect here.

Chapter Nineteen

Dinner was great. The hot, steaming veggie soup hit the spot nicely, and Buddy loved the bits of soaked biscuit he was given and he gobbled them down voraciously. Susanna was careful to pull her fingers quickly away from the snapping jaws. A couple of times she looked at Buddy amazed at how fast the bits of food disappeared down his throat, Buddy simply inhaling them. She wondered if he even tasted them before they were gone.

Mrs. Kelly had been delighted to have company for dinner. During dinner, Susanna stole glances at her. She seemed so chipper since she'd been home and it puzzled her. On this day when the world had forever changed, her own sister had disappeared in this very house. How could she seem so unaffected? Then Susanna remembered how she felt when it first happened, how denial had set in so strongly. She figured it was the same with her mom. She was just showing it differently. Even though it had obviously been her that had gotten up Aunt Fran's clothes from the floor, she was, it seemed, blocking that out as, just not letting it register. Susanna noticed she had not mentioned Aunt Fran once since she'd gotten home. But if she felt good, that was fine as far as Susanna was concerned—even if it was the product of delusion.

With a hot dinner in her belly, Susanna felt much better. She decided not to discuss the events coming in the near future with her mother. She wasn't sure her mom could handle it. It might be best for her not to know, at least for the time being, what was ahead. After some time she will adjust—well, maybe.

For a non-believer, Susanna knew the Bible and Bible prophecy very well having learned from Albert and her own research while working for him. She knew what was coming. Even now, she tried not to think about it, determined to just take things one day at a time. Let her mom be chipper; in a way she envied her. And as far as being an unbeliever, that just wasn't true anymore, was it? She believed; she knew too much not to.

Susanna and Tim stood in the living room as her mom cleared up in the kitchen where they had eaten at the table, the help offered by Susanna kindly refused. The dinner was very informal, and they all had enjoyed that. But now it was time for Tim to get back to work.

"Thanks for a great meal," he said, smiling broadly. "That's going to hold me a long time."

Susanna returned the smile. "It was great to have you here. You gotta come back."

"I will ... soon."

"No, I mean you gotta come back, later on, tonight. Can you do that?"

He drew in a slight breath and was about to speak when Mrs. Kelly bounded into the room, a rectangular plastic container in her hand. "Tim, you gotta take this with you," and she handed it to him. "It's homemade fudge brownies. You can snack on 'em as you drive around."

"See, you gotta come back and return my mom's container. Why a thing like that can go as high as a buck ninety-five. You wouldn't wanna commit grand larceny, would you?"

He chuckled. "Okay." And then he looked into those enchanting brown eyes that never failed to captivate him. "I'll be back as soon as I can." He nodded to Mrs. Kelly and turned toward the door.

"Wait!" Susanna exclaimed. "Before you go, let me see your phone."

He handed it over. It was a smartphone very much like her own. She began tapping away at the screen with her thumbs. Mrs. Kelly looked on wondering what in the world she was doing. In a few seconds, she handed it back to him.

"Now you have my number. You can call when the cell towers start working right again." He nodded. "Now, tell me your number."

He told her, smiled and walked out the door lifting hand as a farewell to Mrs. Kelly.

Susanna wrote it down on the pad her mom kept by the landline phone on the table beside the couch. She tore off the page and dropped it into her shoulder bag. She then turned to her mom. "Brownies! Why am I just hearing about this?"

Mrs. Kelly rolled her eyes. "C'mon, I've got more."

She followed her mom into the kitchen; Buddy followed too. He could smell the brownies and wanted a complete investigation into this marvelous new scent.

In a minute, Susanna had again seated herself in the chair; a small plate stacked with brownies lay in her lap. A glass of milk sat on the end table beside the chair. Even though she'd just had a big meal, these were brownies—homemade brownies—she firmly believed no further justification was needed. Buddy sat beside the chair staring at her. A look of absolute want filled his eyes.

She looked down at him and sighed, "Okay," and gave him a broken-off piece. This time, Buddy actually chewed the food for an entire second before swallowing. Susanna was impressed. He then gave her that look again. "Now I know how you got so fat. Poor Mrs. Mac probably didn't stand a chance against that look of yours."

She took a big bite and just then heard a sound she hadn't heard since that morning. Her phone was ringing. The sound came from her shoulder bag sitting beside the chair. She put down the half-eaten brownie and reached for it, careful not to tilt the plate of brownies into her lap. A vision of Buddy hoping into the chair and claiming salvage rights came to mind. She washed down the bite of brownie with a gulp of milk and answered the phone. It was Gail, her roommate at school.

"I've been trying to get through on and off all day. It's just the last hour or so that the cell phone towers have started working half-right again."

Susanna could hear *Don't Fear The Reaper* playing in the background. Even though the song was much older than Gail, even older than Gail's dad, it was not unusual for her to be playing something by Blue Oyster Cult; she loved classic rock. *Wouldn't it be wild if she played something by Red Lobster Cult?* She blinked away the silly thought. She must be getting tired again.

"Where are you?"

"I'm in the dorm. Classes got canceled after this weird stuff started." Gail described how that morning she was on her way to class, walking across the east quad toward the physics building. There, she saw a couple of students going up the steps who just disappeared. Their clothes fell loosely to the ground. She stood there gaped-mouthed and heard a lot of other students crossing the quad yelling and pointing. For a moment, she was too stunned to do anything except stand there and stare. Then she joined the crowd gathering around the empty clothes, everyone buzzing with excited comments. Others came up and asked what was going on. She stood there a long time then simply walked up the steps, through the doors and on to the classroom. She just didn't know what else to do.

"After about twenty-five minutes, an announcement came over the speakers that all classes were canceled for the day. I came on back to the dorm and just hung around watching TV in the commons room. That's what I'm doing now; nothing else to do but channel surf." She paused a moment. "Do you have any idea what's going on? I've been catching some news on TV but they don't really say a lot. The little they do tell, they just repeat over and over."

Susanna paused and said, "Gail, you remember that book project I was working on with that old guy? You remember us talking about the Rapture?"

"Uh, yeah, I think."

"Well, that's what happened."

For a moment, there was silence. Then, "You mean that's going on? That's why those people disappeared?"

"Yeah." Susanna looked at nothing then glanced down at Buddy now lying on the floor looking up at her, or rather the brownies.

"Wow, weird." Then she exclaimed, "Quick! Turn on channel six!"

Without pause, she picked up the remote from the end table and turned on the TV. It was already on channel six—her mom, like Albert, a Georgette McMillan fan.

And it was Georgette McMillan that was on the screen. Seeing her earlier that morning on the TV in Albert's study, Susanna figured she must have been on most of the day. But she looked different than she had this morning. A little tired, of course; it had been a long day. But there was more to it than that. She seemed—strange. Her expression lacked the calm demeanor that TV news people usually exhibit. Her face was tense; her eyes were wide and staring. She looked a little crazy.

"I see her," Susanna said into the phone. She stared at the phone a moment as if she was looking Gail in the eye, surprised how she reacted, or rather, barely reacted to the fact she'd just been told the Rapture had taken place. She figured it probably didn't register with her. She was sure that Gail, like she earlier in the day, didn't believe in the Rapture and put no value on the information.

"Looks like she's getting' ready to lose it, don'cha think?"

Susanna stared for a moment at the lady usually so handsome and composed. "Yeah, she does."

Co-anchor Bob McIntyre was saying something about traffic still being manageable despite a large number of abandoned cars everywhere. Georgette just stared into the camera unblinkingly. Bob was putting up a brave front, but it was obvious he knew something was wrong with her. He glanced at her time to time as he spoke and probably didn't know what to do.

Over the phone, Gail said, "He's most likely just waiting for somebody to get her off camera and off the set."

Susanna nodded her agreement and realized that Gail, of course, couldn't see her. "Yeah, I bet."

"Any time now," Gail continued, "they'll do a close up of ol' Bob and drag her off. Watch and see.

The wait was short. The closeup came as Gail predicted and in only a second a full, rich alto voice could be heard faintly in the background. "Stop! Stop! Let go of me!" Then suddenly Georgette fell into camera view and landed on her knees right beside Bob in his chair—a close two-shot.

"Bob! Bob! Don't let them do this to me! All the years we've worked together, I've got the most important thing to say that I've ever said before."

The fact that her reports, like most of those by this news program, were either fluff, the boring banality of local politics or the usual mundane trivialities of traffic accidents on I-40 or what person in the viewing area no one ever heard of got shot today, her most important story could very well be the price of tomatoes in Albuquerque.

Bob was cool. You had to give him that. He faced the camera stone-faced. He sat quietly waiting for someone to drag away this crazy woman. He didn't allow the fact that she was his friend and colleague to get in the way of his professionalism.

Gail exclaimed, "Wow! You seein' this?"

Susanna said nothing. She just sat and watched the unfolding drama before her with a sense of shock and pity for this poor woman. In the past, she had been somewhat critical of her and indeed her type of reporter whom she viewed as a pretender, a poser, just a pretty face to read copy off a teleprompter. Now she felt bad about that. Georgette McMillan wasn't just an image on the TV screen; she was a person, a real human being hurting and needing help.

Georgette faced the camera as hands came into view and gripped her right arm.

"This afternoon, I dreamed I met Satan." She jerked her arm free of the grip. "We talked a little bit."

"Georgette," Bob said, "please. You need to rest. You've been at this all day."

"No, Bob; I need to say this and I'll go. Just let me have my say and I'll go."

The hands came back into view. But before they could reach her, he shouted, "Leave her alone! This is Georgette McMillan, confound it! She was here even before I was and she's the reason this station is number one in this area. Let her be or so help me I'll walk off with her!" He had been keeping cool but now the cracks were showing.

Susanna stared at the screen gaped-mouth. She didn't understand why they just didn't cut to something else. Perhaps, they had their hands full down at the station, maybe much more was going on than the public realized. Maybe they knew something nobody else knew yet.

"This happened when I took my last break a half hour ago, the one I just came back from. I fell asleep at my desk and dreamed about Satan. We talked a little. It was not a friendly exchange." She managed a slight smile at the understatement.

Bob wagged his head. "You and your dreams!" He smiled in sympathy with her. It was evident they were good friends. He was no doubt sympathizing with the end of her career. After this, she'd never work in TV again anywhere, he knew.

Bob turned and put his arm around her. "What did he look like?"

"I can't remember exactly," she replied, her hands flapping in front of her. "It seemed like he was wearing a sort of off-white, loose fitting robe; there was one part of it that was a reddish orange color that draped over his left shoulder and crossed the rest of the garment. His build was about average in size; muscular, he seemed. His face was fierce. His eyes were large and seemed filled with blood and they were wild looking. His teeth were like those of an animal, big and wide filling his mouth to overflowing and they were pointed on the ends like daggers. They looked sharp. His mouth was large with wide lips that came over his teeth easily when he spoke. His hair was reddish and short and in tight curls. His skin had, it seemed, a reddish tint to it."

"It's too bad you can't remember him exactly."

She said, "I don't need no smart aleck remarks right now."

He smiled and nodded, his eyes misting up. "Can you remember anything you said to each other?"

Georgette shook her head. "Not exactly; not all of it. I don't recall just what was said and I'm not sure I really want to remember. I do remember that in the dream I had met some other lesser demons first, then at the end I met, you know—" She shrugged. "I remember the place to be a broad rocky plain. To my right was a tall rock formation that was like a wall. The ground was greatly uneven. Standing in front of me was someone that I understood to be a demon. He looked, as I recall, pretty much like a regular person. He was big, rather fierce. He stood on an outcropping of rock sticking out of the ground at the rocky wall. He was looking down at me. He and I had a verbal exchange of some sort; I don't recall what was said. He went away and then from a rise a short distance in front of me, came the one I understood to be Satan. I don't know how I knew that. I think it was he himself who told me. He came over the rise and took a defiant stance glaring at me. I went to him and confronted him face to face. We too had a heated exchange."

Bob kept looking at her, supporting her, acting as though he believed every word. He nodded now and then as she spoke. Their friendship was unmistakable.

"Just before I woke up, he glared at me and shouted, 'Tell them! Tell them! Tell them! I am coming now. I am taking over now! I shall rule the world!' She looked at Bob and shook her head.

Bob patted her hand that rested on the newsdesk.

"I thought I was a Christian," she said, looking at him. "I thought I was ready for the Rapture. But now that's it happened—" At that moment the screen went blank.

Susanna said to Gail, "Did you just lose your picture?"

"Yeah, guess somebody finally pulled the plug."

Susanna couldn't help notice it was right at the moment Georgette McMillan said outright that the Rapture had happened. Someone at the station didn't want that broadcasted, or perhaps didn't want to hear it themselves. All too well, she understood Rapture denial. In a manner of speaking, she'd written a book on it. It seemed the news agencies and perhaps the authorities didn't want any reporting done on the subject. She wondered how they possibly hoped to cover it up.

A commercial for a car dealership—the staple of local TV news programs—came on.

Chapter Twenty

"You mean you're just going to leave it there?" Mrs. Kelly eyed her daughter carefully.

Susanna sighed. "Mom, I'm sure it'll be okay overnight. It's not like it's downtown or in a bad neighborhood. People who live there park their cars there all the time."

After she and Gail finished their call, Susanna did some channel surfing. She enjoyed watching TV while she snacked and the brownies were waiting. She found a channel not filled with news of the day's events and began watching an old rerun of the 60's Batman TV show. Something silly to help take her mind off something all too serious.

"Buddy, you like Batman?" She looked at the curious beagle in his big brown eyes and began vocalizing along with the catchy theme. "Da-da da-da da-da da-da da-da da-da da-da da-da Batman!"

The dog gave her a look that seemed to say, 'Okay, let's just get on with the brownies, shall we?'

When they had reached the last brownie, Mrs. Kelly came in wiping her hands with a dishtowel. "I was just wondering, what are you going to do about the car?" That question led to a pointed discussion of the advisability of leaving the car—her dad's old car—just sitting out where anyone could get it. The car had sentimental attachments for Susanna, but for her mother, it was like a rolling memorial to her late husband. Susanna and her mother locked eyes as she and Buddy took the last bites of the last brownie.

Finally, she said, "All right!" through a mouthful of brownie. She took a big swallow of milk and washed it down. "I'll call Tim. But first I have to do something."

She picked up her shoulder bag from the floor and carried it into the kitchen. She laid it down on the table and dug out her laptop. It was smaller than the bigger notebook computers so much in use. It was thin and light, web-based in operation and very portable. It was the web-book she used in college like so many other students. Her mom's cable service included WiFi and when she opened the lid it connected at once. Also from the bag, she got out the thumb drive with the files for Albert's videos and the book manuscript and plugged it in. It didn't take too long and she had the videos uploaded to the gigantically successful video sharing site with 'You' in the name. She posted them to her own account; she never did get the chance to set up an account for Albert. She did a search on the word 'Rapture' and saw that countless videos had been already been posted just that day. The manuscript had already been formatted for printing and she uploaded it as a PDF file on several book sharing websites. She leaned back and stared at the computer screen. She was sure Albert would have been pleased to know his work, the information, had gotten out there at last.

***

The people roaming the streets, by and large, were controlled enough not to be threatening. There was an occasional push and shove incident here or a verbal altercation there, but nothing Tim couldn't handle. All he had to do was pull up and roll down his window and in a nice, but firm, manner tell them to knock it off. But the mood was not calm, not truly calm—like the proverbial calm before the storm.

Just like this morning, as he patrolled, he saw plenty of empty, abandoned cars everywhere parked at odd angles along the road. Some were down in ditches; some were sitting on the sides of embankments and had obviously been pushed down from the roads above. Once, he even saw someone in the act; he looked on as a big guy pushed a hatchback out of the road. He didn't interfere. Once or twice, he even saw someone getting into an abandoned car and driving off with it. Tim did nothing to stop it; to him, car thief had too low of a priority in a Code Six situation to fool with. And besides, it actually helped get some cars out of the way.

His phone rang and he pulled it free off his shirt pocket. The screen displayed Susanna's name and number.

"Hello, girl! What's up?"

"How's it going out there?"

A kid on a bicycle cut across the road just in front of him. Tim hit the brakes and managed not to curse into the phone.

"Going okay; 'bout as well as could be expected," he said as he glared at the back of the departing kid in the blue tee-shirt and red ballcap.

"Listen, I know you're busy so I'll get to the point. I'd like to get my car. Can you help a girl out?"

It was getting near dusk now. He would rather she just stay indoors. But if she was determined to get back to Cloverdale, he didn't want her out there without him.

"Sure. I'll swing 'round and pick you up."

"I don't want to be a problem. Are things calm enough out there for me not to get in the way?"

"Yeah, it's not too bad. People are confused and a little scared, but they're not causing any real problems." *And as long as I'm around, nobody's gonna cause you any problems.* "It'll be all right."

It only took him a few minutes to get back to the house. Susanna came bounding out of the front door even before he stopped; she trotted to the car and got in.

"You didn't bring your guard dog?" He smiled.

"Not this time, officer," she said as she snapped her seat belt. "About all he could guard would be a plate of spaghetti to make sure nobody ate it but him."

Tim glanced at the house. "Uh, your mom's not in there alone, is she?"

Susanna looked at him. "No. A couple of the neighborhood men came by to check on her. They're old friends of my mom and dad. They're gonna stick around a while."

As they pulled away, Tim's phone rang. Susanna recognized the ring tone; it was the old *Hampster Dance* tune—Do-do-do-da do-da do-da … Even though this was a very short version, it still had the little chuckle at the end. She looked at him and suppressed a grin. *You're just full of surprises, aren't you?*

He again fished the phone out of his shirt pocket and answered. He listened and said, "Okay," and hung up. As he put the phone back into his pocket, he said, "Looks like we're headed back to Cloverdale, car or not."

"Something going on there?"

He shook his head. "Nothing special that I know of."

"Well, it's good to know the cell towers are working."

"Dispatcher said she'd had to try me a couple of times before she got through. Tower service is still a little hit and miss. Must've been a bit of a priority for her to do that."

"Wonder what it is." She moved around a bit to get comfortable.

"I was told to do a drive through now and do several more during the night, especially around the Curtis house. The owner is concerned that too many people are milling about on his property." He did know the reason he got the call on the phone instead of the radio. It was not necessarily a call-for-service dispatch, and it lasted a little longer than most radio calls. Not something they wanted on the radio; radio calls are intended to be brief and to the point.

In a few minutes, they were back. As they pulled through the entry to Cloverdale, it struck Tim how odd it was he kept ending up here. This was a good-sized town and, frankly, there were a lot higher priority places he could, and probably should, be patrolling. There were the businesses and workshops subject to vandalism, and especially the shops and stores that were so vulnerable to looting in times of unrest like this. Not to mention the richer neighborhoods with wealthy, and therefore more powerful and politically connected, residents. But here he was, again, on patrol in Cloverdale. *Home, sweet home,* he thought, but he kept the remark and the sarcasm to himself.

As they approached the Curtis house, he thought how the Curtis family was one of those rich, connected families. Yet, they did not live in one of the upscale, rich neighborhoods like many of their country club co-members. The simple fact is they didn't choose the neighborhood; it chose them. The family, going back generations, had lived here alone back in the old days and the neighborhood simply built up around them.

But he knew why he was here again. The current master of the Curtis house, Benjamin Curtis, current city council member, former lieutenant governor, and general all-round power broker, had made a call. He wanted to make sure the people wandering around looking for someone, or maybe someone to supply some answers, stayed off his property and, especially, away from his door. Someone might get it into their head that a city councilman might have information they didn't. It was possible they might come to the house and *insist* he share that information with them.

A voice, different from the one Susanna heard before, came from the radio: "All units, all units proceed code two."

Tim said, "That means they want us to turn our police lights on. With it getting near dark, the lights increase our visibility. During a Code Six, we want high visibility, and when people see police lights flashing it makes them think twice about getting out of hand."

She nodded.

He reached for the small panel of buttons mounted in the console and pushed one. Instantly, swirling blue lights reflected off the hood of the car.

They took the same route Susanna used so many mornings going to Albert's house. Soon they found themselves on Curtis Road, the Curtis house just ahead.

Susanna looked out the window and pointed to Jasper's house. "That's where that preacher we saw today lives."

Tim's face became solemn. He looked away.

The Curtis house was just to the right. Tim slowed down making sure he gave the occupants a good chance to see the car. Dark as it now was, the lights stood out brilliantly and the beams washed over the front of the small mansion.

"Tim, can we go by Dora's again?"

"No problem."

He sped up a little and they were at Dora's house in only a minute. From the car, they looked over the place. It was dark inside; not one bit of light could they see. Dora's car was still in the driveway. They got out and Tim laid his hand on the hood. It was stone cold.

Glancing at his watch, he saw it was a little past seven. "Is her husband usually home by now?"

"I suppose so. I'm usually not around here this time of night. But from what I understand from Dora, he's usually home from work by now."

They went again to the front door and tried the handle. Still, the front door was unlocked. This time, they did not enter. Tim just pushed it open a little and called out to see if anyone was there. There was no response. Susanna called Dora's name loudly. Still nothing.

The door left unlocked, the dog dish filled but nothing eaten, she realized now that this meant, for some reason, Dora and the dog left in a hurry. She was certain Tim knew this from the start and didn't say anything. Probably afraid it would upset her more than she already had been that morning. And he would have been right. Silently, they got back in the patrol car.

Before he started the engine, he said, "I want you to stay in the car with me. When my patrol here is finished, we'll ride to your car. You can then drive on home and I'll follow. That sound like a plan?"

"Yes, that'll be fine."

That playful bemusement that had come into her voice after she calmed down this morning was gone again. She, no doubt, was worried about her friend.

He started the car and they began driving slowly through the neighborhood. The houses all seemed unusually dim for a nice residential neighborhood in the early evening. Albert's house was one of the most brightly lit; for some reason, it bothered Susanna. She asked Tim to stop for a minute and she rushed into the house. She made sure the back door was locked and turned out the lights. She turned on a small lamp in the living room so the house wouldn't be pitch dark and perhaps attract looters. The thought of that bothered her. She knew she was still adjusting to the new reality of the world. This was Albert's home and her workplace for the past year. She did this out of respect for Albert and the friendship they had. It wasn't until that moment that she realized how much she was going to miss the old guy.

She pulled opened the front door and stepped out. Reaching inside, she set the lock, something she had neglected to do when she came out of the house earlier this morning. She had been too distracted by the gunshots and the deaths of the Davidsons at the time to think of it. She pulled the door closed and walked away. The outer storm door swung shut behind her. Hearing it close was like the end of a chapter in her life. She felt a sense of loss. She walked past her car—it still looked okay—and got back in the patrol car.

Tim noticed her eyes were moist.

Just then someone knocked on the passenger side window. Startled, Susanna almost jumped out of her seat. Quickly, she swung around and faced the woman standing beside the car.

Tim looked past her at the woman. She seemed about sixty with short blond hair in big curls. He was sure it was a wig. She stood there waving and smiling. Tim was a little angry—not with the woman; she was just doing what idiots do. He was furious at himself for letting someone come up on him unawares. One of his instructors at BLET used to say when one of the trainees fouled up, "That's how the cop graveyard got started." He could just imagine the torrent of abuse he'd be getting now if Sergeant Donaldson were here. And the fact he allowed this to happen during a Code Six only exacerbated his anger.

Little ladies with curly wigs can carry guns too, stupid!

He identified the position of both of her hands, one waving, one pressed against the glass. She wasn't carrying. He pushed a button on the door panel and Susanna's window rolled down a bit.

"Yes, ma'am, how can I help you?"

"Hello," the lady said, her voice slightly muffled by the partially closed window. "My name is Cheryl Milliner. I live just down the street." She pointed to the left. "Actually, officer, I wanted to speak to this young lady."

Susanna leaned back, her eyebrows raised.

"You're that young lady that was working with Albert on his prophecy book, aren't you?"

"Yes… Yes, I am." Suddenly Susanna remembered the name, Cheryl Milliner. Dora had told her about her. She had described her as an interfering busybody who, under the pretense of helping people, tried to get into everyone's business.

"I knew about the book Albert was doing. Once in a while, he'd mention it at one of the neighborhood cookouts."

Cheryl Milliner did manage to get invited to many of the neighborhood get-togethers. Not that anyone was too enthusiastic about having her, but not to invite her seemed mean.

"I know what's happened," she said, staring Susanna in the eyes. "I know the Rapture has taken place."

Uncomfortable under the stare, she replied, "Yes, I believe that it has."

"Then why didn't you go?"

She took a breath. "Because as of this morning, I didn't believe any of this. I do now."

Cheryl Milliner nodded. "Yes, I understand. But what I don't understand is why *I* didn't go. Do *you* know?"

Susanna only shook her head. An answer here would do no good and be too late.

"I mean, if anybody should go it should have been me. All I do is go around the neighborhood trying to help these stupid people."

Tim, even with his lack of religious knowledge, could see why this lady didn't get raptured.

"I mean it's like I've been ignored! And Cheryl Lianna Milliner is not going to be ignored." She gave her head a quick shake. "Well, I can't believe it happened without me. It must be some kind of mistake."

Susanna said, "I don't know what to say, Ms. Milliner. We're all a little shook up."

"Well, let me tell you what I'm going to do! I'm going down tomorrow and get me a lawyer and sue that so-called church I've been going to. That Preacher Jasper said if I supported the church and gave generously I'd be all right." Cheryl Milliner put her hands on her hips.

"Why, there's been times I put as much as ten dollars in the offering plate!" She slowly shook her head. "They're not getting away with this."

Tim thought, *Good luck suing a dead man, lady.* Then he said, "Ma'am, we've got to go. It's probably best you go to your home and stay inside the rest of the night."

She looked around at the now dark neighborhood and at the strangers, who before had been her neighbors, milling aimlessly around. "Perhaps, you're right, officer." She turned and hurried away.

The patrol of Cloverdale didn't take long and was nearly done. They saw people milling about looking for loved ones, lost pets, answers, the usual. And it struck them how odd it was that things had come to such a point in which *that* could ever be considered as the usual. They noticed, however, that fewer people seemed to be out. Tim was glad for that; he took it as a sign that people maybe were finally settling down, accepting what had happened.

"Let's swing by the Curtis house again, come back to your car, and I'll follow you home."

She looked at him and nodded.

In less than a minute they were back on Curtis Road. As they crept along, the lights on top of the police car, flashing and rotating, cast blue beams over the road and adjoining yards. Even with fewer people out, there were still many that roamed the streets. Tim looked right and left looking for any sign of trouble. Hopefully, the presence of a police car, especially with the lights going would deter people from acting up. So far, he saw no problem.

Tim knew that now that it was dark, this was the dangerous time, perhaps the moment of truth. It was the time when things could really get tricky. After dark, that's when some people get restless and often take to the streets to vent their fear and frustration. He recalled so many news reports about a riot that had occurred the *night* before. He remembered how on some of the news footage he'd seen that normal everyday people could go so very crazy under unusual circumstances—like a huge chunk of the world's population suddenly disappearing. Or like some people—not just Susanna but others he'd heard on talk radio while patrolling—talking about a horrendous coming Great Tribulation. He wished that talk would stop even if it were true. Susanna, the pretty little lady in the passenger seat believed it. He hoped she was through talking about it, but he liked her far too much to tell her that.

He glanced over at the lovely profile looking forward at the road ahead. *Why couldn't we've met before now?*

"Look out!" She pointed to a pair of men who had just crossed the road a few yards ahead.

Tim hit the brake. The car stopped and shook them both. He looked at her and nodded. "Thanks. I'm glad I brought you along. Getting a little tired; I could use an extra pair of eyes tonight." The fact the extra pair of eyes were warm, soft, big and brown didn't add anything to their efficiency, but it made looking into them so very easy. She glanced at him flashing those warm, soft, big brown eyes at him. He felt his stomach tingle. *Why couldn't we've met before now?* His mind replayed the thought, but this time with a sharper pang of regret.

Chapter Twenty-One

Susanna pulled her smartphone from her shirt pocket; she wanted to check the news. She wondered if anything new had developed since she last watched—since the on-air breakdown had taken place. Channel six, the channel Georgette McMillan had worked for until that afternoon, provided an online stream of its news broadcasts. Bob McIntyre was on—alone now, his face ashen. This day had been a maddening flurry of mystery and heartbreak for so many, and his friend and colleague had crashed and burned on the air. It was not surprising the fake chipper demeanor common to local TV anchor people was at the moment forgone. Susanna suspected that in the near future as Tribulation events began to unfold more and more it might be gone forever.

Bob McIntyre said, "Reports are coming in of crowds gathering downtown around the city office buildings. Although the offices are long closed, crowds still can be found standing around various locations. Let's go live now to Derrick Heathman who's on the scene."

There came on the screen a man of about twenty-five, clean-shaven with short dark hair. He wore an open collar, long sleeve blue shirt. Microphone in hand, he stood in front of a white van that had the station's call letters WTVR and logo displayed prominently on the side. The sound in the background was saturated with voices that had a decidedly bitter tone to them.

He said, "So far, Bob, everyone here is behaving in an orderly fashion. But it's hard to pinpoint exactly why they are here. I've spoken with several of them and they themselves don't seem to be sure. Whether they're here to protest the lack of information being provided to them or to simply ask questions is uncertain. After the strange events of the day, it's easy to understand their frustrations."

The image changed to a man in a green tee-shirt and red ballcap with a microphone stuck in his face. It was a prerecorded interview with one of the people downtown. A bank served as a backdrop. "I'm here," he said, "'cause I want to know what's goin' on! We all have been waiting all day for some kind of explanation and we still ain't got none!"

She turned off the news program and looked at Tim. "You think any of this downtown business is gonna cause trouble?" She slipped the phone back into her pocket.

Tim's face was solemn. "I don't know. Hope not."

His tone, so serious, gave her pause. Was there something he suspected that might happen that she didn't? She didn't find his answer at all encouraging.

She looked around. With fewer people out, the night was quieter. It was easy to hear the hum of the car engine. Susanna guessed many of the neighbors who had been walking around searching for answers and loved ones had now gone back to their homes to watch the news and, perhaps, stare at front doors for those loved ones who—they were perhaps beginning to realize—would never come through them again. No doubt, she thought, they, like her, were now resigning themselves to the fact that things had changed. It was quieter, but, to her, it was an uneasy quiet, the kind of quiet that hangs heavily in the air just before a thunderclap.

As they approached the Curtis house, Tim looked sharply to the left. Suddenly, he pulled over and stopped in front of the house. He cut the engine but left the police lights going.

"What's up?" she asked.

"Thought I saw someone moving around behind the house. That's kind of unusual under the circumstances. I better check it out." He unfastened his seatbelt. "Be best if you wait in the car."

She nodded and watched as he got out and walked slowly, very carefully it seemed, to the corner of the house and out of view.

Coming to the back of the house, even in the gloom of night and of the shadows back of the property, Tim saw a man of slender build holding a shovel and digging up the ground. He took his small but powerful tactical flashlight from his belt and stepped forward. He shone the beam on the man. "Excuse me. Everything all right?"

He was close enough now to see, with the aid of the light, the man was standing near a few old headstones that were in a small clearing surrounded by bushes and small trees. A family plot, no doubt, from generations past by the looks of it. People don't bury family members in the backyard much these days, but as he understood it, in older times it was not unusual for a family estate to have its own small burial plot on their property. It was obscured from the road by the trees and shrubs; no doubt they were intended for that purpose. The man was digging up one of the graves.

He turned and faced him. "Yes, officer, everything is fine."

"Mind if I ask what you're doing?"

While Tim was busy with his errand behind the house, Susanna looked over the Curtis house as she so often did before. At night it was still as impressive as ever. She agreed to stay in the car but she was sure that simply applied to her not going with him as he checked out the back of the house. She believed he wouldn't mind her getting out and looking at the front. And besides, she needed some fresh air.

She stepped out of the car and stretched her legs. Slowly, she started up the flagstone walkway and stopped to look up. The Curtis house loomed magnificently in front of her. It was nice to see it up close.

Light shone in only one of the windows, dull light that seemed cast from perhaps a single lamp somewhere in the room. All the other windows were dark, very dark. To her, it seemed the house was dark on purpose. Usually, if she had worked late and drove by this house in the darkening twilight, mostly in the winter months when it got dark early, the house would be awash in beautiful soft tones glowing from the windows like candles in the night. After seeing it so well lit and cheerful those other times, it was disarming to see it now so dim, so—secretive. It made the beautiful old house she had admired so many times in the daylight and on those other nights now seem a little ominous. However, under the circumstances, she thought maybe her imagination was getting away with her.

She continued looking at the house. The neighborhood was quieter now though not silent. She still heard faint voices and movements away in the distance. She wasn't frightened of the neighbors or the neighborhood. She knew them and it so well. Even under these circumstances she couldn't help but admire this stately old place. Now this close, even in the dark, she could make out the lines of the stone block sills angled under each window. It was cooler now and she hugged herself as she looked at the cornices and how the blocks there tastefully protruded just a bit.

"Would you like to come in?"

Hearing a voice so unexpectedly, Susanna nearly jumped out of her skin. Stepping back, she looked toward the front door. It was open; only a little light shone out. It took her a moment to make out the lady standing in the doorway smiling at her.

"I think I've seen you before," the lady said, her gentle voice reflecting the smile. "You drive by often and admire the house, don't you?" Like Susanna, she spoke with a slight southern accent. But the lady's accent rang like that of a southern aristocrat. It reminded her of Billy Graham.

Susanna, recovering from her shock, nodded. "Yes. I just love this place."

The lady smiled even more. "Then you must come inside." She looked around and the smile slipped away. "Seems to be getting a bit chilled out here."

Susanna thought the lady displayed more concern than a mere drop in temperature should create.

"I'm Mrs. Curtis by the way." She extended her hand.

Susanna walked to the door and shook hands with her. "Hello, my name is Susanna Kelly." She wiped her feet on the large doormat, the name *Curtis* woven into it and followed her hostess into the darkened house. A thought flashed through her mind: *What are you doing walking into a dark house with a perfect stranger!* But there was something about this lady, a gentleness, a friendliness that assuaged her worries. And it wasn't like she was in some totally strange neighborhood or a totally strange house, or that her whereabouts were unknown. Tim was just in the backyard well within hollering distance.

"Excuse the dim lighting," Mrs. Curtis said. "With all this *whatever* that's going on, we're keeping most of the lights off so as not to attract attention ... my husband's idea." Susanna wasn't sure if she followed the logic of that, but she didn't contradict her hostess. "Such a lovely young lady as yourself is, of course, the exception." Mrs. Curtis beamed a smile, sincere and friendly, at her pretty young guest.

Susanna returned the smile. "Thanks. I appreciate you letting me come inside."

Mrs. Curtis closed the door and Susanna looked over the short, dimly lit hallway. With its dark wainscoting and upper walls covered in what seemed like, in the dim light, a cream-colored wallpaper, the passageway was tastefully appointed, as elegant as she had imagined it would be. A collection of small portraits in elegantly carved cherry-stained frames lined the walls. The gray, red and light blue Persian carpeting was plush and silenced their footfalls.

She thought, *I always wanted to come in here and all it took was the end of the world to make it happen.*

At the end of the short passage, to the right, a set of double-doors stood open spilling light into the corridor. It was that which lighted the passage. Mrs. Curtis led the way and stood in front of it. She held out her hand gesturing for Susanna to enter. To the left there was another set of double-doors that opened unto a large room lit only by the light spilling in through the large front window. She could just make out a white-railed staircase curving up to the second floor

By the glow of a single reading lamp, a bit brighter inside than it had seemed through the window, she saw the room. It was not abundantly large, but adequately spacious to be comfortable. It was a parlor like out of a magazine. White crown molding ran around a tray ceiling. Persian carpeting, matching that in the hallway, covered the floor. Wainscoting similar to what she saw in the hall, mahogany and highly polished, surrounded the walls. On the wall opposite the fireplace stood a small sofa covered in a greenish, silk-looking material. The various other furnishings, Queen Ann tables holding fresh cut flowers in crystal vases and a corner cabinet filled with family pictures in silver frames, all fit nicely with the general air of good taste. The walls held pictures like those in the hall—no doubt, Curtis family ancestors.

Outside, Tim stood waiting for an answer to what was going on. He stepped closer to the man. Now, he could see he was about twenty-eight, blond with a short beard. He wore blue jeans, sneakers, and a black tee-shirt.

"Well, I'm afraid that's going to take a little explaining," the man said, smiling.

Tim just stood there and waited. He wasn't there to chit-chat; he wanted to know what this guy was up to.

The man shrugged. "Might as well tell you. But it's going to sound a little strange."

Tim looked down at the grave the man stood beside. It looked already halfway dug up.

Yeah, strange was the word all right.

"This old family plot hasn't been used in over seventy-five years. Buried there," he pointed to the grave, "is an ancestor of mine."

"Sir, what is your name, by the way?"

"I'm Thomas Curtis. My parents live here." He gestured toward the house. "They asked me to come over and do this for them." He nodded down at the grave. "A hundred years ago, this ancestor, so my dad says, was well known as a very devout deacon in his church. Don't know which one. In light of all this Rapture talk, my dad and mom wanted to see if he's still there."

This took Tim back a bit. "Why!"

Thomas Curtis shook his head. "With all that's happened today, all the talk of the Rapture perhaps having taken place, they wanted to see if perhaps he had gone. It's a test I suppose to see if that has indeed happened."

"You mean the Rapture thing is for dead people too?"

Thomas nodded. "According to what someone told my mom, it's not just living Christians that are suppose to go, or I guess I should say, *were* supposed to go, but dead Christians would also go. Something that has to do with the Resurrection. So I guess you could say we're testing that out."

Tim's brow arched. "But after all this time is there much left to ... examine?"

"Oh yes, there should be skeletal remains if not still something of the flesh on the bones." The man smiled. "I'm a doctor by the way. I've had enough experience with cadavers not to be put off too much by one more."

Tim paused a moment. Another crazy moment of a crazy day. What difference did it make? It was their property. If they wanted to dig it up, he had no objection.

Now in somewhat brighter light, Susanna got a better look at her hostess. Her short blond hair was thick and full, neatly combed into bangs and just covering her ears. It framed her face like a golden halo. Her wide face held only a touch of makeup; her skin was still smooth even though she was not young. A wedding band adorned her left hand, and on the other ring finger, she wore what seemed like a two-karat emerald oval ring. Diamond chips flashed brightly when they caught the light just right.

The elegant lady led Susanna toward a pair of plush wingback chairs flanking each side of a stone fireplace. A low flame danced there slowly. The chairs yawned invitingly. Susanna took the one on the right. Her hostess sat in the other. She looked over the lady's attire and admired the simple and beautiful lounging outfit Mrs. Curtis wore. It seemed to echo back to a former age of home elegance that was long gone from most American households, even the rich ones. This was not some department store matching tee-shirt and shorts a young modern housewife might wear around the house.

Mrs. Curtis wore an elegant ensemble that consisted of a black top with long sleeves terminating in narrow cuffs and matching black pants also cuffed. Top and pants both had small black designs of fleur-de-lis woven into the fabric. Susanna could see them when they caught the firelight. It looked nice and very expensive. Susanna was sure the outfit was pure silk. Her slippers were black to match the outfit and were accented with gold trim—not gold-colored thread woven into the fabric but actual gold as trim.

"So, what brings you here, Susanna?"

"I was riding with Tim, a police officer. Oh, I should mention, he saw someone in your backyard."

Mrs. Curtis smiled. "Yes, that's my son, Thomas. He's doing a little errand for my husband and I. He's a doctor on staff at the hospital; a heart surgeon." She pointed to the window. "I saw the young police officer when he came toward the house. That's why I went to the door. I was going to ask him if I could be of any assistance, but he'd already gone round."

"Is everything all right?"

"With all this strangeness going on, I'm not sure how to answer that. But I'm sure they're fine back there. My son can explain everything to the officer." She checked her watch; the stainless steel case around the Roman numeral face was studded with diamond chips like the ring. "My husband's in the basement getting things ... ready."

That last word was spoken with a tone that made Susanna uneasy.

"He should be finished soon. Why don't we go down and check on them?"

Them? Susanna wondered.

"Unless, of course, you'd like a little tour of the house first?"

Susanna's eyes brightened. "Oh, yes, if it's not too much trouble!"

Mrs. Curtis rose and Susanna followed her into the front hall.

Chapter Twenty-Two

Dr. Curtis looked tired. As Tim well remembered from basic training, digging trenches in combat drills, digging is hard work. He decided to give him a hand. Besides, he too wanted to see what was, or was not, in that grave. He was looking for answers and maybe this could give him at least a clue. He took the shovel from Thomas and told him to rest a bit. He sat beside one of the small trees and held the flashlight for Tim to dig by.

He dug for several minutes and was surprised how hard the dirt had compacted, compressed tightly by the passing of decades. "Man! You've been hard at it, haven't you?"

"Yes, it's been a while since I put this much effort into anything."

This was a member of the prosperous, prestigious Curtis family. He doubted if he had ever put this much effort into anything unless skiing in Aspen, or that sort of thing, is inordinately taxing.

Inside, Susanna and Mrs. Curtis were coming down the curved staircase chatting almost merrily. Susanna had loved going through this wonderful old place and had asked a lot of questions. Mrs. Curtis cut on lights for each room as they went and turned them off again as they left. She still wanted the house dark according to her husband's wishes.

The bedrooms, a couple of which still had four-poster beds, were decorated with a mixture of blankets and sheets of modern fabrics and pillows on the beds and antique furnishings decorating the rooms. The other rooms, including the dining room with its long cherry dinner table and matching china cabinet, the music room with the nine-foot grand, and the other rooms all displayed the fine taste and elegance that befitted the house. Much bigger than the cozy parlor Susanna had first entered with Mrs. Curtis, the large room they now descended to down the stairs was where the entertaining took place when guests came over for a dinner party or some other social occasion.

At the bottom of the stairs, Mrs. Curtis checked her watch again. "Please come with me. I really must look in on how they're doing in the basement and see if my husband has everything ready."

Susanna didn't ask what she meant. It wasn't any of her business. And she knew she needed to get back to the car before Tim missed her if he hadn't already. Just then her phone rang.

"Excuse me," Susanna said as she drew out her phone. The screen showed it was Tim calling.

"Hey, Tim."

"You doing all right?"

"Yeah," she replied. "By the way, I'm inside the house with Mrs. Curtis."

"Okay, just checking up. We're a little busy back here but shouldn't be too much longer."

They hung up.

The two ladies came to the kitchen door, the end of the tour, Susanna supposed. Mrs. Curtis pushed it open and led the way inside. Susanna looked over the sparkling clean black and white checkered tiled floor, the gleaming off-white walls, modern appliances and the round wooden kitchen table with its cherry-stained, high-gloss finish that occupied a corner of the room. In a house two hundred years old, she half expected to see an old wood stove and a pump handle over the sink. She figured she was a century and a half too late for that.

Mrs. Curtis explained it had been totally remodeled years ago and outfitted with all new and modern appliances.

"When I married my husband, it had of course been brought up to date from time to time but it was still a little rustic for my taste. So I guessed it was my turn to spend some of the family's fortune and do a complete remodel. I enjoy looking at antiques as much as anyone, but cooking with them," she shook her head, "not a chance."

Susanna grinned.

"When I told him what I had planned, and what it would cost, he groaned. Just between us, the Curtis family has been known to be a little tight with their money." She grinned.

I guess that's how they managed to hold on to it for so long, Susanna thought.

"They sold most of the land to developers. However, I wished they had kept more of the land directly around the house. Bit of an oversight they came to regret. When my husband heard how much my little project would cost, he probably wondered if it was too late to back out of the marriage." She laughed lightly as she led the way toward the back of the kitchen. "That was thirty-five years ago; I guess he decided it was 'cheaper to keep her,' as I believe the saying goes."

Susanna appreciated her sense of humor and her way of making her feel at ease. She was a smart lady as well as elegant.

Mrs. Curtis stopped at what must be the basement door. She opened it and Susanna felt a rush of cool air brush against her skin. Goosebumps rose on her bare arms. It had a slightly damp, musty scent to it. She looked in and saw that the whole stairwell was constructed of brick, and it was old brick too. Two-hundred-year-old brickwork—had to be the original foundation. The orange clay-looking blocks were chipped and discolored with age. The cement mortar bulged a little. The stairs themselves were brick as well and were quite narrow. They would have to go down single file. And the staircase curved sharply to the right as it wound down. Susanna couldn't see what was waiting at the bottom. That made her a little apprehensive.

"A lot of people have been coming onto the property," Mrs. Curtis said. "My husband is on the city council and some people seem to think, because of that, he knows what's going on." She stepped onto the first step and started down. Susanna, against her better judgment, followed. "Just because he's connected with city government doesn't mean he knows or understands this situation any better than anyone else. Several people have already come to the door wanting to talk to him, one or two getting a little hostile when he told them he didn't know anything more than they did. That's why we're setting up down here to spend the night. You'll see."

As they came down the stairs, she was surprised how cool it was here compared to upstairs. As well as musty, the air smelled old.

Mrs. Curtis took her time going down the steps. There was no handrail but with the walls so close, almost as if they were closing in on them, there was not much chance of falling. Susanna could have jogged down the steps in no time, but she reminded herself that Mrs. Curtis wasn't a young woman anymore.

At the back of the house, the night was especially dark around the old family plot surrounded by the trees. The air was decidedly cooler than before. Tim and Thomas stood looking down into the now opened grave. Tim's powerful flashlight made it easy to see.

The dirt removed, the old coffin, dirty and grimy, lay before them solemnly. There was no concrete vault like those so widely used today. The simple rectangular shaped box was simply put into the ground and covered. To Tim, it seemed to be of solid oak construction, not the cheap pine boxes he'd seen in old TV westerns. And it was a split-lid design like those so much used today. It seemed to be in remarkably good shape, not rotted or broken.

They looked at each other.

Tim said, "It's your family's coffin; you open it."

Thomas Curtis nodded and stepped down into the hole and knelt on top of the lower lid. The old coffin held his weight amazingly well with only a little creaking and groaning as he settled down.

Opening the upper lid was much easier than he had anticipated. The hard oak may have survived well, but the metal clasp of the lid did not. Thomas pulled on the lid, and on the second try, it swung open without much resistance.

They looked inside the box and audibly gasped.

Coming around the center curvature of the brick stairwell, Susanna could now see the bottom of the stairs and the cement basement floor beyond. Once upon a time it may have been simply a dirt floor of a cellar. The cement was in good shape and didn't look all that old.

As they came off the stairs, there was a man about the same age as Mrs. Curtis, whom Susanna assumed to be Mr. Curtis. He was stacking a shrink-wrapped pack of bottles of water on top of several other such packs in a corner. On the wrapper it said it contained twenty-four sixteen ounce bottles. The water was a store brand not a name brand.

The air down here wasn't as bad as she had expected. She saw the gentle flames of scented candles placed around the room and understood why.

The basement had a low ceiling. That probably went back to the days when this was little more than a root cellar. But there was still enough headroom for an average-sized man to stand up and move around without bumping his head. Now with a solid floor of cement, electric lights attached to the joists overhead, it had at some time not too many years ago been updated to look like a proper basement. There was a blue wooden partition about fifteen feet from the stairs that extended from the right wall about ten feet. What was behind it, Susanna had no idea. It was on this side of the partition where it joined the brick wall to make a corner that the bottles of water were stacked.

On this side of the partition, there were three army style cots set up all neatly made. Susanna could see the basement was being outfitted to serve as a kind of bunker. She supposed they wanted to spend the night down here in the event things got out of hand upstairs, to give them more of a sense of security. She thought it was not a bad idea.

Mrs. Curtis stepped toward the man and Susanna followed. She asked him, "How's everything going?"

He turned and glanced at Susanna. "Got lots of canned goods over there." He pointed to several boxes on the floor against the wall just beside the stairs. "Just brought some more drinking water down. Got a couple of packs in the fridge already along with some ice tea and soft drinks." Susanna looked at the white refrigerator in the corner beyond the boxes of canned goods. "Plenty of snacks over there." He pointed at several tightly packed grocery bags on a small table near the fridge. On the table sat a small portable TV. "We're all set." He nodded in satisfaction.

"Good, Benjamin. That makes us all feel much better." She glanced at Susanna. "By the way, dear, I want you to meet someone. This sweet young lady is Susanna Kelly. I invited her in and just gave her the grand tour."

As Benjamin Curtis smiled and nodded a hello, a familiar voice rang out from behind the partition. "Susanna! Is that you!"

Thomas looked up at Tim. "Empty!"

Tim moved the light closer to the empty coffin. They saw an old black suit, musty and moldy with age, an old fashioned white shirt—the kind without a sewn-in collar— all buttoned up, a collar with a wide blue necktie, a floral pattern woven into the fabric, still attached lying on the white silk-looking lining of the old box. The coffin didn't even offer any offensive odor.

Thomas was so close he could smell the oak it was constructed of. "Well, I guess we have our answer."

He stood up and began climbing out of the grave. To Tim, it was like something from an old zombie movie. He thought maybe he'd seen too many spooky movies.

"You want me to help you fill this back in?"

Thomas shook his head. "That's all right. I'll just wait till tomorrow and do it when it's light. Besides, it'll be a lot easier putting the dirt back in than it was getting it out."

Tim nodded.

Around the end of the partition, Dora came running to greet her.

"Dora! What are you doing here!"

She stood facing Susanna. "Barbara told me to come in early today."

"Barbara?"

"Yes, Mrs. Curtis, here." She nodded toward the lady.

"You work for Mrs. Curtis?"

"Yes, Dora works for me part-time a few hours a day," the lady interjected.

"All the times you heard me talk about this house and you never told me you worked here?"

"Well, I don't say much about it around the neighborhood. People are all the time wanting to get in and talk to them. I was afraid they would start bugging me about helping them to get in and see them."

"But why are you here now?"

"Mrs. Curtis called me a while after you left and told me to come on over. She told me to even bring some clothes and be prepared to stay at least the night." She lifted her eyebrows. "With all that's going on outside, I'm glad she did."

"How did you get here? I came by your place to check on you and your car was still there."

Dora nodded. "I didn't want to drive with all these people milling around. It kinda freaked me out. So, her son, Thomas, came over and picked me up."

"How about your husband? Is he here?"

"Yes, Robert's here. He's back there in the bathroom."

"Bathroom?"

"Yeah, there's a bathroom over there." She pulled Susanna a little way toward the center of the room and away from the partition. At this angle she saw another addition that had been made to the basement; a small room had been built onto the rear back wall."

Dora said, "It has a toilet, sink, and even a shower. Mr. Curtis explained to Robert that it works on something called a sewage ejector system. See that round black thing? It's a tank that pumps the sewage up and out of the basement and into city sewer drains."

To Susanna, the tall round tank sitting to the side of the bathroom looked like a big trash can.

They heard movement behind the partition and Dora said, "Uh oh, we got company."

Just then her husband's dog, Horatio, came around the partition toward them.

Despite Susanna's frequent stops by Dora's place, she had not actually seen the dog but occasionally heard him barking from inside the house. Usually, they just stood outside and chatted, and when she did go in for a quick cup of coffee at the kitchen table, Horatio was either gone or down in the basement where he usually slept. He was a Schnauzer with a long, scraggly beard and not nearly so ugly as Dora had made him out to be.

The big dog came and stood beside Dora and looked up at her. Susanna scratched the top of his head, his eyes beaming, tail wagging.

"That's the great things about dogs," Susanna said. "They're so honest; no pretense with them."

She gave the big dog a cheerful hello and he wagged his long tail even more, returning the greeting.

"Where's Robert's car? Why didn't he drive you?"

"He put his car in the shop on the way to work this morning. It's near his job. He got a friend from work to drop him off here after I called him and told him the plan."

After they talked for a while, Susanna said, "I've gotta go. Tim will probably be waiting on me by now and I can't hold up a police officer."

"Tim?" Dora inquired

"Yeah, a ... friend of mine. Real good friend."

"Tim, your friend. Oh, I see."

"He's the police officer in the backyard?" Mrs. Curtis asked.

Susanna nodded.

Thomas and Tim stepped out of the family plot. Tim had managed not to get himself too dirty with the digging, but his hands needed washing. Thomas, however, having been inside the grave, was smudged all over.

"I gotta go in and get cleaned up. You wanna come?"

"Well, I'd like to wash up a little if it's not too much trouble. I've got to be getting back to duty. I've been away too long already."

"Sure, the kitchen's just inside."

They headed for the back door.

Susanna stepped out the front door of the Curtis house. Mrs. Curtis had escorted her up and to the door. They exchanged farewells and Susanna headed down the flagstone walkway back to the police car to wait on Tim. She half expected to see him already in the car waiting for her but he was not there.

After just a few steps, she came to a stop. People, neighbors, had gathered from houses nearby and others scattered throughout the neighborhood. They were there, Susanna figured, in hopes of running into Mr. Curtis to see if he could give them some information. They eyed her steadily. Miss Jensen was there. She gave Susanna a hard stare looking at her almost hatefully,. Mr. Davies too. They stood in the glowering darkness glaring at her, most holding flashlights.

One of them asked, "Who's she?"

There came a hushed whispering among them. Miss Jensen's voice was dominant.

"We hear you might know something of what's going on," one of them said, a fat bald man she didn't recognize. "Something about a book you've been working on."

She looked at Miss Jensen with bitter disappointment. The older woman who she thought she knew so well, whom she had believed to be a friend, glared at her coldly, her gaze decidedly unfriendly.

Someone else spoke up. It was a man in a white tee-shirt and khaki shorts; his potbelly hung amply over the waistband. He wore a baseball cap colored sky blue. She thought his name was Garret. "Yeah, something about this Rapture thing people are talking about."

Susanna began feeling a little threatened. It was almost as if they were blaming her for what had happened. Even though she was young, she'd seen enough of human nature to know that some people always wanted to blame someone else when things went wrong; they had an innate need for a scapegoat.

As they drew closer, her anxiety rose. She took a step back.

Chapter Twenty-Three

Inside the kitchen, under better light, Tim saw his hands were a lot dirtier than he had thought.

"Go ahead and help yourself. Everything you need is right there. Thomas pointed to the sink." He walked to the backdoor. "And thanks for helping me out." He reached for the handle and turned the lock. "I don't know how long it would have taken me on my own."

"No problem." Tim looked at the sink and saw a bottle of hand soap and a clean white hand towel hanging from a rack.

"Filthy as I am, I'm just gonna hit the shower. When you're done just let yourself out. Pull the door shut behind you and it'll lock itself."

"Sure. Thanks for letting me use the sink."

Thomas nodded and walked out of the kitchen.

At the sink, he began the task of cleaning up. It took him a good minute to get his hands good and clean the way he liked them. He took the towel from the rack.

As he blotted his hands dry, he heard voices coming from somewhere. He saw the other door near the back door and figured it was the way to the basement. He walked over to it wondering if somebody down there needed help. He gave it three firm raps.

After a moment, a man's voice asked, "Who is it?"

The voice was faint; he barely heard him speaking. He pulled the door open about a bit. "Hello! I'm a police officer. Everything all right down there?"

"Yes, officer." He could hear better now. "Come on down."

Tim stepped onto the stairway leading down and pulled the door closed behind him.

Outside, Susanna now stood surrounded by the crowd. For the moment, they weren't doing anything except glaring at her, silently. A few more strangers had joined them over the past minute but they were just onlookers wondering what this was all about. She looked around and felt panic welling up. Their looks were so hard they were almost like blows. She wondered if that was what they had in mind.

Finally, Miss Jensen spoke up. "You can tell us something about this. I mean, good lord, girl, you wrote a book about it!"

Susanna hugged herself. She couldn't believe this was happening! To see these people, so many of them neighbors she had seen so often on her walks, several she had so often spoken with, treat her this way was incredible. Mr. Davies and especially Miss Jensen who, at one time, she honestly believed to be her friend.

"I know you're all upset," Susanna said. "I'm upset too. Yes, I worked with Albert and pretty much wrote his book for him, but I'm really just an editor. The content, the things the book is about, is all Albert's material, not mine. I just put it together into a book." She looked them over. For now, thank goodness, they seemed to be listening.

"Yes, Susanna," Miss Jensen replied, "but you had to go over all that material. It's like you took a crash course on the subject."

"Just to the point of putting it together into a readable form. Albert kept a close watch on what I was doing and made sure I didn't diverge from his views, and they were his views, not mine. I don't know all the scriptures behind these beliefs; Albert did. All I know is what I learned from him and his material."

"That's what we're talking about!" Miss Jensen shouted. "You did learn something. We want to know what it is!"

"But what do you want me to tell you! That the Rapture has actually taken place? Okay, I do believe that! In fact, I'm sure that's what happened."

Shocked, they took a step back as if she had struck them. She wondered if being so blunt had been a good idea. With everyone so upset, there was no way she was going to tell them about the Tribulation that was still to come.

With the mob circling her, there was no way to get back to the door. Even if she could, Mrs. Curtis and the others were all in the basement by now and would probably not hear her pounding on the door. And if they did, it would take them too long to get to her and help. She began breathing quickly.

Mr. Davies, his eyes bloodshot, stepped forward. "C'mon girl, if you know something about what happened to my wife, I want to know about it!" He stepped even closer. "And I want to know right now!" His outstretched, curled-up hand had the index finger pointing down.

This close, she could smell the alcohol on his breath. He had been somewhere for drinks, and judging by this hostility, it must have been a lot. She would never have imagined this nice man could be this mean, this man who apologized so sincerely this morning for splashing her with water, and in such a friendly way. Now, he looked at her like he wanted to kill her.

"I've been searching all over the neighborhood for her since I saw you this morning and there's no trace of her; not one person has seen her and I want to know why!"

"Why do you think I know!" she replied breathlessly. "I told you already what happened."

"This Rapture thing? Is that what I'm s'posed to believe?"

"Mr. Davies, it's the only answer I've got!"

In the basement, Mr. Curtis had shown Tim all the preparations and asked his opinion. Tim told him the precaution of staying the night down here was a good idea and he'd done a good job of setting up the basement. He saw no firearm. He did not recommend Mr. Curtis get one, but if it had been him, there, sure enough, would have been one there.

The few passersby moving along the sidewalk paid her and the mob little attention. Just twenty-four hours ago these same people would have been on the phone with the police calling for someone to come help this poor girl.

Mr. Davies reached behind him and pulled an old-fashioned hip flask from his back pocket. Maybe this drinking was not something new. Had he always been a heavy drinker? He took a long pull from it eying her the whole time. He took a step forward and spewed the mouthful of bourbon all over her.

No one protested.

She snapped her eyes shut and threw her hands defensively in front of her.

"Plenty more where that came from!"

To Tim, the most interesting part of his trip to the basement was meeting Dora. He'd been to her house twice to check on her and was glad to finally see her. He was glad she was okay. He wasn't expecting her to be as pretty as this. Her husband beside her eyed him carefully. He wondered if he'd picked up on his admiration.

He asked about Susanna and Mrs. Curtis told him she'd escorted her to the front door. She assumed she was in the car waiting for him. He wanted to get back to her and told them goodbye.

With disgust, Susanna wiped her face and then rubbed her wet palms against her pants. She saw the look of near madness in his eyes and took three steps back until she bumped into someone standing behind her.

Miss Jensen shouted, "What are we supposed to do now!"

Her mouth and eyes wide, Susanna stared at the mob, the literal mob that stood all around her, and stayed quiet. At this point, there were no correct answers.

From behind, someone pushed her hard and she fell to the neatly manicured lawn.

Tim came back up the stairs into the kitchen. He closed the door after him and hesitated a moment. He heard the satisfying sound of the lock clicking. Mr. Curtis and the others had neglected to put on the lock when they went down. When Tim suggested he do that, he had explained it totally slipped his mind since they never lock that door, and had forgotten it even had a lock.

Just them Thomas came into the kitchen wearing fresh clothes and clean sneakers. His shower was brief but effective.

Quickly, Tim turned and banged on the basement door. After only a few seconds it opened again.

"You got another tenant, Mr. Curtis."

He looked at his son. "Oh, Thomas, are you ready to come down?"

"Yes, I'm coming," he said as he walked toward the door.

Mr. Curtis said, "Before you go, please help yourself to anything in the fridge. I so appreciate you checking up on us."

Tim thought, *I bet you do since you put in a call to downtown and specifically asked for it.*

"Yeah," Thomas said. "Lots of great sandwich items there, and just about any kind of bread you want in that cabinet." He pointed to the one to the right of the sink. Again, he pointed at the fridge. "And there's some great provolone in there too. Help yourself."

Tim nodded, gratefully. "Yeah, maybe I will."

Mr. Curtis turned and started down the stairs. Thomas followed and closed the door. There was a muffled voice and then Tim, again, heard the lock click into place.

On the ground, she laid perfectly still, shock and disbelief momentarily paralyzing her. She looked up and saw them staring down at her not one bit of concern or sympathy in their hard eyes.

She got to her knees and stood up. Whirling around, taking them all in, she shouted, "What are you doing! Leave me alone!"

He'd had a big meal not long ago and one of the brownies while he drove. The rest he was saving for later; the plastic container waited in the glove compartment. He really wasn't all that hungry. But provolone cheese? Always room for something like that! He decided to take advantage of the kind offer and went to the fridge. After he opened the door, he saw, as advertised, a big hoop of cheese. The plastic wrapping had already been opened and closed again with a big plastic clip. The label was in Italian. He was sure this cheese had originated on the other side of the world. He could only understand the word *Provolone*. Standing at the fridge, he opened the wrapping and pinched off a small chunk and popped it in his mouth. As he chewed, he thought about it and decided he really didn't have time to sit around and take a long break. Susanna was waiting. He broke off a good-sized chunk, held it in his teeth like a dog carrying a bone, and resealed the provolone. At the sink, he started to reach for a paper towel to wrap it in but stopped. Instead, he tried his luck and opened the drawer below the countertop and found plastic bags. He put the cheese in one and stuck it in his front pocket.

"Hey, girl!" someone spat.

Susanna whirled around and faced the man in the white tee-shirt and sky blue baseball cap; his hands rested on his wide hips. "We want answers from somebody! Do you understand that!"

She kept her mouth closed and breathed heavily through her nose. She eyed him without blinking.

Another man standing beside him stepped forward. "Listen, we don't want to hurt nobody but we all lost somebody today." His thin voice went with his thin body. "Can you understand how upset that makes us?"

She nodded but said nothing. Then several of them began to walk toward her and she drew in a deep breath.

The bit of cheese was nice; it made him look forward to finishing the rest later on during this long night. He stepped out the back door and pulled it shut behind him. He twisted the door handle and made sure it was secure.

It seemed he'd done a thousand door checks in his time and this action was automatic now.

Suddenly, he heard a scream. He heard *her* screaming.

His training and experience in the military and the police instantly kicked in and he stepped quickly but purposefully around the corner of the big house. As he quickly advanced, he unclipped the cover of the holster and drew out his weapon and held it up. He approached the next corner. As he rounded it, he saw Susanna crowded by a throng of about twenty people.

"Okay, what's going on here!"

Everyone fell silent and stepped back from the girl. He could tell by their gaze it wasn't so much the badge on his chest but the gun in his hand that got their attention.

Susanna ran to him. With his free hand, he moved her protectively behind him.

"You people been bothering this woman?"

They gave no response. They stood there confused and disoriented as if they had just woken from a deep sleep.

"I don't know what's going on here, but I want you people all to go home right now!"

He stood glaring at them as they absently looked back at him. They seemed puzzled as to what was going on. Whether they were puzzled by what he was doing or whatever they had just put Susanna through, it wasn't clear.

"You heard me! Get moving!"

Finally one of them spoke. Susanna recognized the voice; it was Judy Winslow, the lady who lived beside Miss Jensen. "Listen, officer, you can't speak to us this way. We have a right to free assembly. I'm a paralegal; I know the law."

"Do you, now? Well, do you know you're on private property without permission? That's called trespassing. Do you know what assault is? It's not just causing bodily harm; it's the *threat* of bodily harm with the means of doing it. I'd say twenty against one fits that."

Less defiant now, she began, "Well, I'm sure none of us really intended to—"

"And also," Tim interrupted, "are you familiar with the city's regulations concerning Code Six conditions? It gives law enforcement officers far greater latitude of judgment and action during a Code Six, which is the department's disaster code in effect right now. *Far greater latitude.*" He spoke the last few words with great emphasis.

The smart aleck had the good sense to shut her mouth. She was at least smart enough to catch the veiled threat Tim had just given her.

He looked them over. "Go home, now, all of you."

A few of them started shuffling away; they seemed ashamed.

Miss Jensen approached Susanna. Meekly, she began, "Susanna, I don't know what to—"

Tim glared at her. "Lady, go now!" He leaned down, his face a foot from hers.

Miss Jensen stepped back and looked at the ground. She turned and walked slowly away.

Susanna looked at her. She knew it would be the last time she would ever see this person again.

The crowd was thinning out more and more. "C'mon," he said and led her to the car. He helped her into the passenger's seat and closed the door. He stood away from the car making himself clearly visible in case someone thought about doubling back.

As she sat in the car, she trembled. She couldn't believe what had just happened. These people confronting her, attacking her … how could they have changed so much? That such a thing could happen in such a friendly neighborhood, one usually so quiet, was surreal. She smelled the alcohol still clinging to her clothes and knew it was all too real. She looked through the windshield at the departing stragglers, Tim standing watch over them making sure they left. She wondered, *Is this what it's coming to?* Her chest began to heave and she started crying. He stood there and waited a few minutes as everything quieted down. When she saw him approaching, she tried to bring herself under control.

He got in the car and saw her crying. "You okay?"

"Yeah, just give me a minute."

He leaned over, took her hand, and kissed her cheek.

Through tear-stained eyes, she looked into his and said, "You smell like cheese."

Chapter Twenty-Four

Buddy loved to play almost as much as he loved to eat, and when the two were combined so much the better. As the man on the couch looked down at him, the beagle eagerly moved his head left and right keeping a sharp eye on his moving hand. The closed fist shifted side to side and his keen beagle nose—that precision instrument that, so far, had never failed him—told him there was a delicious smelling object in there. Buddy eyed the appendage looking for an opportunity to seize the hidden morsel.

Old Ben Hawser usually kept a treat on him. He often treated the neighborhood dogs he encountered when he was in his yard and their owners walked them by. The short game of keep-away ended with Buddy exercising a surprise maneuver and jumping onto Ben's lap. Surprised, he chuckled and tossed the treat to the carpet. Buddy absented it immediately and licked his chops.

Mrs. Kelly sat in the easy chair, recently occupied by her daughter, and looked on with an amused grin.

Ted Nagle, sitting on the couch beside old Ben, said, "That's quite a dog Susanna brung ya!" He smiled broadly, so broadly his dentures nearly fell out.

Just then, Susanna walked briskly, and it seemed to Mrs. Kelly sullenly, through the front door looking haggard and bedraggled.

The grin faded.

Susanna gave everyone a brief, subdued greeting and headed directly for the bathroom. Her mom simply figured she really needed to go.

After she and Tim had gotten back to her car, he got out and escorted her to the car door. When she pulled away, he pulled directly behind her car and followed closely.

On the ride back to her mom's place, the night quieter now that more people were getting off the streets, she reflected on what had happened and stared solemnly through the windshield. It still seemed like a nightmare—exactly like a nightmare, like some strange and alien territory reserved for things outside of the waking world in a dark nocturnal fantasyland. She smelled the alcohol on her; it again reminded her it had all been far too real. Before she got home, she resolved she would hurry inside the house and avoid her mom and go directly to the bathroom and clean up and change. Mom must never know how close her daughter came to serious injury—or worse.

The sky was dark now; the twinkling stars were all shrouded behind the blackness of cloud cover. A storm was imminent. She saw a faint flash of sheet lightning. Yet again, she thought about what had happened and the things that were destined to happen. She knew another type of storm was coming. She exhaled slowly. Fog formed on the windshield a brief moment.

After they pulled up in front of her mom's house, before Tim could get out of the patrol car, Susanna jumped out of her seat and rushed back to him.

"Don't tell my mom what happened. I don't think she can handle it right now. It's best she just doesn't know."

He nodded. "You want me to come in?"

She shook her head. "No, I'll be all right."

A clasp of thunder exploded overhead, sounding like dynamite going off. The lightning accompanying it lit the sky like a photoflash; it was like the world just had its picture taken. Through the window, she saw the two men who stayed with her mom sitting on the couch. She was glad she spotted them. She intended to avoid them as well as her mother. She didn't want any of them to catch the stench of Mr. Davies' alcohol on her.

"Okay," Tim said. "Why don't you go on in before this storm breaks?"

"Yeah," she looked at him a moment, "and thanks for helping me out back there."

"No problem. Anytime you need me, just call."

She turned to go but stopped. She added, "I'm not going to get any sleep tonight; I know that. Later on, if you get some time for a break come on over, okay?"

"Yes, I will!" he said emphatically. "Count on it."

As she headed for the bathroom, she noticed a light flickering in the darkened room to her left. It was the room they used as a den. The TV was on. Her mom must have been in there earlier and forgot to turn it off when she came out. On the screen there were scenes of a Washington D.C. street and a riot was in progress. Several cars were in flames.

The reporter doing the voice-over for the video said that people had assailed many of the government offices in protest of the lack of action to recover their lost loved ones or provide them with any information. The screen briefly showed a close-up of a screaming man, his face contorted, the veins in his neck sticking out. He had a 666 tattoo on his forehead. The reporter went on to say it had been about 40 minutes ago when the protests turned violent and rioting broke out. Police were struggling to contain the crisis.

"A city-wide curfew has been imposed," the reporter said, "and there's been speculation that the administration might impose Marshall law."

The implication of that made her blood run cold. She recalled Albert saying that would probably be the first thing the Antichrist would do during the emergency of the cataclysm of the Sixth Seal—impose worldwide Marshall Law. By that way, he would begin to seize power.

"And now the riots are getting worse and the National Guard will be moving in at any time."

There was a news truck parked there. Susanna assumed it belonged to the local network affiliate. The camera panned to the left a bit and the Lincoln Memorial was in the background. There was someone standing to the side of the truck. "This is Derrick Heathman," the young, slim-built man said into the microphone he held, "reporting from Washington."

She stepped into the room and turned it off. She'd had enough for a while.

In the shower with the cleansing stream of hot water washing over her, she felt a little better. She stepped out and quickly dried herself off and slipped into the bathrobe she kept there for her overnight visits. She stepped out of the bathroom still drying her hair with the towel and headed for her bedroom. Closing the door behind her, she went over to the bed and sat down.

The room was neat and fresh, always kept prepared for her visits, which had been frequent. Her mom would be happy when she told her she was moving back in. She took in a deep breath and slowly let it out. She was feeling upset again. On the drive back, when they came to a stoplight and had to wait for it to change, she felt the effects of the whole day and evening come crashing down on her. She had hoped for a future as a professional book editor. She had envisioned working in a big city maybe even New York and living an exciting, fulfilling life there. Now she knew she wouldn't even return to campus except to get her things from the dorm. She wasn't even going to bother with any withdrawal procedures; she just simply wasn't going to show up anymore. College now offered nothing for her. She gripped the wheel tightly as she realized she would have to start thinking about a new kind of future, a new kind of life—an uncertain future, an uncertain life. She shut her eyes and her face tightened. She was about to cry, but she stopped herself. Now was not the time. She took one hand off the wheel and wiped a stray tear away.

But she was home now and it was time for that cry. She had stopped the emotional onslaught in the car but her trembling lower lip let her know it was coming. She deserved it and she was going to have it. As the tears began to flow, she held the bathroom towel to her face. Her body quivered, wracked with great sobs as she mourned the plans for her life that had disappeared this morning as well as all those people. Her life as she'd known it was over; her hopes for the future were gone. The upset was so strong it almost made her sick.

She was heartbroken, lonely and scared—especially scared. She wasn't sure if there was any power on earth that could help her. She pulled the towel from her face.

She was still crying, but more softly now. As she sat overcome with these overwhelming feelings, she thought about her piano in the other room. Playing always made her feel better.

She rubbed her face, got up and put on some comfortable clothes. She went to the living room to check on her mom and the two men keeping her company.

Her mom sat laid back in the chair. Her eyes were droopy and she appeared nearly asleep. She opened her eyes and turned toward her.

"Oh, there you are," she said groggily.

The men were gone. Buddy lay asleep on the floor.

"Where did the guys go?"

"Oh, after you got back I told them to go on home." She got out of the chair. "I'm going to bed."

"Okay, I'm going to play a little bit. I'll keep it down."

Mrs. Kelly walked toward her bedroom door. "Don't worry about me. You won't bother me at all. Goodnight, dear."

"'Night, mom."

Susanna made her way to the other room where her piano waited. She sat down at the console piano that sat now in what used to be her dad's study just off the living room. The piano had been moved there after her father's death to make more room in the living room. When her dad was alive, he would sit in here for an hour or two and read; it was his favorite activity. And he came here to be alone. As dearly as he loved his family, he needed some time alone every day just to let his mind be quiet. High intelligence isn't always a gift. Sometimes a man could think too much.

The piano was supposed to have been tuned last week. She played a few simple chords and was glad to hear that it had been. The strings, all in harmony, not one discordant out-of-tune note, rang together, sang together, in a flowing, simple expression of the joy of music. For a console, the piano had a big, rich tone. The solid spruce soundboard and mahogany cabinet saw to that. She was glad to be playing again. It had been a while. Most of the time when she played, it was at the music center at school using one of the baby grand pianos in a practice room there, or the digital keyboard she kept in her dorm room.

As she played, she recalled a scripture, a prayer, she had heard Albert quote. She closed her eyes and recalled it. 'Lord, I believe; help thou my unbelief.' She recalled another scripture prayer she had ran across in her work. 'God be merciful to me a sinner.'

She started playing *The Lord's Prayer*. She had always admired the somber melody. After a minute, she began singing along with it. She actually had a very good voice and would have made a fine choir alto.

Buddy came into the room and lay down near his new mommy's feet. He rolled over on his back, the music and her sweet voice entrancing him.

She stopped playing and looked down at him. She felt such a deep love for her new friend. Then, she felt a pang of fear, wondering what would happen now to them both. Her hands trembled.

She closed her eyes. "Our Father which art in heaven," then she looked up, "hallowed be Thy name." She put her hands together in the classic praying hands fashion. "Thy kingdom come." She paused a minute, realizing that's just exactly what would happen in seven years when the Tribulation was over. "Thy will be done on earth as it is in heaven." The Tribulation was a hard thing to take in, she realized, but it was the will of God. It was the will of God as it had been so many times before on so many nations who, in the Old Testament days, had offended the Lord. The Lord had made examples of them. Modern man had failed to take note. *Now it's our turn,* she thought. *Now it's our turn.* She continued, "Give us this day our daily bread." She sincerely hoped that would come to pass. Food distribution in the Tribulation was going to be a big issue. "And forgive us our debts as we forgive our debtors." That point, that part of the prayer struck her forcibly. And to her surprise, she felt that funny feeling she'd felt in the church service that Sunday night when she went with her Aunt Fran. From being around Albert, she learned it was called conviction—a work of the Holy Spirit. This time, she would not turn it away. "Lord, I really don't know much about all this. You were not part of my upbringing. But if I have offended you, please forgive me."

Suddenly, she felt an instant relief like the weight of the world had just been lifted from her. There was a wonderful feeling of total freedom and an overwhelming joy. She put her hands on the piano lid to steady herself. She began to cry again, but this time, it was tears of joy. She looked down at the beagle looking up at her. "Buddy," she said through her tears, "I think I've just been born again."

The dog wagged his tail in appreciation of the attention. He loved her.

She took a deep breath and exhaled slowly. She felt wonderful and smiled broadly; she had never before felt anything like this. All the pain, guilt, and the fear— especially that—was gone. She sat quietly for a minute and started singing, "And lead us not into temptation but deliver us from evil. For Thine is the kingdom … and the power … and the glory, forever. Amen."

After she sat quietly for a while, basking in the glorious feeling of this new life, she felt an urge to read the Bible. She got up and walked to the kitchen where she left her shoulder bag and pulled the New Testament from it that she had gotten from Albert's house. It made her think of him. She saw the thumb drive in there and pulled it out too. She sat down at the kitchen table and got her computer from the shoulder bag. She plugged the thumb drive in, opened the computer and found what she wanted.

It was a video of Albert, but not one of his prophecy videos. It showed him fooling around in front of the camera with his guitar. She had been there when he made it. She had stood off camera trying hard not to burst into laughter. He sang *Home On The Range* in a not too bad baritone. She smiled at seeing him again. She looked at his big, bald head on the screen and thought that he was home, sure enough, but not on the range.

"See ya soon, Albert," she said. "I'll see ya soon."

THE END

A Note From The Author

The purpose of this novel is to raise awareness of the soon return of Jesus to Rapture his Saints. At about the time this was published, I also published a paperback edition of my nonfiction work, *Tribulation Unveiled* originally published on my website walterlane.com. That short work was the inspiration for this novel, and it contains some material taken directly from it.

Tribulation Unveiled is the result of many years of study, reflection, and prayer. It contains my views on end-time Bible prophecy, especially where it concerns the Great Tribulation and the Rapture, which is so very near. I honestly believe the Rapture, and the following Tribulation, are so close that Christians must now awake to the truth that time is running out and we need to alert the world to the impending doom that is coming. That may sound a little extreme, like something out of a disaster movie or novel, but I believe it to be the truth. Those who are not yet born again need to 'seek the Lord while he may be found' as scripture admonishes us, and escape the dire consequences the Rapture will bring on those left here.

I hope this novel entertains readers, but I also hope it will instill a sense of urgency to move believers and non-believers alike to action.

About The Author

Walter Eugene Lane brings a unique and richly textured background to his writing. His life experiences include serving as a pastor, security officer, 911 dispatcher, and police records clerk. He has also worked in factories, mills, and warehouses. He is a North Carolina native, now residing near the Research Triangle area. For more information about his works, visit his website: www.walterlane.com

If you enjoyed The Girl Left Behind, you may also enjoy this novel by the author: Fearmonger.

Emmy wonders if Jack is falling for her. She might not live long enough to find out. Country Music star Emmy Dawson is beautiful, talented—and in grave danger. Jack Nelson does indeed love her, but a demonic force has other plans for him and wants her dead: She is the only one close to Jack who knows how to free him from its terrifying grip. In this supernatural thriller, infernal powers scheme to control Jack's very soul, to kill the woman he loves, and use his very love for her to force him into the ultimate submission. This brooding evil wants to use Jack as the instrument of humanity's downfall and to initiate a global Satanic reign. And the demon is not alone. There is another entity, even more wicked and horrible that Jack and Emmy must finally face. It is the source of all horror, the master of fear. It wants Jack. It wants Emmy. It wants you! Fearmonger.

Printed in Great Britain
by Amazon